W9-AYH-191

Laura was only a few feet from Carl's door when she heard something behind her. But she was alone, the elevator hadn't come back with more passengers. She whirled around, terrified it might be one of those cat-size, inner-city rats.

What she saw, standing where she had just walked, was a bearded man wearing tinted glasses and a leather jacket. She looked quickly around, trying to stay calm, to figure her options. He hadn't come from the elevator, she was sure of that, and he hadn't come from Carl's. Which could only mean that he had been there in the darkness all the time. Waiting.

Now he stepped forward out of the shadows.

Laura backed away. No denying the obvious now. She was alone. And death was staring at her . . .

"Imaginatively plotted."
—*Chattanooga Times*

"A first-class thriller."
—*Publishers Weekly*

THE *Seduction*

ALSO BY ART BOURGEAU

A Lonely Way to Die
The Most Likely Suspect
The Elvis Murders
Murder at the Cheatin' Heart Motel
The Mystery Lovers Companion

ATTENTION: SCHOOLS AND CORPORATIONS

WARNER books are available at quantity discounts with bulk purchase for educational, business, or sales promotional use. For information, please write to: SPECIAL SALES DEPARTMENT, WARNER BOOKS, 666 FIFTH AVENUE, NEW YORK, N.Y. 10103.

ARE THERE WARNER BOOKS
YOU WANT BUT CANNOT FIND IN YOUR LOCAL STORES?

You can get any WARNER BOOKS title in print. Simply send title and retail price, plus 50¢ per order and 50¢ per copy to cover mailing and handling costs for each book desired. New York State and California residents add applicable sales tax. Enclose check or money order only, no cash please, to: WARNER BOOKS, P.O. BOX 690, NEW YORK, N.Y. 10019.

THE
Seduction

ART BOURGEAU

WARNER BOOKS

A Warner Communications Company

This novel is a work of fiction. Names, characters, places and incidents are either the product of the author's imagination or are used fictitiously. Any resemblance to actual events, locales, organizations or persons, living or dead, is entirely coincidental and beyond the intent of either the author or publisher.

WARNER BOOKS EDITION

Copyright © 1988 by Art Bourgeau
All rights reserved, including the right of reproduction in whole or in part in any form.

This Warner Books Edition is published by arrangement with Donald I. Fine, Inc., 128 E. 36th St., New York, N.Y., 10016

Cover art by Doris Kloster
Cover design by Irv Freeman

Warner Books, Inc.
666 Fifth Avenue
New York, N.Y. 10103

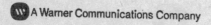 A Warner Communications Company

Printed in the United States of America

First Warner Books Printing: September, 1989

10 9 8 7 6 5 4 3 2 1

To my wife Patricia J. MacDonald . . .
We met under the Biltmore clock,
and it was love at first sight.

"... *Thou shalt not pass by me,*
lest I come out against thee with the sword."

NUMBERS 20:18

THE Seduction

SEPTEMBER

TERRI DiFRANCO closed the front door of the rowhouse and hurried down the steps. Usually when she went out she thought about the black silhouette carriage scene on the storm door, and how her father always teased her mother about it, saying it had been a long time since anyone had seen a carriage in South Philly unless it was at a Mafia funeral, but this time her thoughts were elsewhere.

She paused at the bottom of the steps long enough to adjust the shoulder strap of her purse and to turn up the collar of her jacket to keep out the cool September breeze. The breeze was from the south, carrying on it a hint of the pungent smell of the oil refineries near the airport and bringing a mist that had already encircled the blue-white streetlights in a halo, foretelling the rain soon to come.

Two doors up, Louise Pipari was walking her dog, Willie. Terri waved as Louise bent over and used a discarded potato chip bag to clean up Willie's nightly offering.

When she saw Terri she smiled and sang out, "Thanks for taking in that package for us yesterday. It was a birthday present from Henry's brother in California."

"Anytime," replied Terri with a smile as she turned to go.

At the corner of Second and Morris she stopped at the candy store to get cigarettes. Like most of her friends, Terri had started smoking when she was twelve, but although it had long ago ceased to be a secret, her parents were firm in their resolve not to let her smoke at home. A resolve she found weird since both of them smoked, too.

George Luongo, a longshoreman who worked with her father at the nearby docks, was the only other customer. He had a cassette from Second Street Video Palace tucked under his arm. As she shoved the pack of Marlboros into her purse she caught a glimpse of the title. It was *Mad Max*.

George saw her looking and flashed her a smile which was

missing a tooth on the left side. "Hey, Terri, you're looking good tonight. Got a hot date?" he said.

"Naw, not tonight," she said with a smile and hurried out of the store before he could follow up with his usual line about how if he only weren't married he'd be knocking on her door every night.

Sometimes George would catch her in the wrong mood and his teasing would embarrass her, but not tonight. The compliment made her feel good, for she had tried so hard to look good tonight, carefully choosing from the mishmash of her teenage wardrobe those things that would show her to best advantage, from her high heels and tight Capri jeans to her soft, bright blue sweater, which everyone said made her look cuddly. But that wasn't what made her look good. It was more basic than clothes. Petite in stature and Mediterranean dark, with ebony eyes beneath storm-cloud brows, and full, pouting lips over teeth with a slight gap in the front, she was, some said, a pocket Venus who, at this early, blossoming stage, had not yet come to know her own powers.

Despite what passed for surface sophistication in clothes and manner Terri, at fifteen, was an innocent. Which was not to say that she was without knowledge in the affairs of men and women. She had read her mother's well-worn copies of *Fanny Hill* and *Lady Chatterly's Lover* several times. She knew when to laugh at a dirty joke, basically how couples made love, and had brushed up against what she hoped were male erections several times at school dances. But that was it. Everything she had learned was second hand—until just before Labor Day when all that changed.

Terri quickened her pace. Her destination, near some Water Street warehouses, was at least six blocks away. She was running late, but she considered herself lucky to get out at all. It wasn't so much that her parents didn't trust her. Mostly it was because they were afraid. Over the past few years, teenage girls had been disappearing one by one, without a trace from the neighborhood. Disappearances in a city the size of Philadelphia were, of course, nothing new, and they occurred at intervals infrequent enough that the police chalked them up to runaways who weren't worth the trouble they made. But a growing number of the neighbors, including Terri's parents, thought differently. They feared the girls had been murdered, and because of their fear it was getting increasingly difficult for Terri to get out at night even for a couple of hours.

Tonight had taken a lot of work. She had had to lay the groundwork early in the day, telling her mother that she was going to meet Marie, her best friend, and even then, right up to the last minute, it had looked as if they weren't going to let her go.

But Marie was not the reason she was rushing now—and for the past month. The reason was Peter.

As she hurried past Second and Tasker, with Rachubinski's Funeral Home on one corner and the headquarters of the Avalon String Band on the other, her thoughts went back to that first muggy Saturday night. She had been with Marie at Costello's Cheese Steaks, one of the few places her parents would let her go to any longer, waiting for Joey, a boy she *thought* she cared about. Only Joey was a no-show. At first she treated it lightly, but as the evening wore on, the other girls goaded her until she was anxiously sipping soda, smoking, biting her nails and asking arriving kids if they had seen him.

It did not take long for the pieces to fall into place for her. Joey was with her rival, Lisa, in the backseat of a friend's car. Several people had seen them in the parking lot of the shopping center on Oregon Avenue.

For weeks, in his cute, fumbling way he had been after more than a goodnight kiss, but since his inexperience had matched hers, she had had no trouble keeping him at bay. She thought he had respected her for it, but she was wrong. Now he was with another woman, and everyone knew it. Completely humiliated but determined not to cry in public, she lit a cigarette and started for home. Marie followed, but Terri sent her back and continued up Morris Street alone.

Before she could reach the well-lighted Moyamensing Avenue a sleek, silver Datsun 300ZX overtook her and stopped just ahead. Terri was not alarmed. South Philly was a safe place, and she had seen the car cruising the neighborhood several times recently, so she thought nothing of it.

As she drew abreast of the car, from inside its darkened cockpit a voice asked her for a light. It was a sophisticated, sexy voice full of come-hither, not like the rough, raucous voices of men from the neighborhood.

Had Joey not stood her up, perhaps she would have kept walking, and the past month—the most emotion-filled month of her life—would not have happened. But he had, and she didn't. Instead, she approached the car and offered the driver her matches. As he lit his cigarette she saw he was a real living dream, incredibly handsome, with short, dark hair, a beard, darkly tinted aviator glasses and fine bones that bordered on the delicate.

He wore Italian driver's gloves with holes over the knuckles and, oddly for a muggy late August night, he was wearing a dark leather jacket that looked as soft as butter. Carelessly draped around his neck was a white silk aviator scarf.

"Thanks," he said as he handed her matches back.

She felt him looking at her and, as much to get even with the absent Joey as to please the handsome stranger, she struck a slight pose to give him a better look.

He kept her close to the car by turning up the tape deck so she could hear the opening drum and organ notes to "The Celebration of the Lizard."

"Do you like the Doors?" he asked.

"Sure," she replied with a shrug, but he had scored a point. Music was her language, and even though Jim Morrison had been dead for almost her whole life, the Doors were still a big South Philly favorite on the suitcase-sized ghetto blasters her friends lugged around.

"What's your favorite of their songs?" he asked . . .

Now almost a month later, as she once again rushed to meet him, the thought of the humiliation of that moment when she had been unable to think of the title of a single Doors hit still rankled her.

"'Roadhouse Blues,'" she had finally blurted out after what had seemed like a tongue-tied hour.

He laughed and said, "'Roadhouse Blues,' I would never have guessed that was your favorite. That's a pretty rough song for a young girl."

There was a challenge in his voice when he said the words "young girl," and she bristled at it. One humiliation in an evening was bad enough, and he wasn't going to make it two.

She dropped her cigarette on the street and ground it out. Returning the challenge she said, "All right, which one would you have picked for me?"

"You look like someone who would like 'When the Music's Over.'"

He had been right she remembered now, but she couldn't let him see it. It was too embarrassing to be that predictable, so she played what she thought was the bitch but what later he had laughingly called her "ingenue role."

Gradually they had exchanged personal information. She told him her name, and where she lived. In return she learned that his name was Peter. He offered no last name. Finally, he invited her to get in the car, where it was cool, and to go for a ride with him.

"Maybe it wouldn't be so hot if you didn't go around in that leather jacket," she bantered back.

"It's one of the problems of the job," he replied. "Goes with the territory."

When she asked what job, he produced a badge.

The news that Peter was a cop, especially a handsome cop in a sports car, just like on her favorite television show, was enough to get her in the car, but he refused to give her any more details except to say that he mainly worked undercover.

She watched him with fascination as they turned onto Second Street and for the next half hour drove the same pattern over and over—Second to Snyder, to Front, to Washington, and back to Second. He kept the air conditioning on frigid and the Doors tape loud.

Finally they parked in a dark spot amid the concrete pilings that supported an overhead secton of I-95 near Front and Snyder. He changed the tape from the Doors to a more romantic one by Ray Charles, an old guy who was one of her mother's favorites. It was a misstep on his part. Her system always responded best to the thud-and-thunder of hard rock. It was music you could lose yourself in and words with real meaning. The old Ray Charles stuff made her feel uneasy, like she was sitting in a dark room and suddenly heard a floorboard creak. It was an itchy feeling that made her want to fold her arms in front of her.

Their first contact was even worse. Accustomed to Joey's rougher handling, the gentle way Peter brushed her hair back and the soft whisper of breath in her ear set her teeth on edge. His soft, sensual kisses were almost unbearable on nerves not yet familiar with such pleasure as he sucked and nibbled on her lips until they felt swollen.

She sat perfectly still, wishing that either he would stop or the strange itchiness would go away, but neither happened. Instead, the feeling intensified as he opened her blouse and began to touch her breasts. Before this, Joey was the only one she had ever let touch them, at least bare, but this was different. As with his kisses, before long the pleasure bordered on pain. She felt shame at how easily he took control of her, dominating her until all she seemed able to do was occasionally mutter the expected, "Please don't." Later, when he put his gloved hand between her thighs, she knew she should protest more strongly or even push him away, but it seemed so useless.

After a while he took her back to Morris Street where he gave her a good-bye kiss and said, "Meet me again next Saturday. About eight at the warehouses on Water Street. Know where I mean?"

Suddenly her evening turned to roses. All the liberties he had taken were worthwhile because in the end he had asked her for an actual, honest-to-God date.

Throughout the week her every thought, waking and sleeping, was of Peter. By midweek he had assumed larger-than-life dimensions, and Marie had threatened to kill her if she didn't stop talking about "Peter, Peter, Peter" all the time.

Their second date took a strange turn. She arrived with a thousand questions, none of which he would answer, except to say that he lived in Society Hill. Even this was not news, for she had already decided that there was no other place a romantic undercover cop could live but the most romantic section of Philadelphia.

When she pressed him for details he said, "Look, Terri, in my line of work I make a lot of enemies. People that would go out of their way to get at me or, if they knew about you, to get at me through you. I couldn't stand for that to happen, so you'll just have to trust me and believe it's better if nobody knows about us, and right now you don't know anything about me. That way nothing can happen to you. Do you understand what I'm saying? You're too important to me to put at risk."

Then he had hurt her. Not badly, but enough to make her breasts ache. She could not understand why he was doing it, unless it was to punish her for being too curious, like the way her father had spanked her when she was a little girl, but she sat there unmoving, feeling a closeness and sense of pride, as if he had shown her a new part of being a woman.

When he made her raise herself off the seat so he could pull down her jeans and panties, her hand brushed the front of his trousers and she felt his large erection. It was then that she realized he was feeling the same sort of pleasurable ache that she did, and she knew she was in love.

After he dropped her off she stood on weak and wobbly legs, watching the silver shark with the Bruce Springsteen bumper sticker disappear into the night.

During the week she saw visions of herself dying, lying on the ground with the hard eyes of strangers looking down at her, and she, in a faint voice, saying to bring Peter, and Peter rushing to her side. She cried often and was so moody that her mother let her go out for pizza with Marie on Wednesday.

They had walked almost to Broad Street and then cut over to Passyunk Avenue, leisurely window-shopping and talking: Terri about Peter, Marie about wanting to be thin enough to wear the clothes in the store windows. They stopped at the Metropole Pizzeria in a block filled with Italian restaurants near Ninth. It was crowded with kids from South Philly and couples from uptown, but a short wait got them a table by the window. Being in love and unconcerned with the petty social details of the world around her, she gave Marie the seat where she could see the other customers and took the one facing the window for herself. As she idly glanced out the window, her heart jumped. Parked across the street near Fiorelli's, an upscale Italian restaurant, was a silver Datsun exactly like Peter's. She shifted her chair to get a better look and caught sight of the familiar Springsteen bumper sticker. It *was* Peter's car. He was having dinner right across the street from her.

Her first thought was to tell Marie, but she stopped herself. Marie had been so mean with her teasing. Well, now was her chance to get even. Playing the scene out in her mind, she would just happen to look up and see Peter when he came out of the restaurant. They would nonchantly stroll across the street. His eyes would light up at the sight of her, and they would passionately kiss—right in front of Marie.

But it didn't work that way. Terri was saying, ". . . and I went through all these recipe books because I want to find just the right thing to make him for dinner when he takes me to his apartment. I want him to know I can cook, and not just pasta and stuff like we have at home. I want to make him something nice, like veal, maybe veal marsala. It's not too hard, and my father likes it. What do you think?"

Marie's reply fell on very deaf ears, for at that moment Terri saw two stunning women come out of Fiorelli's and approach the car. One was dark-haired, the other blonde. The dark-haired one got in on the driver's side and reached across to open the door for the blonde. Terri's world ended as she watched the car drive away.

Marie noticed the change immediately and said, "Terri, what's wrong?"

Behind her owlish glasses Marie's eyes had the concerned look of a true friend. Terri wanted to tell all, to pour out her heart, but she couldn't.

"Nothing," she mumbled as she stood up from the table and started for the ladies room.

There was no way she could tell Marie that Peter was married.

Not after all the personal things she had told her over the past week or so. Not only would it make her look dumb for having gone out with a married man, but it would make it look even worse for having let him do all those *things* to her. It was one thing to let him do them when he loved her, but not when he was married and playing her for a fool.

Marie followed her into the ladies room. "Terri, what's wrong?"

"Nothing, I just got my period, that's all."

That explained all. To Marie periods were emotional, sort of sexual, almost voodoo rites of uncleanness to be suffered behind closed doors and preferably in the dark.

The rest of the evening and the rest of the week Terri was torn between standing Peter up for their Saturday night date or showing up for a showdown. In the end she chose the showdown . . .

As soon as she was in the car she lashed out. "You bastard, how could you? Why didn't you tell me you were married? And after all the things I let you do—"

She wanted to hurt him in any way she could—as long as it was publicly and badly. She was unique and alone in the world, feeling an acute and, to her, unique sense of embarrassment, betrayal, disillusionment.

There was surprise on Peter's face as she recounted every detail of what she and Marie had seen from the pizza parlor, but he said nothing until the storm passed.

"It wasn't my wife. It was my sister. I was on duty and loaned her my car. Hers was in the shop."

Terri couldn't believe her ears. It was like he had given her a diamond.

Her dream man wasn't married after all. Relief flooded her and she needed to be held, to be reassured over and over until it finally sank in, but when she leaned over to kiss him he coldly told her to get out of the car.

"But . . . but—"

"Get out of the car."

She wanted to plead for forgiveness, anything, but all she could manage was "Next week? At the warehouse. Please?"

"Perhaps." And he reached across her to open the car door.

Terri spent the early part of the week in torment. She told Marie everything, and Marie tried to comfort her. It did no good. She *knew* she had driven Peter away with her sharp tongue and distrust. She *deserved* to be punished, to spend the rest of her stupid life alone and unloved.

On Tuesday evening the building tension in her house broke free when her father reached the limit of his tolerance when she knocked over a wine bottle and ran crying from the table.

Her mother came to her defense, and the air grew blue with angry words. Her parents fought up the stairs, around the landing and into their bedroom, punctuated by the slamming of the door, while Terri, tears streaming, envisioned her own funeral, thinking how much better off everyone would be without her and yet how much they would miss her as they said good-bye to her little white-clad corpse in its pink-lined coffin surrounded by beautiful flowers.

Gradually the sound of angry words from the upstairs bedroom died down and an uneasy silence settled over the house. An hour later both parents came downstairs looking warm and happy, the fight forgotten, no grudges carried by either one.

She had known for a long time what her parents did behind that closed door, but she had always blocked it out. Until now, the idea of her parents having sex had been too creepy even to think about. Now, in the light of her predicament with Peter, it all made sense. Sex was what kept the wheels turning. She had lost Joey because of it. If only she had the chance she would *not* make the same mistake with Peter.

But once she had reached this decision she felt no peace. The nights were hell. She avoided her parents the rest of the week, feeling that somehow her decision to sleep with Peter made her *look* different and they would know. During her showers she inspected herself for size and depth, thinking about the difference in the huge erection she had brushed against and the slim tampon that fitted her so snugly, hoping that she would not pass out from the loss of blood when he came into her. In bed she lay awake thinking about pregnancy and how she would break the news to her parents and how she would look to her friends when her belly got big and swollen.

The days were her only relief. From the older girls at school she had gotten the idea that sex in cars made a man think the woman was easy. For a man *truly* to love a woman, they had to have a place—a special love nest all their own that she could make with her own hands.

In this pierside neighborhood with so many warehouses, it had been easy. She chose an old railroad depot, long deserted, because it looked like a castle: big, solid and blocky, with turrets on each corner and tall chimneys running up each side. In a freight cul-de-sac, away from prying eyes, she found a convenient rear door with a nearby window. It had been a simple matter to go through the window and open the door.

Each afternoon after school she spent her time cleaning and feathering the nest with blankets and candles, a transistor radio, and even a bottle of wine stolen from home to celebrate with. It was *perfect*.

Now as Terri hurried toward the Water Street warehouses, filled with the hope that Peter would not let her down after she'd arranged the meeting, she was more nervous than if she had to make a speech in front of the entire student body.

There was no sign of him, and ten nerve-racking minutes passed before she saw the headlights of the familiar silver shark of a Datsun. It stopped alongside her and she hurried to get in.

The sight of him made her shiver. She couldn't get enough of looking at his dark hair and beard, his fine bones, his leather jacket and white scarf, his aviator glasses.

She smiled with the thought of finally getting his glasses off and getting a good look at his eyes.

He looked back at her for a moment or two, as if he was reading something in her face. Then he reached for her, and she felt the loving touch of his gloved hand as he brushed back her hair from her face. She leaned forward to be kissed, felt the tip of his tongue, the tickle of his beard, the sharpness of his gun beneath his jacket, and when they broke, her hand brushed the erection in his trousers. She was right, this was the night.

"I've brought you something," he said.

She watched as his hand slipped into the left side of his jacket—the side over his heart—and returned with a chain. It was stainless steel, but to Terri it was silver, priceless silver, the first gift Peter had ever given her, and it happened to be the hottest piece of punk jewelry the older girls were wearing. She had seen them several times in South Street boutiques but had never had the money to buy one for herself.

Each end of the chain had a ring on it, and one end looped through the other, forming a noose like a choker for a dog. He slipped it over her head, tightening it until it was snug around her throat. On the end that dangled like a man's tie was a medallion of a bird. Terri looked at it and thought how beautiful it was.

"I bought this to let you know that you're mine, even though we can't let the world know yet," he said.

Terri was swept away.

After another kiss he put the car into gear. As they pulled onto Water Street, he popped a tape into the deck, and the car was filled with the sounds of Dire Straits playing "Telegraph Road." Over the snaky guitar of Mark Knopfler he said, "Light me a cigarette."

She opened the fresh pack of Marlboros and searched for a light. In her hurry at the candy store she had forgotten matches. Seeing her problem Peter handed her a pack of matches. They were black with only the word "Lagniappe" in gold on the front. Naturally, she thought, the city's most chic restaurant would be Peter's hangout, and soon maybe hers too. She lit two cigarettes, putting his in his mouth, and dropped the matches in her purse.

At the corner they stopped and she said, "You don't have the only surprise tonight. I've got one for you, too."

For a moment Peter looked surprised, but his smile quickly covered it.

"What is it?"

Terri smiled back at him and gave him directions.

As he spun the wheel and shifted gears she thought about how nice it would be if someday he would teach her to drive so she could use the car for lunch and uptown shopping trips.

At night the old railroad depot with its turrets and boarded-up windows looked more like a castle than ever, and the tracks and weed-grown field around it looked like a battlefield where soldiers had died.

She directed them to the cul-de-sac, where they stopped, the car hidden from view, the first drops of rain beginning to splatter on the windshield. For a brief moment Terri's Catholic upbringing told her to wait, to reconsider.

Peter seemed to sense her hesitation. "I know what you're thinking, and it's all right." It was enough.

He waited while she walked up the freight ramp, opened the window, and climbed inside. Using the matches he had given her, she lighted a candle and, with the candle, lighted other candles until their light encircled the pallet of blankets like a frame of flickering gold.

She opened the door and motioned for Peter to join her. He climbed the freight ramp and closed the door behind him, the rain outside coming down harder now.

She was very nervous. If he laughed at her or treated her like a child she would just die. Getting up all her courage, with a sweep of her hand she said, "Well—?"

He didn't answer immediately. Instead he took his time, carefully looking over the room, like he was a movie director checking out a location.

Terri's hand shook as she unscrewed the top to the bottle of Folonari white wine and poured them each a cupful.

"Marie helped me. Do you like it—the place, I mean?" she said, lying about Marie's help to cover her nervousness. She had told Marie about the place but hadn't shown it to her yet. That would come later.

When Peter finally finished his inspection he turned and in a mock-serious voice said, "What we have here is a clear-cut case of breaking and entering. I'm afraid I'm going to have to take you in."

For a second Terri's heart stopped, then she saw his smile. And as he approached her with handcuffs gleaming she knew he was of course teasing, so she only put up a little girlish resistance when he pulled her hands behind her and snapped on the cuffs. Strangely, the restraint comforted rather than frightened her. Now she was no longer in control and responsible for what she was going to do. No longer was she the seducer; now she was the seduced—the captured queen of the castle—and the role, with its blamelessness, pleased and calmed her.

He took her in his arms, kissed her with sharp, biting kisses that sent tiny needles of pain through her lips. She did not flinch.

"You know you're in big trouble, and your only chance is to make me happy, very happy," he said in a hoarse whisper.

"I'll be good, I promise," she whispered back, playing the game.

His hands went over her body, touching her everywhere, each touch seeming to light fires inside her. When he lowered her jeans and panties, he touched both her vagina and her anus. She gave an involuntary start when she felt his gloved finger slip inside her rear, but after that she stood still. With her nervousness gone, everything felt so good that she hoped he would never stop.

In time he led her to the pallet and motioned for her to kneel down. It seemed a little strange to her that by now he had made no move to take off the handcuffs. This wasn't the way she had pictured her first time. She had thought she would lie on her back, gloriously but shyly nude in front of him, and then he, also nude, would lay his beautiful body on top of her, and they would be joined down there in a pure, white and perfect union.

But handcuffs . . . ? Well, maybe this was the way the uptown women of Society Hill did it, and she didn't want to appear unsophisticated. Besides, Peter was her man; she trusted him. This night she would not back away from him, no matter what. When he left her, he would know he had really been loved. And she would be a woman.

Kneeling was difficult, but with his help she obediently leaned forward until she was on her knees with her head on the blankets.

She heard him lower his zipper, and held her breath waiting for the pain to come. But it didn't. She felt the hardness only penetrate her slightly and then withdraw. Peter did this over and over until by his gentleness, rather than force, he gradually broke through all her physical resistance and filled her.

As she became accustomed to feeling Peter inside her, she began to respond, pushing back, and trying to match his rhythm. It was awkward for her, but she was dead set on being the best damn lover that ever was.

Soon she began to feel his body jerk and to hear him moan. Even though she had never experienced it before, she knew what was happening. It was the magic moment, and pregnant or not, she was happy and proud.

When she finally felt him relax against her, she knew she was no longer a girl. Now she was a real woman, and the tears began to flow.

When he took hold of the dangling chain and proceeded to tighten it, Terri's last thought was of the warm look on her mother's face when both the fighting and the loving were done.

OCTOBER

CHAPTER 2

COCAINE GAVE the night snap and tingle for Missy Wakefield, ripping away her blues. Gone momentarily was the depression that had dogged her every step since her father's recent death, and in its place was a rush that heightened her senses, giving the lights and action of Second Street in Society Hill, with its street peddlers and glut of Saturday night celebrants sporting bright colors and bright smiles, the blue-white crystal clarity of a glass of gin.

Of all the drugs she had tried over the years, and there had been many, cocaine was her favorite. With it, so far, the best of the best was even better, and the worst of the worse was nothing to worry about. It was an almost valley-proof high, like makeup: a little at the right time always made you more beautiful, especially in the right light.

A few doors north of Chestnut Street, in front of Sassafras, an old man wearing a blue cap with gold braid and sitting on a milk crate caught a glimpse of her and began to play "Give My Regards to Broadway" on a harmonica, accompanying himself on the spoons; they sounded like a set of wind-up false teeth.

Stapled to the utility pole beside him was a poster that pictured a dark-haired, teenage girl and offered a five-hundred-dollar reward for information concerning her whereabouts. The girl's name was Terri DiFranco.

Missy did not notice the poster as she deposited a couple of bills in the old man's coffee can and kept walking. In the middle of the block she paused long enough to give Tem, the tall Mongolian doorman at Lagniappe, a chance to get rid of two suburban couples who were trying to get into the in-club that was not for the likes of them. As they walked away one of the women was grumbling at her husband for not standing up to the doorman. When she saw the amused expression on Missy's face she flashed her a look that could kill weeds. Fueled by the cocaine, her mind echoing with her father's dictum never to run from a fight, Missy did not look away, nor did her expression change. The other woman did not rise to the challenge.

After they had gone Tem opened the door and gave Missy a smile of welcome, but where his smile was usually tinged with a touch of desire—she knew Tem wanted her—tonight it was different. Tonight he smiled concern.

He seemed clumsy to her, the way he dropped his eyes and shuffled slightly from one foot to the other. "I'm sorry to hear about your father. I know he was a fine man and you'll miss him—"

She silenced him by putting a finger to his lips as if to say, *Ssh, enough said, more will only bring back the pain.*

Thursday and Friday of the preceding week—September 23 and 24—had been the worst days of her life, and now she needed to put that part behind her.

On Thursday her father, Cyrus Wakefield, M.D., had been struck by a massive coronary while strolling from Brooks Brothers to lunch at the Union League and had died right there on Broad Street, his Brooks Brothers' bag with two shirts and three ties instantly snatched up by someone in the crowd. By midafternoon, in accordance with his known wishes, his medical colleagues had stripped his body of any transplantable parts, and what was left had been cremated even before Missy could say a short good-bye to the man with the hawklike visage, the salt-and-pepper mustache and the great tufted brows. With Friday morning had come a short service for a few select friends, the scattering of his ashes in the garden of the Chestnut Hill home and a buffet afterward—at which Missy had acted badly.

The sight of people sipping white wine and lunching on crab claws, smoked salmon and cold lobster had been too damn much—too civilized—and made her own grief seem out of place. There had been too much vodka, a drive into town she could barely remember, a bottle of pills and then, almost too late, a frantic call to Carl Laredo, who had found her nude and unconscious.

Well, get hold of yourself. You're a good actress. Act. "Is Carl here tonight?"

"He's in the back at his usual table," said Tem.

"Good." She turned toward the bar.

After her release from the hospital she had gone to the family condo in Marigot, St. Martin, for some healing sun, but within days the peaceful solitude was driving her crazy. To work through her grief she needed to expend energy, not to sit and stare.

She walked through the crowd, paying no attention to the sleek men and beautiful women around her as they flashed their predatory eyes and switchblade smiles, pursuing one another with the bartering carnality of Armenian rug merchants.

At the bar she pushed into a space between two women and motioned for Marc, her favorite bartender.

He hurried down, leaned across the bar and took her hand. "Darling, you look scrumptious tonight."

He was right. The Gucci blue-and-gold bolero jacket worn over a darker blue silk blouse with a turned-up collar fit her perfectly. Highlighted by a turquoise and old silver necklace and bracelet given to her by Carl and completed with black pleated evening pants and Charles Jourdan shoes, the outfit showed her athletic leanness with enough style to raise the hackles of every woman in the room. It was too New York, too competitive, too daring for Philadelphia, where women still made fashion statements with simple little two-piece suits and black pumps. It was too *haute* bitchy, but she was the woman who could carry it off.

Her short black hair was moussed and tousled. She had beautiful high cheekbones but without the cadaverous look of fashion models. Lips that were just a trifle too thin but with skillfully applied makeup still had the glistening fullness to give a primitive growl to most men's thoughts. But her eyes were what kept them at bay, eyes dark and shiny as a black onyx soul.

She thanked him and, more out of courtesy than interest, said, "How are things with you?"

She waited patiently if abstractedly through his reply.

When he realized that Missy was only half-listening to his paean to yet another sullen-looking blond boy with whom he had had his way, he quickly got down to business.

"You want the usual—Stolichnaya and soda?"

She nodded, looking not at him but at the crowd.

"Shall I send it over to Carl's table?"

"Oh, Carl is here?" she said as if it was news to her.

Tanya Tucker was belting out "Bed of Roses" on the stereo system, and Lagniappe only played that tape when Carl was there. They did it partly to flatter him, partly to josh him about the torch he still carried for her, dating from her days as a teen heart throb.

Cyrus Wakefield had never approved of Missy's relationship with Carl, but then he had never understood what an interesting relationship theirs was. They had met a few years earlier at a Locust Street art gallery. Carl had just returned from five poverty-filled years studying in France and was taking his first career move as the artist-in-residence at the Philadelphia art school, the Walker Academy. As soon as she saw him, it was like seeing the right fur coat. She just had to have him.

The reason she had to have him was simple in a complex way. He gave off signals, subtle but obvious to her, that he wanted to be possessed by her. She was more than receptive.

In exchange for his devotion and submission to her whims she offered sex, money and a place to sell his paintings through her society contacts. It was a devil's bargain for Carl . . . one she broke according to her mood. His going along with this unequal pact was most pleasing to her, somehow a confirmation of his devotion and love. She needed that, needed it badly. She might grieve for her father, but she'd received precious little show of affection from him . . .

So Carl became boy friend, girl friend, confidant, supplicant, savior, sinner, and she cherished him like a favorite doll from her childhood.

Glancing around the room she saw several people she knew, including the blonde hostess of a TV talk show who nodded for Missy to join her. Her attention, however, was fixed on finding Carl's table, and when she did she was furious.

Four were seated around the table: Lagniappe's owner Justin Fortier, blond, smooth-shaven and still deeply tanned from a summer on his boat, next to him a man she did not recognize, then Carl, and next to him a woman who was obviously with Carl. Carl could be so tacky with his flirtations. No taste at all. A discreet little fling was one thing, but she would not have him bringing one of them here and embarrassing her.

Most times she was more tolerant. It even amused her to see him involved in one of these flirtations, knowing his secret: he had almost no self-control—a fact he felt ashamed of, but one that pleased her no end. She used this knowledge to replace conventional, prosaic coitus with blitzkreig-like encounters in hallways, bathrooms, kitchens, taxis—anywhere but bedrooms. She liked to keep him on the edge, usually with her hand, occasionally with her mouth, until he would whimper and even beg like a child. Something she was certain his little pieces were incapable of provoking.

But tonight she was in no need to indulge him. Tonight she was still reeling from her father's death, and she needed a role reversal, needed Carl to be the strong one for a change and look after her.

Justin was the first to see her and stood to greet her with a flirtatious smile. The unknown man next to him also stood, and for a moment Missy's eyes were drawn to him. He was a shade under six feet, darkly handsome with a neatly trimmed beard and the lean body of a runner. He was wearing a double-breasted suit of Italian cut, a white shirt with collar pin, and a red-and-gold club tie. No question, he reeked of poise, but there was something about him that made him seem considerably more than a pretty male in a pretentious whiskey ad. There was something very . . . physical . . . in the way he looked at her that both unsettled and attracted her. Like her father . . .

Carl was on his feet, too, and for a moment she compared him with the stranger. Both were dark and slim, had beards, but there it ended. There was something obviously soft, pliant in Carl—none of that in this new man.

She kissed Carl lightly on the lips, Justin on the cheek, and shook hands with the stranger who was introduced as Felix Ducroit, a friend of Justin's from New Orleans.

A waiter brought her a chair, and only then did she acknowledge the presence of the other woman across from her. She was in her mid-thirties, with reddish-blonde hair of that in-between length that meant she was letting it grow out. Her skin was soft and delicate, the kind that begged floppy hats and cool shade, but the tracery of wrinkles around her eyes indicated a careless disregard of its delicacy. Her eyes were clear and deep blue, but underneath were dark shadows that made her look tired and drawn.

Carl introduced them. "Laura Ramsey, this is Missy Wakefield," and Missy was irritated even more. By introducing Missy to the other woman, rather than vice versa, he made it seem as if Missy were the intruder, and not, as of course it was, the other way around.

Missy smiled through cocaine-clenched teeth and managed a perfunctory "Hello."

"Would you like a—" Carl started, but before he could say "drink," Violet, a pretty waitress with a gentle look and flowing hair of a sixties flower child, appeared at her shoulder with a Stolichnaya and soda.

It gave her a small sense of satisfaction when Violet leaned over to say, "We missed you, but your tan looks great. Did you have a good time?"

"Yes, but it's good to be back."

"Where were you?" she heard Laura Ramsey say.

Missy let the question hang for a moment while she settled back and lit a cigarette. If there was one thing a lifetime of breeding and manners had taught her, it was how to keep everyone waiting.

Finally she said, "St. Martin."

"Did you stay on the French side or the Dutch?"

"The French. The Dutch is too much like a bad weekend in Atlantic City."

"It's a great island. I managed to get there two years ago for a few days. How long were you there?"

"Only a week this time, unfortunately."

"What she means, Laura, is that the reason she was there was unfortunate," Carl said. "Missy's father just died, and she was at their family place down there recovering from the shock . . ."

In fact, she hadn't intended to mention her father's death, at least not in front of two strangers, and she resented the way Carl seemed to be, deliberately, asserting himself by stepping on her toes.

"I'm sorry to hear that. Were you close?" Laura asked, the sympathy in her voice sounding sincere but too near pity for Missy's comfort.

"Yes," she said flatly and then hurried to change the subject. "Now, folks, bring me up to date on what's been going on around here."

"To be honest," said Justin, "when you arrived we were talking about the South Philly runaways."

"The what?" said Missy.

"I guess you haven't seen the papers," Justin went on. "Yesterday one of them, I forgot which, had an article about it. It seems that teenage girls have been disappearing without a trace from South Philly. Almost a dozen of them . . ."

Carl put in, "it wasn't that many, more like a half-dozen—"

"Half a dozen, a dozen," said Justin. "People are beginning to take some notice."

"Well, South Philly seems like a good place to disappear from," said Missy with an edge in her voice. This *wasn't* what she wanted to talk about now.

"They ran pictures of the girls, and they were all quite pretty, so young and fresh—"

"And Justin has been trying to get me to admit I know something about it," said Carl, smiling nervously.

Missy smiled back. *You'd better be nervous,* she thought. *Making me sit here like this with another woman at the same table, right here in front of everyone . . .* Still looking directly at Carl, she said to Justin, "If it has anything to do with teenage girls in white panties, Carl could just be your man . . . Sorry, darling," she said and leaned over to give him a proprietary peck. "Just *joking.*"

Carl clearly didn't appreciate the joke.

"It's supposed to be a classic fetish," said Justin, sounding unaccustomably pontifical.

"Thank you, Dr. Freud," said Missy, still looking at Carl and enjoying the way he looked away from her. "But surely South

Philly strays aren't why you're all gathered here tonight," she said, this time shifting her attention to Laura, Carl's new one.

Laura said nothing.

There was a silence at the table as attention shifted to Carl. Finally he said, "We're having a . . . little celebration—"

"What are we celebrating?" Missy asked, as if any birthday cake within sight would surely conceal a ticking bomb.

Again silence, and then in a voice, for him, remarkably cold and strong, Carl said, "We're celebrating my moving to New York."

The shock of that, combined with the cocaine, gave her a heart palpitation so strong that it felt as though someone had jabbed her in the chest with a thumb. For a moment the shapes and colors in the room seemed to shift out of sync, and her skin broke out in droplets of sweat.

She took a drag on her cigarette to calm herself and tried to ignore the trickle of sweat between her breasts.

"I think I must have come in on the middle of this movie. Now tell me again, slowly. You're doing what?"

"I'm moving to New York, Missy . . . Laura has been helping me to set up a show there—"

"And just how has Laura been doing that?"

"Laura works for a paper here. She was on assignment up in SoHo and met the gallery owner. She was good enough to mention me. He'd heard of me and agreed to look at my work. I guess he liked the idea I was from Denver . . . a rustic American from the hinterlands . . ."

"Which paper?" said Missy, zeroing in on the heart of the matter.

"The Globe," Laura told her.

"How did you two meet? In a museum, I just bet."

"Yes, as a matter of fact, we met at the Philadelphia Art Museum when they were having that exhibition of Texas art and culture. I was covering it for the paper."

Turning back to Carl, Missy said, "I believe that was last year . . ."

When she got nothing from him, she turned back to Laura. "Then you're the art critic for the Globe?"—knowing full well that she wasn't, since she already knew the Globe's art critic.

"No, I do features—"

"But you just happened to be in New York on assignment where you met a gallery owner who just happened to be interested in Carl's work—"

"There's a bit more to it than that, but I guess that's pretty much it."

The damn woman was too cool, and she, Missy realized, had been losing hers. "Well, Carl, you said he looked at your work and liked it. What does that *mean*? Is he going to give you your own show or just take a couple of canvases on consignment and maybe never pay you?"

"I thought you understood, Miss, he's giving me *my own show*, and it's a good gallery so I know he's *not* going to cheat me—at least not any more than any other gallery owner cheats."

Missy squashed out her cigarette and immediately reached for another. Anything to keep her mouth busy, to keep her from turning geek and leaping across the table to bite the head off that meddling bitch.

As she fumbled for a light she heard a calm voice say, "May I?"

For a moment the words didn't register. Then, turning slightly, she found herself looking into the eyes of the newcomer, Felix Ducroit. Now the resemblance to her late father seemed stronger, and it first startled her, then quieted her. She put the cigarette between her lips and he lit it with a silver Dunhill lighter.

Forcing a more cheerful note, she said, "I think it's good about the show." With the possible "I" she tried to reassert herself. "We've thought a lot about getting a New York show. I'm really happy about it, but I don't understand this business about moving there."

"It's not immediate. The show's not until spring so I won't be going for about a month . . ."

"But, darling, I don't understand why you need to go at all. Here you've got friends, an established career, a good life, a nice loft. Why don't you do the show but stay here?"

"Missy, I can't. This is my chance to move up. I've done all I can here. If I want to make a bigger name for myself I have to go to New York. It's the same for actors. If you want to be in the theater, it's New York. Movies, it's Hollywood. For an artist, no question, you have to go to New York."

"Thank you for the lecture. I'm not exactly a stranger in the art business—"

"Then please don't act like one. I wish for once you'd think of somebody besides yourself and be happy for me."

"Like Miss Laura here?"

"I think it's time for a bottle of celebratory champagne," Justin cut in, ever the diplomatic *mein* host.

Missy ignored him. "I still don't see why it's necessary to move there so soon for a spring show. Couldn't you wait and move there, say, in March?" She knew she was pushing it, losing control but couldn't stop herself—and she hated this fucking Laura for being responsible . . .

"The gallery owner," Carl said, now trying to calm matters, "wants me there through the holidays, for parties and so forth. It's a bore but he says if I'm a no-show there will be no show." Nicely put, he thought.

"I think some champagne would be just right," said Laura enjoying the byplay even though it did make her uneasy. Actually there was nothing between her and Carl, not the way Missy Wakefield thought. But it was up to Carl to enlighten her.

"So you're just going to pick up and run out on your friends like you've done with everything else in your life."

"Whoa, time out. You're understandably upset, Missy, but enough is enough," said Justin, raising both hands. He hated scenes in his establishment, bad for business.

Missy looked at him. "You're right, Justin, enough *is* enough," and she picked up her purse and headed for the ladies room.

Moving away from the table, she thought she had never felt more *alone* and betrayed. Goddamn them all.

She slammed the door of the ladies room behind her. She needed some privacy to regain her composure, but instead found Lois Fortier, Justin's wife, a striking redhead in a simple, black Halston. She was standing at the sink touching up her makeup and didn't glance in Missy's direction at the sound of the door; she let the mirror do the work for her.

"From the look on your face I'd say you've heard the news," said Lois not unkindly.

Missy locked the door and walked toward the sink. "What news?"

"About Carl moving to New York?"

"Oh, that," she said as she fumbled in her purse. "Yes, I've heard about it and I think it's very exciting. This is the break we've been waiting for all along."

Lois turned and looked at her.

Missy took out her compact, opened it, and laid it on the edge of the sink.

"Of course, there's nothing I want more than to see Carl become the biggest and most famous artist in the world—"

. . . *And move in with Laura,* Lois thought but didn't say as she smoothed her dress over her hips and leaned forward to make sure there was no lipstick on her teeth.

"Look, dear, I know the way men are. There's no use fighting it. You just can't trust them. Soon as you turn your back they're trying to replace you with a younger model. I keep waiting for Justin to trade me in. Of course, if I ever find out he has I'll throttle him . . ."

While Lois was chatting on, trying to make Missy feel better, Missy took a small packet about the size of a stick of chewing gum out of her purse and was carefully pouring some white powder from it onto the mirror of her compact. When she heard the words "younger model" she felt no special comfort, even though this Laura could be ten years older than she was. In Carl's case the older woman seemed an attraction—though a pretty damn sudden one, considering his obsession with teeny-teens in white panties . . .

"That's not the way it is at all," Missy said. "She's just a friend from the paper who's trying to help out." Which, ironically, happened to be the case.

Lois nodded, not wanting, like some others, to rub it in, but not convinced either.

Missy, needing relief, not an argument, lowered her tone and smiled. "Want some?" she said as she took the cover off a matchbook and began to divide the white powder into lines on the compact's mirror.

"Maybe just a line," said Lois.

"Like I said, this is what we've both been working for, and

we're *both* happy as can be. Oh, I'll miss him, sure, but New York's just a train ride away so we'll see a lot of each other and I'll get to meet a whole new group of people in New York," she said, rolling a twenty dollar bill into a tube and handing it to Lois, smiling until she felt her face would crack. Crack . . . not for her, for the peasants . . .

"I must say, Missy, you're taking this a lot better than I would," Lois said. "When you took Carl Laredo under your wing he was a hick. Without you, he'd still be a pig's ear."

Even in her anger Missy knew this was not strictly true. When they met, Carl had just come back from living in France and knew more about food, art and wine than anyone she'd ever known. Including herself.

Lois, who had bent down to the powder on the compact's mirror, looked at the rolled-up twenty and straightened up. "Don't you have anything larger than this? I never like to snort with anything as small as a twenty. You can never tell whose nose it's been up."

Missy threw back her head and laughed a loud, genuine laugh. "Lois, did anyone ever tell you that you can be a cunt?"

"Only Justin, and that was in the heat of passion," she said with a demure smile. "And speaking of passion, or an approximation thereof, I saw Felix at Carl's table. What do you think of him?"

"He's . . . nice-looking but I didn't pay much attention . . ."

"Oh, well, I just thought you might have noticed him. He's an old friend of Justin's from New Orleans. Made a fortune developing real estate. I believe that's what he's doing here, some big project or other. Of course there's more to it . . . his ex-wife lives here and Justin thinks he wants to get back together with her."

Missy had no comment, finished her cocaine and put her compact back in her purse.

Lois, though, wasn't finished on the subject of Mr. Felix. "You probably know her . . . Susan Ducroit? She lives in the Locust Towers on Fifteenth Street and owns the Pine Street Charcuterie."

Missy nodded abruptly, picked up her purse, took a glance in the mirror to be sure her makeup was fresh and no telltale powder was clinging to her nostrils, and started for the door . . .

An uneasy silence settled over the table, and she knew immediately they had been talking about her.

Once she was seated Carl leaned toward her. "You okay?"

Not looking at Laura, she said, "Of *course* I'm okay. Aren't I always, darling?"

Laura was looking at Carl. "It's getting late, Carl. Don't you think we should go back to your loft to make sure the caterer is finished? The crowd from the Spectrum should be arriving any time now."

"What crowd from the Spectrum—?" Missy could have bitten her tongue. It was the damn cocaine loosening it.

"The rock group Fraternization is playing there tonight," Carl said uneasily. "They're coming over after the show for a little get-together . . . Why don't you and Felix here come around—"

She and Felix? What a nervy thing to do. Well, she wasn't someone to be laid off on a stranger . . . even one that strangely moved her . . . like a three-eyed cousin. Not after all she'd done for him. Lois was right—he *was* a hick, all the acquired French *culture* notwithstanding.

Truth to tell, below her anger she had never felt more vulnerable in her whole life than at this moment. Mostly she was the strong one, in charge, and the one time she *needed* someone, humiliation was what she got. Men. . . .

Felix saved her. They were now the only ones still at the table. He reached across and put a hand on her arm in a gesture that was both possessive and protective. It startled her. His hand felt almost exactly like her father's . . . when she was little he would do the same thing, put his hand on her arm just that way whenever she'd get upset, and when he did she'd know everything was all right. At least until the next time when he got mad at her and made her scared and miserable all over again . . . Felix's eyes, they were so like how she remembered her father's . . . she'd noticed it when they were introduced but it hadn't really registered until now . . .

"I don't know about you, but I haven't eaten. Would you stay and have dinner with me, or at least keep me company?" Looking at Carl he added, "The party will still be going on a while, won't it?"

Missy didn't bother to hear Carl's answer. He had made his bed. He was now a nonperson as far as she was concerned. Except, of course, for the payback.

"Good, we'll join you later," Felix was saying, and thereby taking matters out of her hands.

Felix was a pleasure, in control, on top of the situation. A regular Cyrus Wakefield, early edition. As she turned back and saw Carl and company walking away through the crowd, she thought, *We won't be joining you—not now, not ever.*

Tonight she had come to Lagniappe looking for Carl and some support, even comfort. Instead she had found, it seemed, something better. Something she had given up looking for . . .

A man to match her father.

CHAPTER 3

LAURA RAMSEY woke up with a start, heart pounding. Once again she had had the too familiar nightmare . . . She was on the operating table. Masked faces were looking down at her. She was conscious but unable to speak or move. One of the faces was saying, "It has spread; we're going to have to take more," and then they began to cut off her arms and legs . . .

Usually when she had this nightmare the sight of her cozy bedroom with its white walls and blue woodwork was enough to quiet her, to remind her that she was safe in the little house she loved so well. But not today. It took her a moment to realize why, and then she understood. It was the sound of the sirens.

She took a ragged deep breath and pushed back the bedclothes. Tugging at the bottom of the white T-shirt she slept in, she crossed the room and opened the window.

Her bedroom faced onto narrow, tree-lined Emily Street. By leaning out her window she could see nearby Front Street, the concrete pilings of the overhead section of I-95 and almost to the Delaware River beyond. From the way the police cars were racing down Front to Snyder under I-95, and up Water Street on the other side, it looked like something big was developing.

Laura pulled on a pair of corduroys, a bulky sweater, and stepped into a scuffed pair of Tony Lama cowboy boots. She stopped in the bathroom just long enough to run a comb through her hair, brush her teeth and put on a little lipstick and eyeliner. Downstairs she grabbed her tape recorder and purse and was out the door.

Neighbors were emptying from their houses and making their way toward Water Street and the screaming police cars. Rushing along with them, Laura once again felt the strong sense of neighborhood that had first attracted her to this section of South Philadelphia near the docks—a sense of belonging, even some mutual concern not possible for an apartment dweller.

She followed the crowd until they came to the normally deserted train depot between Water Street and Delaware

45

Avenue, which now, ringed as it was by at least a dozen police cars, was far from deserted. Uniformed officers were busy trying to keep back a small but growing crowd.

Stopping at the rear of the crowd near a silver-and-white coffee truck already doing a brisk business, Laura found herself next to a long-haired young woman holding a baby in one hand and a cigarette in the other. On the back of the hand holding the cigarette she noticed a small flower tattoo.

"What's going on?" Laura said, out of breath and standing tiptoe to get a look over the crowd.

"Beats me. I just heard the sirens and come over. Probably found a body in there. Nothing else'd bring this many cops. The Mafia, somebody probably got smart with them and got killed for their trouble . . ."

"Who you kidding?" said a young woman in a tank top. "It ain't the Mafia, the Mafia don't work like that. They just shoot 'em and leave 'em on the street like the rest of the garbage that don't get picked up in this neighborhood. It's those missing kids. Their bodies are in there. Every last one of them. Mark my words . . ."

Laura pushed on into the crowd until she got to a uniformed cop. Behind him she could see unmarked Plymouth sedans and a blue-and-white van labeled "Crime Lab" scattered near a cul-de-sac with a freight ramp. Fishing in her purse she found her press credentials and flashed them at a young officer. He had a grim look on his face.

"Officer, what's happening?" she asked, hoping that the woman was wrong, that it wasn't a building full of bodies.

He glanced at her credentials and stonewalled. "I don't know, ma'am. You'll have to ask the lieutenant about that—"

"Where is he?"

"Inside, *ma'am.*"

All right, he was at least ten years younger than she was but she wished he would stop calling her "ma'am." It also was sort of corny, like an old TV show. Well, she wasn't here as a critic.

"Can I see him?"

"Soon as he comes out I'll tell him you're here . . ."

She turned away from the next "ma'am" and moved down

the line. As she did she noted the tight, grim faces. From her experience it took a lot to affect a cop. Something really terrible must have gone down in that old depot.

She saw detectives come out of the building, all with handkerchiefs over their noses and mouths. As she stood there she felt a rough hand on her arm and turned to face a woman in her forties with short hair and hard eyes.

"You're that reporter, the one that lives over on Emily Street, right?"

There was an angry look on the woman's face, too, but unlike the police hers was not a controlled anger—it was the look of someone who was ready to blow and looking for a place to do it. For a moment Laura was intimidated by her ominous presence, but she pushed it to the back of her mind.

"That's right . . ."

"I thought so. Me and my husband, we saw you at Walt's having crabs. You were by yourself. The waitress told us who you were. You're going to write about this, aren't you? Somebody's got to do something about it."

"I don't know. What's going on?"

"They found a body in there, we think it's Terri DiFranco. You know, the latest missing girl. It's a sin. They ought to shoot the sonofabitch that did it."

Laura knew, all right. She had a collection of handbills from the neighborhood, all with pictures of missing teenage girls and reward offers. This Terri DiFranco was the latest. For months she had tried to interest her paper in doing a story on them but had gotten nowhere. Without bodies they were just runaways, she'd been told. They weren't news. No one was interested. Including the police.

Another paper, though, had done a piece on the missing girls as a fill-in on a slow newsday. That was last week, Saturday— the day she and Carl and the others had been talking about it at Lagniappe.

"How do you know what they found?"

Another woman, of similar stocky build and haircut but wearing glasses, chimed in, "Because Lennie Carnelli and his pal Mike knew her. They were laying outa school, playing hooky, and gonna spend the day in there. When they broke in they found her—"

A tall blonde in her late twenties interrupted. "I don't know if you know, but there's nine cops that live in the one and two hundred block of Mifflin. When they found her they ran up Mifflin looking for my Jim, both of them sick as dogs. But Jim's on days so I sent them across the street to Walt Kramer. He's the only one in the block on nights right now. And he went down to have a look. Sadie, that's his wife, called me later and told me that when he come back to call it in she'd *never* seen him look worse. She asked him what happened and he wouldn't say anything about it. But she did hear him call Louise Pipari, she's the DiFranco's neighbor, and tell her to stay close because they might need her. When Sadie asked him again what happened all he'd say was if he got his hands on whoever did it he'd kill him himself."

"They ought to shoot the sonofabitch that did it," repeated the first woman.

"Shooting's too good for a bastard like that," said a woman in a red satin warm-up jacket. "I heard he tortured her. They ought to chain him up, right in the city hall courtyard, and cut his nuts off. And not with a knife, with a saw so it'd hurt more. Ever cut yourself with a saw? Hurts ten times worse. Isn't that right, Flora? That's what they ought to do, chain him up and saw his nuts off."

Flora was a shapeless woman with a gray complexion and wrinkled bags under her eyes. She wore a tattered cardigan and a dress that looked like it had been made from a mattress cover decorated with little blue flowers. She was clutching a handbill with a picture on it, and there were tears in her eyes as she stepped forward and handed Laura the crumpled handbill.

"She was a good girl," she said, "went to Mass every Sunday and never did anything wrong. She's Italian but she always call me her Polish grandmother. Sometimes she stop by after school to see me and tell me things and we would talk. But lately she too busy with this new boyfriend she has, and she don't stop by so much more. I tell her he's no good for her, he's too old, but she just laugh and tell me that grandmothers always say that." The woman's face twisted up and the tears overflowed her eyes.

Laura saw that the picture on the handbill was poorly repro-
duced, as though it had been run off from a cheap copying
machine, but the snapshot was clear enough to show a dark-
haired, nubile beauty with a faintly sullen cast to her face. It
occurred to her that if she'd ever had a child it would have been
about the same age . . . "But we don't know for sure that it's her.
It may not be her at all." True or not, she wanted to give the
women some hope while they waited, but the hard-eyed looks
she got back showed little gratitude. And Laura knew that with
that one remark she had gone from being a neighborhood
insider with an interesting job to an uptown outsider to whom
doors would now be closed.

Anxious to turn away that image and keep the women talking,
Laura pushed ahead: "What about this boyfriend you mentioned? What's his story?"

The woman in the satin warm-up jacket was the first to speak.
"She told Flora he was an undercover cop and drove a silver
sports car, and that he was handsome and wore a beard and had
dark glasses—"

"That's bull," said the blonde. "There's no undercover cop
that lives in this neighborhood, and if he did he sure wouldn't
be driving no silver sports car."

"That's what I said," agreed the woman in the warm-up
jacket. "I *said* she made him up. You know how kids are."

"Maybe he just told her he was cop, trying to impress her,"
Laura said.

"What do you think about that, Flora?" said the woman in the
warm-up jacket.

"His name's Peter, that's all I know, and he's real enough."
This from the old woman.

Laura looked at the picture again. Something in Terri DiFranco's expression, maybe it was her eyes or the stormy look on her
young face, made her believe that Terri had been telling the
truth. Yes . . . Peter was real.

She felt a touch on her arm and turned. It was the young cop
who had been so formal a few minutes earlier.

"The lieutenant will see you now, ma'am," he said.

"We'll be right here," the woman told her. "Come back and
tell us what you find out."

Laura handed the handbill back to the old woman, who refused to take it.

"No, you keep it. So you can tell us if it's her."

Laura nodded and turned to follow the officer.

He led her past the ring of cars to where a group of detectives were talking near the freight cul-de-sac.

"Here she is, lieutenant."

Laura immediately recognized the balding man in the blue blazer from softball games between the department and her paper. George Sloan. As the leader of Seven Squad, the homicide squad assigned to the city's trickier cases, his presence meant that whatever was inside the deserted depot was a considerable hot potato. As she came closer she noted that he looked sallow and drawn.

"God, George, you look like hell." And indeed he did.

"Thanks a bunch, Laura, I needed that. It's just a touch of flu," he said, managing a weak smile. "I didn't know Will had assigned you to the crime desk."

"He hasn't. I happen to live nearby and heard the sirens. You ought to take some aspirin and a slug of brandy and get into bed before that stuff kills you."

"I'd like to, believe me, but there's no time . . . I didn't know you lived around here."

"Yes, in the one hundred block of Emily Street . . . George, what the hell's going on here?"

"Looks like a rape-murder but we won't know for sure about the rape until the M.E. finishes his examination later today."

"Who is it?"

"Can't be sure until she's been identified by the next of kin."

"Is it a young girl, a teenager?"

"Yes . . . how did you know?"

"Is it this girl?" She showed him the handbill.

When he looked away she knew the answer but asked again, for the record. "Is it, George?"

"Like I said, we won't know for sure until she's identified, but it's possible."

From the way he said it, Laura felt sure the search was over for the family and friends of young Terri DiFranco. She took a deep breath and got on with it. "How did she die?" Her mind was filled with visions of a body with countless stab wounds, like so many rape victims one read about.

"Strangulation."

". . . Anything else?"

"From the looks of things, he didn't torture her, just raped and strangled her."

Laura was glad crime wasn't her beat. Now, though, by accident of circumstances, it was. "Do you think she knew her attacker?"

"Difficult to say. There's evidence the attack was premeditated, but whether it was meant for her personally or she was an unlucky, random victim we don't know yet. But this may be our first break . . ."

"What do you mean?"

"Up to now we've had to carry these girls on the books as missing persons because there've been no bodies." He pointed to the handbill. "This one, Terri DiFranco, she's the latest. If the body in there proves to be her it could help break this case."

"You think there's a serial killer loose in South Philly?"

Sloan dodged it. "We don't know that."

She tried another tack. "You mentioned some evidence a minute ago. What kind?"

"The way the room is set up."

"What do you mean?"

"The room she was killed in was picked in advance and decorated like a love nest. Her body's in the center, there are damned candles all around. Weird."

"And he lured her there to rape and kill her?"

"Could be."

"Then how could you say you don't know if it's a serial killer? Girls disappear. You find the body of one of them in some sort of love nest. What else could it be?"

"Someone she knew, a boyfriend—"

"George," she said, grabbing his arm, "while I was waiting to see you I got to talking with the neighbors. One of them, an elderly lady, said she was a good friend of this girl . . . of Terri's, and she was telling me about a boyfriend, an older boyfriend named Peter. She didn't know his last name, but Terri had told her he was a cop. An undercover cop."

"We've already heard about this boyfriend from people who knew her. So far we haven't been able to locate him."

"What about him being a cop? Have you checked that out?"

"*Yes*, Laura, we're not all asleep here. We checked, and we feel sure there's no truth to him being an officer. It's common for a rapist to pose as a cop, happens all the time. That's often how they get their victims to go with them. But it usually happens quick. They see their victim, get her in the car and do it. But we know that Terri was seeing this guy for at least a month. That much we're sure of from the missing person's investigation. If he was going to do this why'd he wait a month? Doesn't sound right."

"Any ideas?"

"You asking as a reporter or a friend from our ball games?"

"Does it make such a difference?"

"It does, because now we're getting into speculation. You're new to this beat. There are some rules. It wouldn't help if you printed a bunch of speculation. Just get people stirred up, cause a lot of problems . . ."

Laura looked at the crowd behind the police line and understood what he was saying. The angry crowd could turn ugly.

"A real hot potato, right?"

"The hottest . . . otherwise why do you think I can recite chapter and verse from a bunch of missing persons reports? I've been living with these cases, just waiting for an excuse to wade in."

"I'm asking, George, as the worst left fielder you ever struck out." She even allowed herself a demure smile.

"All right, all right. I'll try to trust you. One possibility is the guy might have been trying to impress her. Say he was a security guard somewhere. They have badges, handcuffs. They know enough cop lingo to fool a teenager. It wouldn't be hard for him to pass himself off as a cop. Of course, that's just one possibility . . ."

"Meaning?"

"Enough with the Lois Lane. I've already told you too much."

Laura was looking at the building. "George, take me inside. I want to see it—"

"No, you don't. Believe me—you don't."

"I need to see it, George. How else can I write about it?"

Sloan sighed, turned to one of the other detectives. "Rafferty, let me have your bottle."

Rafferty reached inside his jacket and handed him a small bottle that he then offered to Laura. "Here, take this."

"What is it?"

"Men's cologne. When we get inside it's going to smell real bad. Hold this under your nose and sniff. It'll help. A little."

As he turned to lead her in she suddenly wasn't so gung-ho. What the hell was she doing? Her beat was rock stars and art shows and openings . . . not rape and murder. Well, she'd complained long and sometimes loud to her boss that she was tired of that stuff. So suck it in, girl, fish or cut bait, and whatever other awful mixed metaphor you can think of . . .

Sloan looked over his shoulder. She swallowed hard and followed him as he led her away from the cul-de-sac and around the building.

"Wait, I thought it happened back there," she said, pointing toward the cul-de-sac.

"It did, but I'm giving you the tour to give you the feel of the place. Atmosphere for your piece." He obviously wasn't enjoying this, even resented what he was doing, although he'd always liked her personally. They paused at the door long enough for him to say, "Whatever you do, *don't* touch anything. The fingerprint man can't do the place till they remove the body—"

And then she wasn't hearing anything. The smell overwhelmed her other senses. She would never be able to forget it, never be able to describe it, either. The death smell of a young girl . . . it seemed to coat her from head to toe like a second skin.

Sloan took out his bottle of cologne, used his handkerchief to cover his nose and mouth while he sniffed it. Laura, watching, quickly did the same. The rooms of the old depot they passed through were still filled with furniture: old-fashioned oversize desks, wooden swivel chairs, filing cabinets and a freight scale. Papers were still strewn on the desktops, and the wire in/out baskets were still full. Only the thick layer of dust, grime and cobwebs showed they were not in some sort of time warp where everyone was out to lunch.

The door and window to the freight room were both still open for maximum ventilation, but by the time they got to it the smell was overpowering, even with the cologne. The people from the medical examiner's office were coming through the open freight door now with their stretcher and body bag, but Sloan motioned for them to wait outside.

Laura looked about the room, taking in everything but the central figure of the tableau. Unlike the rest of the building, this room had been dusted and swept clean and was as Sloan had described it: candles, giving it the feel of the setting for some sort of secret rite, a ceremony; a bottle of wine; a transistor radio—that last somehow did not fit in.

Finally—how long could she avoid it?—Laura forced herself to look at the victim. The body was in deep shadows, but Laura could see she was in a kneeling position, her head resting on some blankets. She was not nude but her pants were down, her blouse pushed up and her hands fastened somehow behind her.

As she edged forward, she felt Sloan's hand on her arm, ignored it and took another step. A gleam of light from the open window cut across the body, and she saw the girl's hands were secured behind her back with handcuffs.

Another step gave her a clear view of the body, and it was all she could do not to scream. The swollen body had burst open and—

Enough.

Sloan grabbed her and quickly led her out the freight door. "Now you know why I didn't want you to see it."

"George," she said, almost afraid to breathe normally, "you've *got* to get him. He can't get away with it. My God . . ." Whoever had done this was a sickness, a virulence that had to be stamped out before it could spread.

Sloan took her arm and led her away from the depot. "I promise, we'll get him. Now go on back to the paper and I'll call you as soon as the identification is complete."

As she walked toward the crowd she was certain of one thing . . . no boyfriend could have done this, no matter how kinky he was. And no ordinary rapist, if there was such a thing.

No, this was special. Beyond the pale. Sick, yes. But evil too. And the word rang in her ears, melodramatic in most situations, the only right one for *this* . . .

CHAPTER 4

ON THE way across town to the paper Laura mentally composed her story, and when she came off the elevator at her floor she was ready to write it. She went straight to her desk, flung down her purse and began: "She Died Without Pain," was her lead.

The story came easily. In fact, in a rush, as if it had to get out. No struggling for words as when trying to justify the existence of yet another skinny, tattoo-encrusted rock-and-roll zillionaire or phony titled hustler from Dubuque who had hooked a titled European hustler living on the proceeds of tourist payments for the privilege of viewing his fallen estate. This time the words were genuine, and when she was finished she knew it was the best piece she had ever written. She just hoped the editor, Will Stuart, agreed.

She checked her messages and went to the cafeteria for a cuppa. When she returned to her desk she called Will and asked to see him, took the elevator to his office and waited while Martha—Will's tall, thin, sixtyish secretary—lit an unfiltered Camel, patted her tight curls and went in to announce her.

When she came back she touched the ruffled collar of her white blouse and said, "He's on the phone, but go in."

As they passed each other Laura could smell the familiar lavender sachet that caused Will to refer to her with affection as the "moll for the Lavender Hill mob."

"What's his mood like today?" she asked.

In a cigarette-roughened voice Martha said, "I wouldn't pay too much attention to him today. I think his hemorrhoids are acting up."

Will was still on the phone, so Laura took a moment to look around. She always liked his office. It was decorated like a men's club with lots of well-worn leather chairs and sofas scattered about. The wood furnishings, the coffee tables, the end tables and his massive desk all gleamed from the daily coat of paste wax given them by the custodial staff. The room was paneled in a dark wood, but there the resemblance to a club ended; where in a men's club the walls would be decorated with animal heads from bygone safaris, Will's walls were adorned with trophies of another kind—photos of male ballet dancers—and one he made no attempt to hide.

When he saw Laura he quickly said, "I'll get back to you later, dear," and hung up and greeted her. Will was a dapper, portly man in his mid-forties with a moon-shaped face, brown hair and a small mustache. Sleek was the word Laura always associated with him. Besides young men in ballet troupes, he listed among his other weaknesses a love of custom shirts, wide ties, suspenders and a lime cologne imported from the Caribbean, all of which were in evidence today.

"Sit, sit, darling," he said, waving Laura to a wing chair in front of his desk. "How are you? You feeling all right?" Asked in a conspiratorial tone.

"Fine, Will, just fine." She appreciated his concern, but also wished she had never had to let him know about the operation. At least he didn't know about the nightmares . . .

"Good, so what can I do for you?"

She told him about her morning. ". . . And I'd like to get off features for a couple of weeks to follow up on it. Less time, of course, if the killer is caught quickly."

"Laura, I won't mince words with you—no pun intended. The answer is *no*."

Before she could protest he began the underline: "I pay you a fair stipend to hobnob with the swells, and what do you try to sell me—mean streets, that's what you're trying to sell me, but I'm not buying. Lord, I already *know* about mean streets. *Everybody* knows about mean streets. No news down there. Whatever has possessed you?"

"It happened in my neighborhood, Will. I heard the sirens and got curious—"

Now out of his chair, he began pacing. "Laura, if I want stories about a little neighborhood tease whose boyfriend killed her because she wouldn't put out, I've got two ex-cops with brewer's droop I can send forth. But ask me if I can send them over to the Palace Hotel to interview Prince Ranier or Mick Jagger, just *ask* me."

Laura took a deep breath. "All right, I'm asking you, Will." And now a touch of anger had edged into her voice. "And you're not being fair. This was no neighborhood tease. This was a kid who kept old people company after school. I've tried to get you on this before . . . teenage girls are disappearing in South Philly. As soon as the identification is complete you're going to see she was the latest. Will, for Christ sake, she was raped and murdered. And I'm betting they're going to find the same thing happened to the others. This is big. George Sloan and Seven Squad are on it. There's a serial killer loose in South Philly . . ."

He sat back and seemed to be reconsidering. "You say George Sloan's on the case . . . ? Well, doesn't signify." Pointing to a framed photograph of Glen Caruthers, the billionaire who owned the *Globe,* he said, "Laura, you know our policy here. We leave the national and international stuff to the *Inquirer,* the local to the *Daily News,* and *we* stick to human interest. The kind that titillates, not upsets. And, I might add, we've done very damn well following that policy."

"But this is human interest—"

"Yes, but not the right kind. If they were rich kids from Bryn Mawr, fine. But not teenagers from *your* neighborhood. Besides, I read that story on the weekend and I'm not sold that the disappearances are related."

"But we *did* get scooped. Don't we care about that? Remember, I was the first one to pitch the story to you . . . By the way, what's so wrong with my neighborhood?"

"What's wrong is you're in it. You insist on living down at the docks like you were into rough trade. You could have a place in Society Hill, or a condo on Rittenhouse Square, or a carriage house on the Main Line. But you insist on living down there. Beats me why."

He flopped in his chair and swiveled until his back was to her. "Laura, sometimes you make me feel just like your mother. After I go to all the trouble of getting you all dolled up, you go out and roll in the dirt."

She shook her head. He knew exactly how to get to her. What he was reminding her about was that his was the lone voice speaking up for her when Caruthers' legal eagles wanted her fired as a "potential corporate liability" on account of her operation. Indeed, when the agreement was over, not only did she still have her job but she had her leave of absence, too.

And during those awful months after the operation Will was her best friend, no question. At her blackest moment he appeared on her doorstep bearing a white Afghan he had crocheted for her bed, then came back more than a few times with tea and sympathy. He always had the filthiest joke imaginable for her, or a shoulder to cry on. She owed him, no question. All he had to do was ask—any time, any place. Except now. These "missing" girls, plus the murdered Terri, took precedence, at least temporarily.

"Will, you're not fooling me with all this smoke about what *we* do and what *they* do."

There was a moment's hesitation, and then with his back still to her, "You're a smart lady, I always say that. What I want you to do is a little digging and then give me a piece on a man named Felix Ducroit. I need it ASAP, by Halloween at the latest. That's the last day of October, if memory serves."

"Felix Ducroit?"

"A real estate developer—"

"I know who he is, but why?"

"I've gotten some calls from people who are very interested in Mr. Ducroit."

"What about the girls?"

"Laura, sorry, but right now this is more important to me."

"Will, I've met Felix Ducroit. I can't imagine he's more important than the lives, and deaths, of these girls. But I'll make a deal with you. Let me follow up on the girls and I'll do the other for you, too."

Will swiveled around to face her.

"What gets priority?"

She knew what the answer had to be or there would be no deal.

"Felix Ducroit."

"And remember one thing when you write it. I want no mention of a serial killer. I want this treated like an isolated incident. People start to panic at the mention of serial killers, and neither I nor our revered owner wants to be responsible for that."

* * *

Sloan, feeling just a bit like Hill Street Blues, called the meeting of Seven Squad to order. The room was thick with stale smoke, and the detectives slumped behind metal desks looked as tired as they felt from their morning at the old depot.

"All right," said Sloan, head so stuffy that his voice sounded in his ears as if from a tunnel. "Let's go over what we've got."

He glanced at the file on the desk in front of him. "The lab work's not in yet. Evans, where is it?"

Evans, a stocky man whose tie fell short of his belt by a good six inches, said, "Like you told me, I took it to Wakefield and Pollack. It won't be ready for a couple more hours."

On account of a heavy weekend of crime the police lab was jammed, and he'd okayed that Terri's specimens be sent to a private group, Wakefield and Pollack. They were the best. No problem there.

"Each of you has copies of the rest of the stuff. The remains have been ID'd. The deceased is Terri DiFranco, one of the missing girls. I'm betting we've got a serial killer here and that this Peter is our man. In addition to the deceased, we know from missing persons Peter's name was linked with at least two other of the missing girls. From what they could turn up, he courts them a while, then one bad night they just disappear."

An officer raised her hand.

"Kane, what is it?"

"We haven't found a trace of any of the other girls. Why do you think he broke the pattern with this one?"

"I don't know. Maybe for once he did something spontaneous instead of premeditated."

A boyish detective with curly hair and glasses asked, "What about the other bodies?"

"Right now, Spivak, I don't know, but it doesn't surprise me we haven't found them. There are lots of places . . . hell, ten blocks of Fifth Street is deserted, so is a lot of Seventh. They could be stacked, buried, bricked up, in any of those old houses. We've searched some of them but we've got to do more. There's also both rivers. There's North Philly. You could lose a damn army there. And of course, let's don't forget Jersey and the pine barrens. So I don't know. I'm not too worried about that right now, though. We've got a body, people. Finally. We've got a murder-one charge. Now we need to find Peter and pin it where it belongs. I'm sure you follow." He looked down at the file again. "We have a description here but it's all third hand. Nobody seems actually to have ever seen Peter. Just hearsay stuff . . . dark hair, beard, tinted glasses, leather jacket. Could be half the buddy boys in town. It also might be a disguise, of course. Guy could be bald as yours truly. Evans, check out the costumers on Walnut, get names of people buying wigs and beards. Two other things, though. He drives a silver-gray sports car. No make or model—yet. And he tells the girls he's an undercover cop."

"Don't they all," said Rafferty, digging at his nails.

"He's been perfect up till now, but it appears he may have made a little mistake." Sloan held up a black matchbook with the word "Lagniappe" in gold on the cover. "We found this in the purse of the deceased. It's from Lagniappe, the restaurant in Society Hill. Fancy place. Rock stars, sports figures, politicians, artists, you know what I mean. Not exactly the kind of place you'd find a teenager from South Philly in. She had a pack of Marlboros in her purse. Two cigarettes missing, and no other matches. According to her parents she did smoke but they wouldn't let her do it at home. So a possible scenario—she kept the matches when our man gave them to her to light a cigarette. Maybe she lit one for each of them."

"That seems thin to me. She could have gotten them any number of places," said Spivak.

"You're right on, Spivak. It's the old thing about the bottle being half-empty or half-full. I'm choosing to think of it as half-full. This is the first lead of *any* substance we've had on this guy. We're going to follow it up *all the way to the end*. I want you and Kane"—he nodded at the female detective—"to hang around Lagniappe. Get known as customers. See what you can come up with."

"On expense account?" said Kane.

Sloan ignored it.

"What about me and Rafferty?" said Evans. "That's a gravy

assignment. You'd think a couple of vets could get in out of the rain once in a while."

Sloan allowed a smile. "With the faces on you two, they wouldn't let you in the door. Besides, Evans, your wife would skin me if I sent you into a dangerous situation like that."

"Dangerous?"

"To you, genius," growled Rafferty. "He's right. Agnes would kill you if she found out you were hanging around a slop chute like that without her. Case or no case."

Sloan let the banter run its course, then brought them back to business. "I'm sure I don't have to tell you," he said to Spivak and Kane, "don't tip you hand. The last thing we want is to get our man in motion before we're ready."

"Anything more about the place we ought to know?" asked Spivak.

"I asked around before the meeting," Sloane said. "It's not exactly my turf. No drugs or hookers. A reputable establishment for the rich, the famous, and the upward-mobiles. There is one thing, though. Couple of years ago one of the waitresses accused the owner of trying to rape her. The complaint didn't get anywhere because it turned out the owner"—he paused and looked at the file—"Justin Fortier's his name, had just fired her for stealing. Probably means nothing, but check it out. It's at least a place to start."

CHAPTER 5

MISSY GLANCED down at her gold-and-diamond Piaget wristwatch with some annoyance as Felix Ducroit stopped the car across from the Rothstein Medical Tower at Seventeenth and Pine. Quarter past ten. She'd be late for work, and her first morning back. Never mind, Felix was more important . . .

The man really was something the doctor ordered, especially after the humiliation Carl had handed her at Lagniappe with that sickening-sweet society reporter who was going to fix up his wonderful career for him. Jesus, and after all she'd done for him . . . Well, bye-bye, Carl; hello-hello, Felix. She rested her hand on his thigh, looked up at him, waiting for a reaction. She felt edgy, strongly drawn to this man and also resentful of him. He was nice, no question, had listened to her the way Carl had never bothered to do, or been able to do, when they sat around her place after leaving Lagniappe. She found herself talking about her father to him, letting her feelings out more than she had with anybody, ever, and she'd just met him, for God's sake. Maybe that was what made it easier, that he was a stranger. But he also seemed to bring down her guard, and at the same time she welcomed that, it also made her feel uneasy, wondering if she could trust him. The ways she'd so often felt with her father—though that last thought never surfaced, only had its effect on her emotions, mixing them.

She was impressed that he hadn't tried to bed her, but curious . . . more than curious . . . annoyed that he didn't. Not even a move or gesture. And it was the same thing now, sitting here in the car . . . She moved her hand up his thigh, just grazing his cock, felt it respond. Well, he's at least all there in that department, she thought. He was also, no question, wonderfully handsome, all bearded and stern-looking. She felt much better. In control again.

"See you tonight?" It was more a request than a question, and without waiting for any answer she took her hand from his cock, leaned over and brushed her lips lightly on his cheek, quickly

got out of the car, waving with her back to him as she proceeded into the medical building.

Missy Wakefield was smiling to herself as she got on the elevator and rode it to the tenth floor offices of Wakefield and Pollack, urologists specializing in male sterility and sexual
dysfunction.

Kate, the red-haired receptionist, looked up from her work
and smiled nervously as Missy pushed open the glass double
door. "Welcome back."

"Thanks." Missy glanced around the waiting room. While
most of the doctors were still making rounds at the hospital the
place had filled with patients. She recognized several of the
faces; others, the nervous ones accompanied by their wives,
were new patients. But what especially caught her eye, today
even more than when he was alive, was the oil painting of her
father. His stern face seemed to command respect and obe-
dience even now.

She went behind the receptionist's desk and looked over
Kate's shoulder to check out the appointment book. Three
names immediately stood out, each there for his final consulta-
tion before entering the hospital in the afternoon. One was an
aging Hollywood sex symbol, a former crooner whose lifelong
battle with drugs and the bottle had caused permanent nerve
damage. He was there for a surgical implant, a miniature
hydraulic system. After the implant he would be able to sum-
mon an erection, just press the small bulb in his scrotum and it
would pump air into the system and, presto, an erection. Nerve
damage would prevent an orgasm, but he would be able to
maintain his old reputation as a stud of studs. God, what vanity,
she thought. Cocksman of the world using a device to get it up.
Well, and she couldn't help smiling, *modern science can be wonderful,* she thought. *And nobody the wiser . . .*

The second name belonged to a gay British rock star whose
sexual behavior was notoriously compulsive. His psychiatrist
had prescribed a small battery pack similar to a pacemaker
implanted in his lower abdomen; when matters got out of control, it would allow him to administer a mild shock to his genitals to cool himself down.

The third was a Middle Eastern oil nabob who had contracted a case of genital warts from one of his numerous wives. It was rumored that he had had her hacked to death and her parts then spread across the desert.

Pointing to them, she said to Kate, "I assume you had them brought in by the private entrance."

"That's right. The office limo has been busy all morning going back and forth to the airport to pick them up."

"They're back in the examining rooms now?"

"Right."

A pause, during which Kate was waiting for her to begin some girl talk, to share confidences of the past month. It didn't come. It was enough that Missy knew Kate was sleeping with one of the younger physicians in the practice and didn't fire her. No reason, she figured, for them to start sharing picnic lunches and lipstick.

Walking to the linen closet, she thought about how different it was going to be here without her father. The practice had been like an oasis . . . in her mind their Tara—he the master, she the mistress. He'd wanted her to be a doctor, something she couldn't possibly do . . . it meant putting herself on the same level with him, exactly what she *didn't* want, couldn't and didn't presume to. Besides, it wasn't medicine she cared about, it was him, being near and pleasing him. He, of course, never understood her resistance, and she had never been able to repress it.

She wanted them to be a team, to work side by side, which was why she became a nurse and ran the administrative functions of the practice. Yes, here they were a team, father and daughter . . .

In the linen closet was a stack of her father's lab coats, the name "Wakefield" embroidered in red over the left pocket. She traced the name with her fingertips, then on impulse put it on, turned up the collar and turned to look at herself in the mirror on the back of the door. How long had it been since she'd worn anything of his? Twelve years ago. She had just turned sixteen, and as a birthday present he had taken her to their cabin in the Poconos for a fishing trip. The first day a rainstorm had come up and he'd given her his jacket. What a special feeling that had been, walking back to the cabin all bundled up, his arms around her . . . She thought now of wearing the lab coat, in his memory, but quickly rejected the notion, feeling guilty even considering it. He would never have allowed it . . . nothing like that sort of intimacy had been possible after that trip . . .

What had happened, she'd told herself again and again over the years, was not her fault. It was that damn Roy Curtis; the seventeen-year-old son of the banker who owned the next cabin. He'd made it happen and she got the blame.

She only wanted to go fishing with her father, be with him. But everywhere she turned there was Roy, a pup in heat. Actually she'd willingly lost her virginity three years earlier to a twenty-seven-year-old cowboy on a Montana dude ranch and wasn't much interested in sex. Horses and being with her father took precedence. Roy, though, wouldn't back off or even be discouraged. He buzzed around her as though he was a fly and she a honeypot. Finally, to get him off her back by her getting on it, she gave in.

It happened in the boathouse, and Roy was as inept as she knew he would be. She was doing her best to move with him, help him finish and get him off her when she idly glanced at the window to see her father's face. Their eyes met and held as Roy pumped away on her. She wanted to die, would have welcomed that as an out. And by the time her father turned away she was ill from the terror building in her. When she was finally able to push Roy off and run outside, her father was gone. In more ways than one.

Hours later, when she gave up hiding and slunk back to the cabin, he was sitting there. The car was packed. Not a word was spoken. She huddled in her corner of the front seat the whole trip, cold and sick. If only he'd wrap her up in his old fishing jacket and tell her that it was all right, that he forgave her. But of course he didn't. Didn't even look at her, didn't speak . . .

In the twelve years since that day, no matter what she did, he had not forgiven her. She took off the lab coat, folded it carefully and put it back on the stack with the others. Before she could take a fresh nurse's uniform from the stack the door to the linen closet opened and one of the secretaries stuck her head in.

"There you are. Dr. Pollack would like to see you before you change."

"I'll be right there," Missy said.

Nathan Pollack, her father's partner, was not alone in his office. Waiting with him was his wife Beverly, whose stare was frigid. In Missy's view God had never created a more repellent couple than the Pollacks. Why her father had chosen him as a partner was beyond her. As a couple the Pollacks reminded her of Laurel and Hardy, minus the humor. Nathan Pollack was the straight. She had never heard anyone, including her father, call him "Nate." He was a small man who wore glasses with the kind of mock aviator frames favored by men who carried pockets full of pencils, a man who wore T-shirts under his Izod on the golf course. For Nathan Pollack a spontaneous act was to drive his black BMW into town without an umbrella on the back seat. But Nathan was a regular peach compared to Beverly, who offended Missy's sensibilities with her abundance of facial hair, two hundred and counting pounds and smothering breasts.

Nathan rose from behind his desk and indicated a chair for Missy as though he was trying to sell it to her.

"Sit, sit, please."

His voice sounded shaky. She wondered why.

He sat back down. "Let me say again—and I'm sure I speak for everyone in the practice, especially Beverly and myself—how sad we are about Cyrus."

She instantly resented his using her father's first name, reserved for a few close friends. Nathan might have been a partner but never a friend or confidant.

"I hope the time off helped some."

"Yes," she said, holding back to keep from saying it didn't help to see his wife bulling her way through the buffet with a crab claw in one hand and enough food to feed Philly's homeless in the other.

"Good . . . well, to bring you up to date, while you were gone we have made a few changes—"

"What *sort* of changes?"

"As you know, your father was a brilliant physician—"

"Yes, I know. Can we cut to the chase, Nathan?"

"I beg your pardon."

"Sorry, just some jargon I picked up."

"Yes . . . well, as I was about to say, without your father the practice will undoubtedly suffer. And to avoid future financial problems, we dismissed four of the girls in the office."

This was what he was so tentative about. When her father was alive he generated enough work for at least four girls; without him there was no need to keep them. It made sense but the way they did it bothered her. She had little doubt firing them while she was away was Beverly's idea.

"If I remember correctly, you only own twenty-five percent of the practice," she said.

"Not anymore. When your father died I bought out his share of the practice."

"What? That doesn't make sense—"

"I would have thought you knew we had a buy-out agreement. Whichever one died first, the other bought his share."

His tone was the same pseudo-compassionate one he used in telling testicular cancer patients that their balls had to come off. His bad-news voice. It made her sick.

"Tell me all about it," she said, trying to sound calm.

"It's simple. We had an agreement and insurance policies. When Cyrus died the insurance company paid your mother two and a half million dollars, and she signed over to me your father's stock in the practice."

"What about the other assets, the property?"

"Your townhouse and car went to your mother. All according to the agreement. The rest—the cabin, the house at the shore, the condo in St. Martin—stays with the practice."

"And you own it all—"

"Which brings me to my next point." Oh, he was loving this. The *segundo* now *numero uno*. "In the interest of cash flow, our accountant has recommended that Beverly take over running the office and you be in charge of the lab."

"The lab?"

"You're a registered nurse. It will work out fine . . . And now I'm afraid we're going to have to cut this short. This morning the police brought in sperm samples from the body of one of those missing South Philly girls. They need the test in a rush."

Missy shook her head. "Let them wait. I want to hear the rest of this."

"If you wish. As I mentioned, you'll be in charge of the lab, including the employees who work there and the work done there, subject, of course, to our supervision. With the way the business is growing from our outside work and our city contract I'm sure in a short time you'll pass your old salary."

"Pass my *old* salary? What do you mean by that?"

"I'm afraid your present salary of a thousand a week, along with the benefits your father gave you, no longer justifies itself. But as the lab business grows we will increase your salary until you're back up there and beyond."

"And what is my new salary?"

"We feel twenty-two thousand would be more in keeping with the job. Naturally, as a stockholder you'll also be entitled to any bonuses or shareholder salary increases."

There but for one word they would have had her. "Shareholder." Nathan didn't get all the stock with his buy-out. He only got her father's shares. With his original twenty-five percent, plus her father's sixty-five percent, there was still ten percent unaccounted for—the ten percent her father had given to her. Don't panic, live to fight another day. She forced a smile. "I guess I'd better get to work."

She could see they were disappointed in her reaction. Good, that's how she wanted them. She did not go back to the linen closet for a nurse's uniform. Those days were over. Instead, she went straight to the lab.

The technicians looked up when she walked in. Nobody seemed surprised at her demotion, and while she was gone they had moved her things from her office to a corner desk with two windows. Maybe it wouldn't be so bad to spend more time here. Lab work had always been her favorite part of the practice anyway . . .

"Are you okay?"

Looking up she saw Gladys, one of the technicians, standing in front of her desk.

"Of course." And then, changing the subject, "what's happening on that police work Nathan mentioned?"

"The sperm sample from the dead girl, one of the teenagers missing from South Philly?"

"Could be," said Missy.

"Terri DiFranco's her name. They're all done, but Dr. Pollack wants to sign the report himself in case the police should need his testimony."

Of course, anything to get his name in the paper, she thought but did not say. "What else do we have, Grace?"

"There's a patient in number two examining room. Dr. Pollack wants you to see him."

The patient, dressed in work clothes and boots, was reading a copy of the morning edition of the *Globe* A lunchbox and hardhat were next to him on the examining table. His chart said that his name was Roland Morris and that he was there for a sperm count.

When he looked up from his newspaper uneasiness and surprise crossed his face. She was accustomed to dealing with patients embarrassed at dealing with a woman. She introduced herself and said, "Mr. Morris, your chart says that you're here for a sperm count. Do you have a sample of your semen?"

"Uh, yeah, sure."

He opened his lunchbox and brought out a small jar that contained about a teaspoonful of white liquid. The substantial volume was a possible but not certain indicator of a low sperm count. She held up the jar to the light and noted that the contents were separating.

"Mr. Morris, when did you do this?"

"Last night . . . just before I went to bed."

"And where did you keep the jar last night?"

"In the refrigerator. The lady I spoke to said it would be all right."

She didn't ask which lady. That was no longer her job, at least for a while. Instead, she went across the small examining room and took a fresh vial from beside the sink.

"I'm afraid we're going to need another sample."

"You mean right *now*?"

"I'm afraid so. For us to do an accurate test we need a fresh sample, not more than an hour old, and one that's been kept warm not cold. It's kind of like hatching eggs. Everything's got to be warm or it doesn't work."

"Where do you want me to do it?" he said, the sound of Waterloo in his voice.

"Right here. I'll leave the room and when you're finished just bring it back to the lab. I'll do the work and Dr."—she looked down at the chart that listed the name of one of the younger physicians—"Dr. Baker will give you the results."

Walking back to the lab with the old sample in her hand, she was tempted to take the fresh one and smear it on the toilet seat just before Beverly used it, then listen to her try to explain a black baby to Nathan.

While she waited for her patient she called her mother. Careful not to say too much with people around, she merely asked if she could come out for a drink in the evening. Her mother said, "Yes, of course," but there was a moment of hesitation, as if she were going to have to rearrange some plans to accommodate her.

Next, she called Felix, reaching him at his construction site. She told him that she had to see her mother early in the evening, but would he come over for a drink later, around midnight? He agreed, although he seemed a bit distant. Must be because he was on the job, she decided . . .

Some ten minutes later her patient was back in the lab with a fresh sample. She sent him back to the waiting room and got to work.

She was humming as she poured the fresh sperm into a small graduated cylinder to measure its volume in cc's, then checked the pH balance to determine if it was acidic or alkaline. It was mildly alkaline. Next she placed a drop on a slide and checked the motility of the sperm under the microscope. Noting that approximately seventy percent were active, she turned her attention to the morphology, the shape of the sperms, which gave the configuration of the heads. Sperm with small heads, pinheads as the technicians called them, tended to be too weak to fertilize an egg. Not the case here. She skipped the vicosity test, feeling sure it would properly liquify in an hour but not wanting to spend the time. Then she diluted the sample with five grams of sodium carbonate, one milliliter of Formalin and enough distilled water to bring the liquid to a volume of one hundred cc's, inactivating the sperm so that they could be counted. The count came to slightly over eighty million, which was on the low-normal side. Coupled with the mild alkaline quality, this could explain the family's conception problem. If they were lucky, all that would be necessary for the wife to get pregnant would be to douche with a mild solution of baking soda and water before intercourse.

Missy was just finishing the report when her phone rang. It was Kate, the receptionist: "There are two policemen out here about some lab work."

"Oh? Well, have them wait a moment," and she sent Gladys out to bring them back to the lab.

Both men were in plainclothes—one balding, the other stocky. The balding one introduced himself as Lieutenant Sloan, and the stocky one as Detective Evans.

"What can I do for you, gentlemen?"

"We're here for the lab work on Terri DiFranco. We called and were told it was ready," Sloan said.

"Gladys, has Dr. Pollack signed that report yet?"

"Yes, here it is."

Sloan nearly tore it from her grasp in his hurry to see the results. When he saw them a look of disappointment crossed his face.

"What you hoped for?" said Missy.

"Not by a long shot," replied Sloan.

CHAPTER 6

L AURA COULD not get the sight of that girl's body off her mind long enough even to begin work on the piece about Felix Ducroit. All she could think about was the deserted depot and the room with its candle-encircled pallet. And what went through the girl's mind when Peter's hands closed around her throat.

She looked at herself in the mirror, her blue eyes red-rimmed. "You look a mess, like you've been on a three-day drunk," she said aloud to her image. She went back to her desk, the sights and sounds of the newsroom all around her but far away.

Up to the moment she asked Sloan to show her the body, her interest in the missing girls had been professional. A chance for a good story. Afterward it became personal. She felt the pain, the fear of death. It wasn't difficult for her; if anything it was too easy. The breast cancer and the operation had seen to that. She knew, she understood . . . She and the girl, she felt they were drawn together by common secrets. She shook her head, trying to clear away the thought. *Be careful,* she told herself. *You won't do anybody any good getting morbid about this. The girl is dead, you survived. Remember that little detail . . .*

The jangle of her phone brought her back to the press of the immediate. She looked at her watch. Realistically she couldn't expect to hear from Sloan for some time yet . . . who knew how many details had to be worked out before he was ready to talk to the press. Until then, there was her bargain with Will Stuart— first deliver the piece on Felix Ducroit; then go for the Terri story.

She made some calls—first to Justin and Lois Fortier at Lagniappe, and to Carl Laredo, the artist. Talking with them, she was reminded of the evening they'd spent together, about how Felix Ducroit with his grace and graciousness had saved the day, or night, by taking a raving Missy Wakefield off their hands. No doubt Felix had his own reasons for doing it . . . whatever variety of bitch Missy Wakefield might be, she fairly poured sex appeal. Damn her . . .

As it turned out, Carl wasn't able to help much. Neither was Lois, except to remind her that Cynthia Ducroit, owner of the Pine Street Charcuterie, was his ex-wife. Justin was a different story. He and Felix had been boyhood friends, went back as far as either could remember. Tales of playing cowboys and Indians and how Felix always wore a black hat and he always wore a red one and of a wooden horse Felix's father had made for them from a sawhorse and a barrel were charming but not much help. Still, she was personally taken by the image of these two very adult and handsome men as children, Felix so dark, Justin so blond.

All Justin's tales were about a carefree Felix, a quality hardly evident at Lagniappe the night they'd met. He had been so quiet, apparently deep in thought. She found herself speculating on what was on his mind, what was bothering him. More than that, his preoccupied air attracted her. No surprise . . . brooding men often affected her that way. "Too much *Wuthering Heights* as a child," she would tell those who noticed and asked about it.

After she finished talking with the Fortiers she called Cynthia and made a lunch date. The two were casual friends, had been ever since Laura had done a piece on female-owned businesses in Philadelphia—which was when she had originally heard the name Felix Ducroit . . .

When Sloan finally called, she had just finished talking to a fellow reporter from the New Orleans *Times-Picayune* who assured her that she would send on anything they had on Felix Ducroit. Sloan was calling from police headquarters, the "Roundhouse," as it was called, and told her to meet him at the Liberty Bell in twenty minutes. She grabbed her coat and was on her way.

She parked in the underground garage on Fifth Street across from KYW television and the Bourse shopping complex, then proceeded across Independence Mall in the chilly drizzle.

The Liberty Bell was housed in a small brick, metal and glass building shaped like a paper airplane. She went inside and while she waited for Sloan, half-listened as a park ranger explained to a high-school class that the crack in the bell was not what was important. Pay attention, he said, to the words about liberty engraved near the top and think about what they meant to all the different groups in America throughout its history. The kids were in good spirits, and neither the drizzle outside nor the lecture inside had dampened their real enthusiasm—it was a day off from school. Watching them, so full of youthful piss and vinegar, she couldn't help think about one of the missing—a young girl whose body had been moldering in an old depot in South Philly.

Her thoughts must have shown in her face, because the first thing Sloan said when he arrived was, "What's wrong?"

"Nothing. I was just thinking about the girl . . . Terri DiFranco, wasn't it?"

"Come on, let's walk," he said, taking her arm. Then as an afterthought, "You don't mind, do you? I mean with the drizzle and all."

"I don't mind. You're the one with the flu."

Outside he stopped long enough to turn up the collar of his single-breasted London Fog, but Laura noted he was still hatless, rather unusual for a man with so little hair.

Sloan didn't seem in a hurry to talk about the murder. Instead, as they strolled among the rows of park benches still at least half-filled with people, he said, "It takes more than a little rain to drive them out of this park. You know, if you come here anytime, day or night, unless there's two feet of snow, you'll nearly always find people here. I've never been able to figure out what makes this park different from the others in Center City." When Laura didn't reply he chattered on, "Once, too damn many years ago, I met a girl at closing time at Doc Watson's and convinced her to go to one of the Greek places around the corner for breakfast. Afterward we came down here, you know, to be alone, and at four in the morning there wasn't a single empty bench in the whole park."

Laura kept staring out toward Independence Hall, the tower hazy in the mist and drizzle.

"Anyway . . . getting to what you're waiting to hear, we've pretty well wrapped up the first stage of the work on the girl." He hesitated for a moment, then said, "The parents just left before I called you. The ID's positive. It's Terri DiFranco."

"My God, the shape her body's in. How could you put them through *that*?"

"We didn't. We first took the clothes around and her mother recognized them. Then we got the name of the family dentist from her, borrowed the kid's records and ID'd from them. But when we went back to the parents—she'd called the husband and he'd come home from work by then—*they* insisted on seeing the body. I tried to talk them out of it. It was no-go. They insisted."

"How did they take it?" Stupid question, she realized, as soon as it was out of her mouth.

"Bad. So if you can do your story without seeing them, at least for a couple of days . . ."

"What were they like?"

"What were they like—parents, what else?" A touch of anger was in his voice, and she realized with some force that she wasn't alone in the way that day had affected her, that even someone in Sloan's business needed to compartmentalize, to get at arm's length from something like this or he couldn't function, either.

He began again. "She—Terri—was the oldest, with a younger brother. Her parents are South Philly born and bred. They live on Second and Morris. The father's a longshoreman, the mother works as a checkout clerk a couple of days a week at the Pathmark on Oregon Avenue. They're in their thirties, I'd say, Catholics who no doubt go to mass every Sunday at Sacred Heart. The mother is pretty: very Italian-looking but still trim with dark hair cut short. The father's got dark hair, too, except it's like mine, about all gone."

He paused, then: "You don't have any kids, do you?"

"No, I'm not married." What had made him ask that?

"Me neither . . . I guess to really understand this, what they're going through, you have to be a parent."

They walked for a few minutes in silence. The drizzle now turned to light rain, but the park benches, as Sloan had said, remained at least half full. The only ones going for shelter seemed to be the tourists.

Finally Laura broke the silence. "What did you tell them happened to her?"

"The truth, that the autopsy showed she died from strangulation, and that she'd been raped."

"Considering the condition of her body . . . I mean, how could you tell for sure about the rape?"

"There were still traces of sperm."

Sperm, such an antiseptic word, Laura thought. It conveyed nothing of the violence that was done to her.

"Also, for whatever it's worth, mostly to the parents, I guess, she was a virgin."

"That's so damn sad, whether you're a parent or not. Maybe you have to be a woman to understand . . . What about fingerprints?"

"Only the victim's."

"So you still have no leads to the killer—"

"I didn't say that." Defensively.

"Well, what do you have?"

Sloan pulled his coat tighter around him. He'd already told her more than he probably should have, but she seemed a straight lady; he liked her . . . oh, he didn't have any illusions about anything happening between them (or did he?) . . . and sometimes it helped to have somebody besides the folks at the shop to bounce things off of. He didn't have anybody like that, no wife, no kids, so the hell with it, he was only human . . .

"Okay, Laura, it goes like this, and I have your word you won't print anything unless I give you the go-ahead. What we have here is sort of the normal procedure in reverse. I mean, in a case like this the two things that help get a conviction are sperm and pubic hair. I said 'get a conviction,' not catch the suspect. Once we have a suspect in custody sperm and pubic hair can yield important pieces of evidence. In this case we have some evidence from them but no damn suspect. But hey, you take what you get and hope to match it up with the guy when we nail him."

"So what have you got?"

"Well, first of all we checked the sperm for V.D. and found none. Our boy is clean—"

"How nice for him."

"Yeah . . . well, you asked for what we had and I'm trying to tell you. I can always spare you the boring details—"

"I'm sorry, Sloan, please . . ."

"Yes, well, the next thing we did was check for blood type. The ABH factors in the blood determine blood type—A, B, O, AB, positive or negative. Mine's A positive." He felt sort of foolish telling her that. Was that the best he could do to make a connection?

"Mine's O." She even smiled. Things were really heating up.

"That's the most common," Sloan said. "Now it gets a little more complicated. In about eighty percent of the population these ABH factors are water soluble. That means they turn up in every other body fluid as well as in blood. So we can get blood type from sperm, urine, saliva, even tears. People with water-soluble ABH are the 'secretors.' In the other twenty percent the ABH factors aren't water soluble and can only be found in actual blood, which is the only fluid that yields up the blood type. People in that twenty percent are 'non-secretors.' The lab tested the sperm found in Terri for ABH factors and first found out whether our boy was a secretor or a non-secretor, whether he was in the eighty or the twenty percent."

"And . . . ?"

"Off the record, your absolute word on it?"

"Come on, Sloan, I already gave you that. But if you need it again, absolutely off the record until you give the word."

"He's a secretor."

Laura thrust her hands deeper into her trenchcoat pockets. "So he's one of your eighty percent. That's a lot of territory. I guess you'd have preferred he be a non-secretor."

"At first when I got the results I reacted that way. But it's a mixed deal. Sure, if he'd been one of the twenty percent it would have theoretically narrowed the field by plenty. But we would also have had to stop the testing right there. We'd have needed his blood to get the blood type. The semen wouldn't have told us anything. As it was, we could test for the type and get it. So we've got two pieces of important information—he's a secretor and we know his blood type from the semen. Any suspect we bring in, the first thing we do is give him a saliva test, easier than the sperm and just as good. We're testing similar liquids. He's got to match up with the finding from the sperm in Terri. If he does, it's a strong—not conclusive, but strong—piece of evidence against him. Probably more important, if he doesn't match up, he's scientifically eliminated and in the clear. It can help to know who *isn't* guilty, too."

"I feel like I just had a session in the crime lab. Please, there I go again, sounding smart-ass. It's helpful, very helpful to me. But what's the killer's blood type? You didn't say."

"That I won't tell you."

They were crossing Chestnut Street, where horse-drawn carriages were pulled up, and continued on toward Independence Hall.

"You mentioned pubic hair. What can you tell from that?" Laura asked.

"Theoretically a lot. Aside from hair color, sometimes you can tell sex and race from it, but it's not always reliable." He was warming up. "Take for instance the Jeffrey MacDonald case— you remember, the Green Beret captain convicted of killing his family. The prosecution identified a strand of hair taken from MacDonald's sweatshirt as belonging to him. Later it was proved that it wasn't from him at all but from their *pony*."

"Sure doesn't sound too reliable, but the way you mentioned it earlier I get the feeling you were putting some importance on it."

"Well, there's an interesting angle to it here."

"Tell me."

"Still off the record . . . we didn't find any. Not one damn pubic hair."

"And that's unusual?"

"Very. It's almost impossible to have sex without leaving a few around. And a rape creates even more action, almost sure to dislodge at least a few hairs."

"Maybe the killer shaves himself."

Sloan stopped, took out a handkerchief and wiped his face.

"Maybe this walk wasn't such a good idea after all. I'm starting to feel a little worse. Mind if we head back toward Race Street?"

"Sure, fine." Obviously he'd given her as much as he felt he could. *Don't push too hard,* she told herself. As they turned and began to retrace their steps, Laura said, "What about the crime scene, and that awful stuff he used . . . the chain around her neck, and the handcuffs?"

"A sticky area."

"Meaning?"

"Look, Laura, I can't stop you from writing about the handcuffs and the punk necklaces, but if you do, you bring up images, perverted and weirdly romantic images that in a town this size would almost certainly provoke copycat attacks, something none of us needs.

"I understand that's a possibility, but maybe you better spell it out."

"Simple. I'd like you to use real discretion in your article. Except for the two kids who found the body you're the only person outside of the cops who was at the scene, saw these things. It's okay to say she was bound and strangled, but please don't turn it into a fashion show. It could wreck an important part of our case as well as put others at risk."

"From copycats."

"Right."

"Okay, no handcuffs or necklaces. But have you been able to turn up anything on them?"

"We're checking shops around town to see if anyone remembers anybody buying them but we aren't holding our breath . . . they're common enough items. The parents didn't recognize the necklace, and of course they didn't know anything about the cuffs. We're assuming the killer had them with him. He probably gave the necklace to her as a present. That way he got it around her neck in advance."

"That sounds like you've decided she knew him," said Laura.

"Well, when we went over the place we didn't find the killer's fingerprints, which didn't surprise us, but we found *hers* all over the place—the walls, the doors, everywhere—so we had her parents look at the radio. It belonged to Terri."

This was a three-sixty turnabout.

"Wait a minute, I'm not following you . . ."

"I'm saying it looks like the place was Terri's idea, along with the lovenest and the candles. *Not* the killer's. And that may explain why the body turned up this time."

"This time? Then you do think it's connected to the other disappearances; not just a case of a boyfriend, uncle or neighbor," she said, quoting from an earlier lecture from Will Stuart.

"Right now we're looking for a dark-haired man with a beard who wears tinted glasses and answers to the name of Peter. As you know, he *was* reportedly Terri's boyfriend. He was also reportedly the boyfriend of at least two of the other missing girls. Of course, the beard and the glasses could be a disguise. He could be a blond, or he could be clean shaven. We don't know yet. But we are going on what we have until we know different."

"It *is* a serial killer," said Laura, remembering he'd said this Peter had posed as a boyfriend to several other girls.

"It would seem so. And he doesn't follow the usual pattern. He's not spontaneous. He calculates. First he dates the girls for a while, then—"

"Is this on or off the record?"

"On," he said.

"Boy, that wasn't how you felt when we were at the depot."

"That was before I had the facts I now have. Based on them, I can say, I have to say, there's a killer at work here, and the people have got to know that. We owe it to them. Just handle it with care . . ."

CHAPTER 7

MISSY TOOK the winding curves of boathouse row on East River Drive like a five-time winner at Le Mans. Normally the drive up the Parkway, decorated with its flags of all nations, past the majesty of the art museum and onto the tree-lined drive along the river relaxed her. But not tonight. Tonight all she wanted was to get to Chestnut Hill and her mother as quickly as possible, have it out with her and get out.

Trees and shrubs carefully tended by an array of gardeners concealed the large stone house from the view of nosy passersby. Which was standard for houses in Chestnut Hill, all very large and all very private.

The family had lived in this house for as long as Missy could remember. She had learned to swim in the pool in the back near the croquet court and to ride at the nearby Hillsgate Stables, where she still kept a horse.

As she pulled into the driveway, her lights illuminated the shape of the house with its two stories of stone, shutters and carved masonry. It seemed, as always, a somber house. She parked and walked to the kitchen entrance at the back. With its six bedrooms and servants' quarters the place was really too large for the three of them, plus Edgar, her father's major domo, who, as the lone live-in servant functioned with the hats of butler, cook, and valet. The only light in the kitchen was the small fluorescent one over the stove. As she passed through the kitchen and into the hallway that led to the dining room on one side and the living room and her father's study on the other, she encountered Edgar. Edgar Kirby, tall, thin, white-haired, who had been with the family almost as long as they'd been in this house. Missy had no love for him, though at one time she had called him "uncle." "Your mother's in the living room; she's expecting you," was all this ex-"uncle" had to say.

Her mother was sitting at one end of a green velvet sofa. Missy kissed her on an offered cheek, then flopped down in one of the armchairs and threw her feet onto the coffee table covered with a stack of art and travel books.

"When did you get back?"

"Last night."

Helen looked directly at her. Meaning she knew better.

Both mother and daughter were tall and lean with erect posture. Their faces were similar, except Helen's was heavily lined from age, too much sun and too many cigarettes and martinis. The essential resemblance always made Missy uncomfortable, looking at her mother was seeing herself old, gray and on the downside.

Edgar, unbidden, arrived with drinks, a martini straight up for Helen, gin and tonic for Missy.

Missy took hers without looking at him. For some fifteen years she had known that her mother was having an affair with Edgar. She'd sensed it for a long while, and then she *knew* it. Of the two, she blamed Edgar more. At least at the time. He was her father's friend and he had betrayed him. There was no forgiveness for that. As for her mother, in a sense, and secretly, it pleased her because, she felt, it strengthened her own bond with her father. Little girls believe what they choose to believe . . .

Her mother took a sip of her martini and got down to business. "To what do I owe the honor of this visit?"

"I think you know. Why did you sell out to Nathan? Without even *consulting* me?"

"Why would I want to consult you?"

"Because you know damn well Dad and I *built* that practice. We slaved to make it what it is today, and then as soon as he's gone and my back's turned you sell out—"

"It wasn't quite like that."

"What *was* it like?"

"As you doubtless know . . . you were, after all, closer to your father than I . . . Nathan and your father had a buy-out agreement, with an insurance policy on each of their lives. It was your *father's* idea. Nathan simply executed it. He got my stock; I got the proceeds of the policy."

"So I understand. And where does that leave me?"

"You mean, why aren't *you* running the practice."

"That would make sense, considering that Dad and I—"

"Don't be naive. No one is going to work for you. You aren't even a doctor. Don't you remember, your father wanted you to be a doctor but you refused. You wanted to be a nurse and serve by his side, I think that's how you put it. Like a lady in one of those frightfully romantic Hemingway novels. Well, you served, and you have your reward, nurse."

Missy couldn't handle that part of her feelings just now, especially with her mother. She returned to the matter of the practice and her consignment to the lab and Beverly having been given her job. "They cut my salary by over *fifty* percent."

"You have your house and your car. I have the title to both of them and I'm not going to charge you rent. And if it's not enough, I suggest you find yourself another job."

That almost stopped her. "You . . . don't understand. I can't find another job, not like this one . . ."

"You're saying that a comparable job wouldn't pay what you're accustomed to? Or that for some reason you can't get another job?"

"I can but they don't pay. *You* know how cheap doctors are."

"Then from what you're saying, Nathan only brought your salary in line with what the job is really worth on the market."

"You're enjoying this, aren't you?"

"No, I'm just trying to point out the realities all around—"

"Screw all that. You and your toady are—"

"Don't use that kind of language to me. Your father may have thought it was cute that you have a mouth like a sailor. I don't."

Missy backed off slightly; tactics indicated it.

"I'm sorry . . ."

Helen ignored it. "Your father had an odd sense of humor, if humor is the word for it, where you were concerned. I remember how *pleased* he was when he learned about you chewing *tobacco* at camp."

It was true, Missy and her father had laughed together many times over the incident. That was before the fishing trip . . .

Helen took another sip of her martini. "Enough of happy family reminiscences. I want you to understand that I am not going to support you. You are twenty-eight years old, smart and quite beautiful. You can take care of yourself."

"You don't understand, my salary's not enough to live on—"

"Then you'll simply have to make other arrangements, won't you?"

"That's not what Dad wanted—"

"It's *exactly* what he wanted. He understood that you were too unstable to trust with money. You have no discipline. You drink too much. I suspect you take drugs. Also, you have the worst taste in men. To give you an income would be inviting folly."

"That's crazy—"

"I don't think you really understood your father very well."

"You know we were close." Defensively.

"Oh, I don't blame you for it," she said, ignoring Missy's response. "I was the same when I married him. He was a young, handsome doctor, swept me off my feet, as they say. That, of course, was before I knew the kind of man he really was. He hated women . . ."

Missy started to rush to his defense, even though she knew her mother was right. Hadn't he meant her to be a boy, turned on her, away from her, after that one time he saw her acting out as a female . . .

Still, Missy was damned if she'd give her mother the satisfaction of openly agreeing with her. Besides, his elusiveness, even rejection, was a challenge to overcome. Even though she'd never managed it. But ever since, the men she'd chosen to be really close to, like this new one, Felix Ducroit, were like him . . . attractive, enticing and yet distant and rejecting. Damn them. God-*damn* them . . .

Her mother had paused and was looking at her as if she expected Missy to interrupt. When she didn't Helen went on, letting loose feeling she'd bottled up for years. "When I found out I was pregnant I was incredibly happy. I was giving Cyrus what he wanted most in life, a child—or rather what I *thought* he wanted most. We were *so* close during my pregnancy . . . He would hold me and pet me . . . It was when we started talking about names for you that I had my first clue that everything might not be okay, just peachy, although I didn't pick up on it at the time. He would only talk about boy's names, wouldn't even consider the prospect of a girl. Well, I rationalized, most fathers wanted a male child, but if he got a girl he'd be happy too. My first *real* sign of trouble came about the seventh month because I'd ignored all the earlier ones. That was when I decided on what your name would be if you were a girl. I waited for what I thought was the right moment and one night I told him. He'd been under a lot of strain at the hospital, and he accused me, incredibly, of trying to turn you into a girl before you were even born. This from a *doctor*. Then he hit me in the face. I fell against the corner of a table and started to hemorrhage . . ."

Missy couldn't believe what she was hearing, except she could . . . The look in his eyes watching her with that boy was definitely a look that could kill . . .

"He rushed me to the hospital," her mother was saying, "and it was touch and go for a while. They thought they were going to have to do a Caesarian, but in those days, care being what it was, with me barely in my seventh month, you probably wouldn't have lived. I said no, wait, and finally it worked out.

"Your father was shaken, was actually contrite. But when I finally went into labor again and he was driving me to the hospital he kept saying things like 'Think positive, think boy, everything will be fine.' Even between pains I thought how absurd that was. Your father the doctor, the trained medical man who knew perfectly well that your sex had been determined months before, was carrying on like someone doing a voodoo rite. In a way it was touching, but it also scared me. As they wheeled me into the delivery room I actually said a prayer that you would be a healthy baby and that Cyrus would not be disappointed, whichever sex you were . . . But when he heard the news he just walked out of the hospital. At one time he even made noises about putting you up for adoption—"

"What?"

"It's the truth. And who do you think stopped him? Me. Your terrible mother. He never stopped punishing me—or you. Even from the grave."

Missy didn't want to believe it. Hated to, hated her mother for telling it, even as she realized it seemed to be true. Oh yes, damn him, god*damn* him.

Her mother paused, forced herself to go on. "The one time I had some hope for you was when your father caught you sleeping with that boy up at the cabin. I was actually proud of you, for once you were acting like a girl your age should, not like some tomboy to please your father. You were experimenting with womanhood instead of trying to figure out a better way to tie a trout fly. Maybe if he hadn't caught you, or maybe if you'd come to me for help afterward, you and I might have grown closer. But you didn't. You just tried even harder to win him over and pushed me further away . . . I said he was punishing you from the grave. He was, by leaving you nothing. You never stopped being a girl . . ." She didn't add that she was sure Cyrus desired his daughter almost as much as he resented her. That much she would spare Missy . . .

"What happens now?" said Missy, thoroughly shaken.

"Winter is coming, and tomorrow Edgar and I are closing the house and leaving for Rio."

"Why Rio?"

"Neither of us has ever seen it. I fancy a little sun, and Edgar, bless him, has become quite enchanted with this bathing suit they call the String. He wants to see *me* wear it where it originated. I think that's sweet of him, considering my less than stunning figure and skin these days."

"How long will you be gone?"

"Hard to tell. We've rented a house there and intend to stay at least six months."

"What if I hadn't called? I wouldn't have even known you were going—"

"Oh, we would have sent you a postcard . . . By the way, if you'll take a motherly piece of advice, even though I know you place little stock in my opinions, I would suggest that if you can't make it on your own, then you should find yourself a husband and marry well. It may not be what it's cracked up to be, but it does have its moments." She said it with a straight face.

CHAPTER 8

SLOAN GOT up from his desk, put the folders on the missing girls and the dead one in his file cabinet. Well, at least they had a body now, a description of Peter, true or false, and lab tests that at least eliminated twenty percent of the male population. Nothing conclusive but a beginning. Fire to let the pot heat up. Time to get out of here.

He pulled on his coat and started for his car. With each step he seemed to feel worse. This flu bug was killing him. He decided to stop by Doc Watson's on Eleventh Street for a Scotch and head home to bed.

The cold plastic upholstery of his car felt like ice against his back, and he began to shiver. He turned the heater on high, the first blast of cold air making him shiver even more. As he drove through the rain he tried not to think about the case, but it was no use. Detectives Kane and Spivak might still turn up something at Lagniappe, something more, he trusted, than an owner who was accused of rape by a discharged employee. Standard stuff. Still, nothing was too obvious or farfetched to be discounted.

A couple of times during the drive he noticed the same car in his rearview mirror and wondered if he was being followed. Who the hell follows a cop? He parked on Eleventh Street near Jefferson Hospital and walked in the rain to Doc Watson's. The car that had been behind him was nowhere in sight. Getting jumpy in your old age, he told himself.

Inside Doc's he got a booth near the front window and waved to Barry Sandrow, the owner. He read over the dinner specials while he waited for his regular drink. When the waitress set it in front of him, he heard a voice say, "I'll have the same."

He looked up to see a young woman standing beside his booth. She was dressed in a denim jacket, leather skirt and boots, had streaked red hair cut punk-style and was wearing sunglasses. He indicated the empty seat across from him. She didn't introduce herself, didn't need to. Sloan knew her.

When the waitress returned with her drink she raised her glass. "Here's looking at you." Sloan nodded and raised his glass to her.

"What are you doing here?" he said.

"I followed you from the Roundhouse. A man in your line of work really should be more observant."

"It's probably the flu," he said. "I picked up your tail, decided it was my imagination."

Her name was Delores Inverso, beloved daughter of Nicholas Inverso, near the top of the Philadelphia mob. Which could change at any time. Both her brothers had already died in the eight-year-old intra-family quarrel that had already taken a toll of some forty prominent mob figures. Many of her father's interests, as he liked to point out, were legitimate, and among other members of the family his was regarded as a voice of reason.

"You're wearing your hair different," Sloan said. "What does your father think of it?"

"I'm in art school now. He digs artists have to be free to express themselves."

"I'd heard you were in some school. How's it going?"

"Good, except Dad wants me to get to where I can paint church ceilings. You know, a lot of fat nudes."

"You don't like to do nudes?"

"Boring. Fabric design is my thing."

"A good field. If memory serves your family has some interests in the garment industry."

She stiffened at his remark. "That's history, Sloan. You should know that."

He smiled, blew his nose. The mob didn't much like to use women, but since her brothers were killed he'd heard Delores had been filling in. A capable lady.

"Look," she said, getting to business, "we know about you finding this Terri DiFranco's body. We want to know what you're going to do about it. People from the neighborhood have been around to see Dad. He's very interested in clearing up this missing girls business, plus nailing the DiFranco killer.

Typical, Sloan thought. Like most of his brethren, he still lived in South Philly, in the blue-collar neighborhood he was raised in. They liked a low profile.

"Tell your father we're on the job. As he knows, until we had a body there was nothing we could do."

"He's glad you're on the case," she said.

"Tell him thanks."

"He wants to know what you're going to do about this Lagniappe connection."

Sloan was surprised, quickly realized he shouldn't be. The mob had more informants than he did. For the record he said he didn't know what she was talking about.

She took a sip of her drink. "Dad said you'd say that. He also told me to tell you he did some checking. He said there's a man . . . he'd rather not mention the name . . . who approached a man Dad knows about getting him some young girls. Twelve-, thirteen-year-olds. You know the deal."

"And this man hangs out at Lagniappe?"

"I can't say any more. We don't want to be connected to this on any of your records—"

"Wait a minute. Cut the damn tease. You dangle some unnamed creep who buys teenagers and then you clam up. Tell your daddy for me that thanks for nothing and you can pay for your own drink."

"Simmer down, we do what we can and I know what you're trying to do and it won't work. I won't be baited. You get all I can give you. We want this cleaned up, and we want it fast. People like to blame people like my dad for all kinds of lousy things and it hurts business. So good luck, Sloan, and we'll be watching to see how you do. If you don't make the play your way we'll make it ours and you can read about it in the papers. And for God's sake, take care of that cold. We *need* our police . . ."

She even pecked him on the cheek as she tossed a tenner on the table and ambled out.

CHAPTER 9

IT WAS just after eight when Laura Ramsey finished the story on Terri DiFranco. What had seemed so easy earlier in the day had turned out more difficult than expected. Eventually the writing came down to a series of judgment calls—what to tell to sell papers, what to hold back to allow the family some privacy and dignity.

The rain was still coming down as she walked to the parking lot for her car, and once she'd begun the drive down Spring Garden Street toward Delaware Avenue she told herself that she should go home, open a can of soup, take a hot bath and go to bed. But what she really craved was some junk food. She might pay for it later, but right now it was definitely the ticket: something wonderfully unhealthy washed down with a cold beer. If she'd been home in Texas, Mexican food would be perfect, but not here in Philly.

Passing the Pier 30 tennis courts on the Delaware River, she considered driving down to Oregon Avenue for a hot sausage sandwich and a bag of chips from the Doggie Diner but decided against it because it was too early. She liked to save the Doggie Diner for those uncontrollable cravings that come in the small hours of the morning. Instead she turned off at Washington Avenue, taking Front Street to Costello's Cheese Steaks, found a parking place three or four car lengths away and walked slowly to the entrance, head down, too beat even to hurry out of the rain.

Costello's: sheet paneling, drop ceiling, fake Tiffany lamps, two video games, jukebox, cigarette machine the size of Kansas. The place was quiet except for a covey of teenage girls gathered around the jukebox, which was playing Madonna's "Live to Tell."

Laura went directly to the counter to give her order to a brunette with Annette Funicello hair—a double pepper, mushroom-and-cheese steak with pizza sauce, fried onions and hot peppers. She hoped she would have the control to eat only half and save the rest.

Waiting for her order, she heard one of the girls at the jukebox call out, "Hey, ain't you the reporter who was there when they found Terri this morning?"

"Yes."

Turning to her friends, the girl said, "See, I *told* you it was her."

The pack moved over to Laura. All three of them wore skin-hugging jeans and tight sweaters. The one who had just spoken was wearing short boots with her jeans tucked into the tops; the other two wore sneakers. Two were smoking, and the one who wasn't was holding a pack of Marlboros.

Taking a drag on her cigarette, the leader said, "My mom told me she saw you there this morning, you know, when they found her . . ."

Laura wondered which woman was her mother.

"You going to write about it for the paper?"

"It'll be in tomorrow's edition."

She waited for them to press her for details, but they didn't and then she understood that with the neighborhood jungle telegraph they probably knew more about the case than she did.

"Do you think they'll catch the guy?"

"The police think so."

"We hear it was the boyfriend that done it," said the girl with the Marlboros.

"The police aren't saying. What's he like?"

"All we know is what Terri used to say. None of us ever saw him but if you want to find out more about him you should talk to Marie. I don't think she ever saw him, but she was Terri's best friend. She knows more about him than anyone else," the leader said, pointing to a girl hunched over the jukebox.

Marie turned out to be something of an ugly duckling, with spiky red hair, glasses and a body that had not yet outgrown its baby fat. She was wearing sweatpants, sneakers and a football jersey several sizes large for her. The jersey was green and white, the Eagles' colors, with the number seven on both sides and the name "Jaworski," the great quarterback, on the back. The girls practically forced Laura toward the jukebox to meet Marie.

"Hey, Marie, this is that reporter we were talking about."

"I know." She didn't look up, kept her eyes on the jukebox selections.

Laura, feeling exhausted, just went along. "Hello, Marie."

Marie didn't speak, and the leader put in, "We were just telling her how you was Terri's best friend and if anybody knew anything about her boyfriend it'd be you—"

"I was right *here*. I *heard* you. I wasn't in *Camden*, you know."

"Don't pay attention to her. She's upset. Wouldn't you be if your first day back at school you heard they found your best friend's body?" said the leader.

"You were out of school?" At this point Laura was just being conversational.

"Yeah."

"Were you just out or did you have a touch of the bug that's been going around?"

"I had the bug."

"How long were you out?"

No answer.

"She had a bad case of it. She was out a couple of weeks," the leader said.

"That's a long time to be laid up."

"Yeah, well, I had it, then I got over it, and then I got it again. Jesus."

"I hope it's better now."

"It's better."

Marie was giving no easy openings, so Laura decided to bull ahead. "I was there this morning and I saw Terri's body. I've written a story about it for tomorrow's paper and I'm going to write follow-ups until they catch the guy who did it. But I need to know things about her, things other people don't know. What I'm doing isn't going to bring her back, but maybe it'll help the police catch him, or at least keep some other young girl, like yourself, from getting herself into the same terrible situation. Will you help me?"

"Would I get my name in the paper?" Still looking down at the jukebox.

"Do you want your name in the paper?"

Marie now looked at her. "God, *no*."

"Then it won't be. I guarantee it."

Marie shrugged. "What do you want to know?"

"Why don't you just tell me about Terri? What it was like to be her friend?"

What she got was a picture of lifelong friendship, of youthful high jinks, of two girls who were tight as only adolescents could be. When she mentioned "Peter," Marie almost physically cringed, and only reluctantly told how Terri had met Peter, how much she had loved him, and how upset she was the night they were having pizza and she saw the two women get into Peter's car.

Laura pressed on. "But *you* didn't see the women get into the car, right?"

"That's right."

"What about the car, did you see it?"

"No, Terri didn't tell me about it till later so I didn't see the car."

"Still, you must have seen the car at some other time. I mean, as close friends as you were and as many dates as they had, you must have seen it . . ."

"No, Terri wanted to show him off, but him being an under-cover cop, she said he couldn't afford to have people in the neighborhood get to know him."

"Do you believe he was an undercover cop?"

"I guess not, not now. But Terri did."

"Did you know about the depot and what Terri was doing there?"

"No."

"You were her best friend. You must have known about it."

"Hey, I don't lie. I was sick, that's when I got the bug."

"Wait a minute," said the leader. "We had an English test that week. You didn't get the bug then, you got it later. I remember you were there for the test—"

"Look, I'm telling you what happened. If you don't want to believe me then to hell with all of you. I'm going home."

She pushed her way through the other girls and was out the door before Laura could stop her. Laura threw some money on the counter and hurried out, her cheese steak forgotten.

She could see Marie running ahead, crossing Front Street and going toward the ice-skating rink built under I-95 near Federal Street.

"Marie, wait," Laura called as she hurried after her.

Marie slowed down, as though she wanted Laura to catch up with her at the rink.

Laura, winded, was relieved that the deserted rink was at least out of the rain, under the overhead section of I-95.

Marie waited for her, leaning against the waist-high yellow rail around the rink. Laura approached her cautiously. Marie knew more about Terri's death than she was saying, that seemed obvious. The question was, why was she holding back? Didn't she want to help catch Terri's killer? After all, Terri was her best friend . . .

Laura realized she had no good idea how to begin with Marie, to get some answers. For all the contact she'd had with teenagers, they might as well have been Martians. As for how she'd felt as one, that was too many years ago in dusty Texas, years with about as much relevance to this girl and her situation as a "Gunsmoke" rerun. But she knew one thing—she had to make the first move. She took a deep breath and said something she realized was inanely chatty; "Thanks for slowing down. I don't know about you, but I've had enough exercise for a year."

Marie gave it the silent treatment. Laura said, abruptly, "it hurts to lose someone you love. Is this the first time for you?"

"Yes." A small voice.

"It's never easy."

Not surprisingly, Marie didn't respond to that profound statement. Laura was getting edgy. *Come on, Marie, give me a break* . . . But Marie wasn't about to make it easy. *Okay, then we'll go back door* . . .

"Marie, do you believe in God?"

"What? God? Sure . . . what's that got to do with—?"

"Do you believe that this was how God wanted Terri to die?"

"No, I mean, I don't know," Marie said, turning away from her to hide the tears she felt coming.

"Well, I do. This was *not* God's intention. What killed Terri was evil and deserves to be punished for it."

"I know that."

Laura figured she just couldn't stop sounding stupid. Of course Marie knew that. She'd rushed this like it was her first interview. She needed more time to win Marie's confidence, but she also felt she'd painted herself into a corner. There was nothing left for it but to cut the stuff and get to it . . .

"You have to help, you know."

Silence.

"Whatever it is you're holding back is making you very unhappy. You'll feel a lot better if you get it out."

When she'd just about given up hope, Marie said, "I saw the car. It's a silver Datsun 300ZX with a Bruce Springsteen sticker on the rear bumper." The words came in a rush.

Laura was excited, but had to probe. "Do you know a lot about cars?"

"No."

"Most girls don't. In fact, most of us don't know one car from another. How did you know it was a 300ZX?"

"*Because* there's a little sign on the back that says that's what it is," Marie said, and turned away.

"But how could you see a little sign at night on a silver car?" Then, waking up . . . "Unless the car was stopped?"

Grabbing Marie by the arm, she spun her around, and looking in her face saw she was right. "You saw the car when it was parked, didn't you? Where? Where did you see it?"

In a voice filled with shame, "At the depot."

It took a moment to sink in. "Oh, my God." She resisted asking why Marie hadn't spoken up sooner. This wasn't the moment. Instead, as Marie burst into tears, Laura drew the girl to her and put her arms around her.

When the sobs quieted, Laura said, "Tell me what happened."

Marie took off her glasses, wiped her eyes with her sleeve. "You were right. I knew about the depot but I hadn't seen it. All I knew was that Terri had told me about it . . ."

"Go on."

"Things weren't going like Terri wanted. She wanted to get married but he seemed to be losing interest or something. Anyway, she got scared it was going to be over unless . . ."

"Unless she slept with him?"

"Yes, but it wasn't like that, not exactly. I mean, before Peter, Terri was going out with Joey from the neighborhood, only she wouldn't let him, so he left her for Lisa. Then one night her mother and father got in a fight at the dinner table and afterward they went up to their room and . . . well, Terri knew they were doing it. They did it a lot, I'm talking about a real lot, and it always made Terri feel weird to think about it, them doing it, but not this time. She said this time it all sort of made sense and that's when she decided to do it with Peter . . ."

"Who came up with the idea of the depot?"

"Terri . . . we know that a man won't respect you if he does it to you in the car, and Terri didn't have a place, so she picked the depot."

"But you didn't see it."

Marie hesitated again. "Not then, not when she was fixing it up. I wanted to but she wouldn't let me. She said it was their place and she didn't want me to see it yet."

"And this made you feel a little left out maybe?"

"No. Well, yes, maybe a little, but I wasn't jealous or anything. I just wanted to see it . . ."

"How'd you feel about Terri doing it with Peter . . . what did you say his last name was?"

"I don't know what his last name was. Even Terri didn't know. Peter, that was it. Anyway I didn't like the idea and I told her so. The sisters taught us it's a sin to let a man do stuff before you get married."

"What did Terri say about that?"

"She said it wasn't a sin if you were *going* to marry that person, and that's what she and Peter were going to do."

"So she believed they were going to get married. Then what happened?"

Marie turned and again leaned against the yellow rail surrounding the ice rink. Laura was acutely aware of how wet and cold she was. Her boots were soaked through, water had dripped in around her collar. But it was worse for Marie, who had no raincoat and who was carrying around a load of guilt and grief large enough to chill her insides.

"Then I did a bad thing—I went to the depot."

"That Saturday night, the night Terri was killed?" Laura was afraid to believe what she was hearing.

"Yes . . . look, I wasn't trying to spy on them or anything. I just wanted to see what the place looked like . . . what *he* looked like. After all, I was her best friend—"

"Marie, you did *not* do anything wrong. There's nothing wrong with being curious about the person your best friend is going with . . . Were you outside or inside the depot?"

"Outside. I thought about going inside but I decided it would be wrong."

"Okay, can you tell me about it?"

"I got there early, before they did. That's when I thought about going inside because Terri had told me about the place and I knew how she got in."

"But you didn't."

"No, I found a hiding place where they couldn't see me, but I could see them when they pulled up."

Laura held her breath.

"They came, and he pulled the car up in that little dead end. Terri got out, opened the window and went inside and opened the door."

"What about him, Marie?"

"He stayed in the car till Terri opened the door, then went inside."

"What did he look like?"

"He wasn't real tall but he was taller than Terri. They made a sort of good couple. He had dark hair and a beard, and he was wearing dark glasses. Oh, and he had on a leather jacket and a white scarf. Terri said he always wore them."

"Anything else . . . I mean about the way he looked?"

"Just that he really was good-looking, like she said."

From the description Laura thought he could have been wearing a ski mask, with a beard attached. There was no way even an eyewitness like Marie could identify him for certain with a description like that. Even if it wasn't a mask, the beard could have been a phony, or if it was real he could have shaved it off right after . . .

"What happened then?"

"They closed the door."

"So that's all you saw . . . But what about when they came out?"

"I didn't see them then. It was starting to rain and I thought they'd be in there for a long time, maybe all night, and I didn't feel like getting soaked, so I left."

"What did you think when Terri didn't show up for school on Monday?"

"I was sick then, I didn't go to school on Monday."

"But you already knew she was missing, didn't you? Her parents must have been going crazy."

Laura could see her tightening up and realized she had hit a nerve . . . the reason Marie was feeling so guilty.

"Why didn't you tell anyone about this until now?" Laura said.

"Because when Terri told me about the place and what she was going to do, she made me promise not to tell *anyone*, especially her parents, because if everything worked out like she hoped she was sure she and Peter would run away and get married."

"Didn't you worry?"

"Yes . . ." and she began to cry again. "I was afraid for her, she was my best friend, I didn't want her to do this—"

"Did you talk to the police?"

"Yes."

"Why didn't you tell them, or your parents?"

Crying harder now, Marie said, "I was afraid everyone would *hate* me for what I did. Sneaking around like that, spying . . ."

Laura reached out and put her arms again around the girl.

"Never mind. It's all right. You didn't do anything wrong. You didn't, believe me," and she held her like that until she was quiet. "But you will have to talk to the police, Marie, and this time you'll have to tell them everything."

"I know . . ."

As they walked back into the rain together Laura was thinking that her day wasn't over yet. First she had to call Sloan and tell him about Marie, and then call the news desk. After all, there was nothing in her bargain with Sloan to keep her from using the account of an unnamed witness in her story.

CHAPTER 10

THE CORNER of Broad and Locust was a madhouse as cabs discharged passengers under the flickering gaslights of the Academy of Music. Ordinarily waiting in line for *anything* drove Missy wild—but not tonight. Alone with Felix in the backseat of Wakefield and Pollack's limousine she felt almost serene, an unaccustomed condition for her.

It was also in stark contrast to how she'd felt when she'd left her mother's Monday night. She had driven back into town, crying in rage, bashing the steering wheel, and on the rain-slick East River Drive she had spun out, nearly hitting the stone arch of a bridge abutment, winding up in a riverside parking lot near a closed concession stand. Only her well-conditioned reflexes had saved her from serious injury or death.

Once back in Center City she had stopped at a pay phone and called a connection for cocaine, and after she'd picked it up, had headed for Christian's, a bar on Sansom Street in the same block with the White Dog Cafe and La Terrasse. After throwing back several Cuervo Golds, she'd picked up four Penn students—three cleancuts in their junior year, and a nineteen-year-old female whose black turtleneck, long straight hair and copy of *Atlas Shrugged* had given her an almost timeless coffeehouse-beatnik look. Carl wasn't the only one who occasionally needed younger flesh to prop up a bruised or demented ego. Everyone was getting theirs, including her sainted *mother*, for God's sake . . .

From the bar she'd taken them to her house where, the stress, drugs and alcohol all melding, she had proceeded to undress in front of the four and perform oral sex on each. At first the girl had been reluctant, but with the pressure of more drugs and good old peer pressure she had gone along. And so it had gone through the night and into part of the next day, with the once-reluctant girl becoming a most responsive subject for Missy's ministrations. But when they had finally gone, she'd realized the party was over in more ways than one . . . she had had each of them doing as she wanted, but in the end it hadn't *changed* anything. She'd still been alone, feeling broke, and no one in the world gave a good goddamn.

As she'd reluctantly changed to go to work, she'd flicked on her answering machine and heard a message from Felix. In the upset of the past night and day she'd forgotten their date for Monday night, and his taped voice had sounded both irritated and concerned. He'd called before she'd gotten back to her house with the college kids. As she'd listened to the short message, she'd decided she was wrong; she wasn't alone; someone out there apparently did care.

She'd immediately called him and made a date for the opera that evening . . .

Now together with him for the first time since leaving her mother, she was quiet inside, though part of it was thanks to ten milligrams of Valium, a vodka on the rocks and a new outfit from Nan Duskin purchased only hours before picking Felix up at his apartment.

She was feeling so good and cozy, in fact, that it was a moment or two before she even got the drift of Felix's words as they waited for the traffic in front of them to clear. He was, she gathered, talking about some article in the *Globe* by that awful Laura Ramsey about "an eyewitness to the rape-murder of some South Philly teenager." Missy, still very much in her own cocoon, preferred to think about her new outfit and its expected affect on Felix . . . a Calvin Klein off-the-shoulder top in ivory and a full, belted, black silk skirt with a crinoline and a hemline that ended just above the knee. It had immediately caught her eye, highlighting as it did her lean and leggy figure. The thousand dollar price tag had not caused a moment's hesitation. She had charged it to her mother's account. Served her right for all those things she had said Monday night. Thinking about it, she'd decided not to believe that stuff about her father wanting to put her up for adoption . . . It was just her mother's way of somehow trying to justify cuckolding him with Edgar.

When their limo pulled up in front of the Academy of Music, Albert, the chauffeur, hurried around to open the door for them and they joined the throngs going up the steps and past the posters announcing the opening night performance of Puccini's

Madame Butterfly by the Opera Company of Philadelphia. Glancing around the crowd, Missy took inventory of the number of Evan-Picone and Liz Claiborne outfits. So much money, so little imagination, she thought.

As they moved to the bar it pleased her to think how good she and Felix must look together. No question, he cut quite a figure in his tuxedo. All he needed was a touch more gray in his hair and beard and he'd be just right. That would come in time, she reminded herself. Time they would be spending together.

Before going to their seats they met several dowager types who seemed to know Felix, even though he was a relatively new arrival in town. They made flattering comments on his good works, converting dilapidated warehouses into decent housing, and reserved their most perfunctory smiles for Missy Wakefield.

Moving on, Missy was fuming at the snubs, but took comfort in the fact that Felix, the new boy in town, was clearly well liked and respected. All of which reinforced her growing conviction that he was the man for her.

At the bar, as they sipped their drinks—hers vodka-rocks, his Jack Daniels neat—she noted the abrupt tightness in his face and turned to see what was causing it. Coming toward them was a prim-looking brunette in her early thirties, shoulder-length hair parted down the middle and pulled back. Missy identified her flowered dress as a Ralph Lauren, but with its scoop neckline that accentuated her slender neck and collarbones rather than her breasts it might as well have been a mail-order from Talbots.

"Hello, Cyn, how are you?" Felix was saying.

"Fine, Felix," she said, "just fine."

"Missy, I don't know if you two know each other—everyone else in Philadelphia seems to know each other. This is my, my"—he hesitated for a second—"former wife, Cynthia . . ."

And suddenly Missy was back at Lagniappe on the night she had first met Felix; a series of still images clicked in her brain, images of personal humiliation as she apparently had lost Carl to that bitch reporter Laura Ramsey, the one writing the articles about the South Philly girl, and over it all she could hear Lois Fortier's voice saying that rumor had it Felix Ducroit was in town to get back together with his ex-wife . . . Well, it wasn't going to happen. *She* had the inside track, and this prim little person could eat her dust.

Ignoring Missy, Cynthia fixed her attention on Felix. "I'd heard you were in town . . ." letting it hang there, as if to say, and I've been waiting for your call.

The unspoken was picked up by Felix. "Yes, I've been meaning to get in touch, been pretty busy."

At which point Missy smiled sweetly, to make clear just how Felix had been keeping busy.

Cynthia pretended not to notice. "You're the talk of the town, you know, what with the real estate project you're doing and all. In fact, I got a call from a reporter at the *Globe* to interview me for an article about you."

Felix clearly didn't welcome the news, tried to toss it off with "I hope you'll be able to say nice things . . ."

"You know I will," she said, and for a moment the primness was gone. "Well, it's almost curtain time. I'd better get to my seat." As she turned to go she looked back at him, a smile in place. "If you want to know how the interview went, give me a call."

Felix did not reply, but Missy stood there feeling a tingling at the back of her neck. Ex's, *all* ex's, wives, lovers or whatevers always meant trouble . . . "Your ex-wife is very charming," she said in a tone one might use in referring to a middle-aged woman, a small house or a gay man who could dance well.

"Yes, I suppose she is," he said.

"Were you two close . . . I meant when you were married?"

"In the beginning," he said, taking a sip of his drink.

"I don't mean to be nosy, but what happened?"

"I guess it's more what didn't happen. Children . . ."

"She wanted them and you didn't?"

"No, the other way around."

"Oh. Well, that's sort of unusual."

"I suppose . . ." He seemed to want to explain. "When we met in New Orleans a couple of deals had gone sour and I was flat broke. She didn't seem to care, and even when we moved in together she was the one paying the bills. She had some family money and she had a job managing one of those little hotels in the French Quarter. And she was damn good at it. I really admire her business skills . . . Anyway, I finally put a couple of deals together and they got us out of the woods completely, so it seemed a good time for her to stop working and have a family . . ."

"And she wouldn't hear of it?"

"That's right. I just didn't understand how much her career meant to her, or maybe how uneasy she was about mine. Whatever, I handled it all wrong, pushing so hard for children, and that was that."

Missy, saying nothing, took his arm, squeezed it gently and led him in to their seats. What he had just said told her something about him that pleased her. For all his obvious strengths—financial success, good looks, social presence—Felix was also a man who, thanks to his sensitivity, could be manipulated. And thinking this, she remembered what someone had scribbled on the ladies room wall at Lagniappe: "Sensitivity is when a man does what *you* want." Amen.

As the curtain went up and the audience applauded the set depicting the small town of Nagasaki, Missy paid little attention. Her thoughts were on the man next to her. She'd never had a man affect her quite the way he did. Most seemed fairly shallow creatures, useful to service her and be discarded at whim. Felix was different, more, as she'd felt from the beginning, in her father's mold. The good side of her father . . .

He was the right man for her, no doubt about it. He was handsome and intelligent, rich and well connected. Sophisticated and yet down to earth. And somewhat remote, with a little mystery to him. She liked the challenge of that, though she had little doubt she would more than meet that challenge.

She stole a glance at him. In profile he had an edge—a hard edge? She sensed that when he was ready he would be a demanding lover and shivered slightly in anticipation. His ex-wife, or the story of her breakup with him, had shown the way to what he wanted most—children.

Could she do it? She looked without seeing at the unfolding romantic conflicts of Butterfly and Pinkerton . . . Even the thought of getting pregnant again made her feel sick . . . Much as she resisted it, that one time came back now. It had happened that summer when she was sixteen, the summer when her father had watched Roy Curtis have her in the boathouse. Afterward at home she'd gone on a sexual rampage. She had slept with anyone who asked her, done anything anyone wanted. She hadn't done it out of some need for penance or self-punishment . . . she hadn't cared a damn about that . . . but she'd cared about her father, had been obsessed with getting him, somehow, no matter how, at least to pay attention to her, with breaking through the wall that had grown between them ever since Roy Curtis. It hadn't worked. She'd gotten pregnant.

On stage Butterfuly was singing the aria "Un Bel Di, vedremo" as she waited for Pinkerton to return from a long absence, and the music kept Missy's thoughts where she didn't want them . . . She didn't know who the father was, didn't care. Her mother had been in Europe that summer. Edgar had been on "vacation," probably with her. So she had been alone in the house with her father when she had told him she was pregnant.

In the darkness she felt the scar on her abdomen begin to cause pain and to burn. As always. The scar was twelve years old, but every time she thought about her pregnancy it happened. *Don't think about it,* she ordered herself. *Not now. It'll ruin the evening, eventually ruin your chances with Felix.*

The pain, the burning, only came when she tried to remember what had happened that night she'd told her father she was pregnant. She could remember standing at the door of her father's study, waiting to tell him, feeling terrified. He'd been behind his desk, his hawklike face lined by the light and shadows of a desk lamp. With his tufted brows he'd appeared Mephistophilean. He'd looked up from his papers—and then memory clicked off.

That was the way it always happened. She could remember everything *up to that point.* How she'd fretted, how she'd worn baggy clothes to hide her swelling stomach, how she'd prayed her period would start. But *after* that point, nothing. For twelve years her standing in the doorway waiting to tell him was as far as she could remember. And with each succeeding memory of that night, the pain built in intensity until at a point it became white-hot, so awful it blocked out all further memory, perversely providing its own relief.

The music of the opera swelled around her as she surreptitiously put her hands on her stomach and tried to press the pain away. But it came over her in a wave so intense that it took away her sight and hearing . . . her world turned into a collage of colors, her heart began to race, panic took over. She pushed up from her seat, stumbled past Felix and the others in the row and nearly ran up the aisle to the lobby, where she proceeded immediately to the bar and ordered a double vodka.

While she waited for her drink she swallowed another ten-milligram Valium. Her hands were shaking. Years ago she had been sure she wanted to know what happened but couldn't recall. Now all she wanted was to forget, but she couldn't do that either.

By now Felix had caught up with her. "Are you all right?"

She looked at him, and for a moment she hated him. This was his fault. Everything would have been just fine if he hadn't started with this pregnancy business. That's what had touched off the pain and truncated memory.

"I'm fine," she said lightly, picking up her drink.

"You don't look so fine to me. What's wrong?"

"I'm *fine*," said through clenched teeth.

"You clearly aren't and you're going home. What you need is a good night's sleep."

She said nothing, just stood there while he took the drink from her hands and set it on the bar, laid a five dollar bill beside it, put his arm around her and started for the door.

Outside, Albert had the limousine parked up the street in front of the Bellview-Stratford. While they waited for him, Missy, fighting for control, told Felix she'd really prefer going home alone, that she was sorry she'd ruined the evening, and asked him to call her tomorrow. And before he could respond she was in the limo and telling Albert to drive off and be quick.

As the limousine wheeled into traffic, Albert could have sworn he heard her muttering something like, "Damn you, daddy, damn you . . . I did my best but it wasn't enough, never enough . . ."

CHAPTER 11

DETECTIVE RAFFERTY earned himself no Brownie points, especially with Lieutenant Sloan, being late to the meeting of Seven Squad. Nor did his excuse cut much ice.

"Sorry to be late, lieutenant, just couldn't stand any more of the coffee around here so I stopped at Rindelaub's on Eighteenth, for all our own sakes. The traffic coming cross town was a bitch, you know how it is this time of day . . ."

Sloan nodded and ignored him. In fact, he was grateful to have Rafferty on the squad. Its oldest member, he hadn't lost a step with age, was still as much a handful as ten years ago. Maybe more, with the added smarts. The only reason he had been available when the squad was formed was the fall-out from a West Philly shoot-out that made him a temporary leper in the department. Not that he'd been wrong—no one thought that—but, as they said, publicity-wise it was a bummer. An ice cream parlor near the university, a hold-up in progress when he stopped in, a quick exchange of gunfire and the hold-up man was stone dead on the floor. All very fine, except that the "critter" had been the son of a West Philly ward leader. The department's loss had been Sloan's and Seven Squad's gain.

Sloan called them to order. "Last night I got a call from Laura Ramsey. I'm sure you've all been reading her stuff on the case. It seems she's turned up a witness in the DiFranco killing. Terri DiFranco's best friend, Marie."

The room was suddenly quiet.

"This morning I went out and picked her up myself. Her identification is sketchy. It was night, but she did see him and she has confirmed his description—thin, dark hair and beard, tinted glasses. Right now she's inside looking at mug shots."

"A real break—"

"Which brings me to my next point, Spivak. Before you start clicking your heels in the air, tell me why we need the newspapers to show us how to do our job. This girl was Terri DiFranco's best friend. She's not from outer space. Okay, enough." He

113

checked his notes. "Evans, where the hell is that report on the theatrical costumers? What gives?"

Evans looked like a chastened buddha. "We checked on them, lieutenant. We went back over two years in every costumers' records and pulled all the sales slips for beards or wigs. There's at least four or five hundred of them. Right now we're checking them against the known-sex-offender file to see if we can get a match. That's about all we can do . . . it'd take Rafferty and me a year to check them all out on foot."

Sloan calmed down some. They weren't goofing off; they were doing it by the numbers, only the leads were too damn few and far between. "You're right, I guess, especially since it's only speculation that our boy is in disguise. And if he is, he probably gave a phony name when he bought the beard. But follow up on any sex-offender matches. Who knows?"

Detective Kane stood up. "Lieutenant . . ."

"Speak."

"I went back to Lagniappe again—"

"I thought I told you to give it a rest."

"You did, but you also told us to use our best judgment. So I went back, and I met an artist there, a Carl Laredo. Nice guy. We got to talking and he introduced me to the owner, Justin Fortier. You remember we had a prior complaint about him from one of his waitresses. I figure we ought to check it out further."

"Spivak, you heard her. Rafferty and Evans, get back to those costumer receipts. Kane, come with me. I need you with this Marie, Terri DiFranco's friend. She's still pretty scared, you can help calm her down."

They went to the interrogation room, where Marie was finished looking at mug shots and was now looking at photos of cars. A uniformed policewoman was helping her.

"Any luck in the mug books?" asked Sloan.

The policewoman shook her head. Marie looked up. "I . . . I didn't see him." She picked up a picture of a car. "I did find this, though. It looks like the car."

Sloan turned it over. On the back it said, "Datsun 300ZX." She had said it was a 300ZX before. "Kane," he said, "order a complete run from Motor Vehicles of all 300ZX's in the Philadelphia area. I don't care how many there are. We can't afford to pass up anything. Check the owners against the known-sex-offender file. Hell, see if Mr. Fortier happens to own one."

He turned to the uniformed policewoman. "While Detective Kane and I have a chat with Marie, bring in the police artist. Let's see if Rembrandt can draw us a suspect."

CHAPTER 12

LAURA, A few minutes early for her lunch with Cynthia Ducroit, pushed her way through the swinging doors on Arch Street and entered the Reading Terminal Market. Originally begun in the 1800s as a farmer's market but now expanded over a square block to include restaurants and ethnic food stalls, it was one of her very favorite places in Philadelphia. The smell of barbecued chicken from the Amish section was drawing throngs for lunch, and behind the counters the Amish people with their beards and hats or old-fashioned long dresses were rushing about trying to take care of customers.

She watched for a moment, then strolled toward the center of the Market, stopping at a fish counter to see the catch of the day, stopping again to say hello to Harry Ochs, her favorite butcher. Past his stall, toward the Twelfth Street side, was Bassett's Ice Cream and the flower stall. She walked deeper into the center of the Market toward the Coastal Cave Trading Company, where she was to meet Cynthia.

As it turned out, Cynthia, too, was early and was already seated at the counter talking to Lobster Bob, the owner of The Coastal Cave Trading Company, which specialized in Maine lobster and other seafood delicacies. Laura joined her now at the counter, taking the stool beside her.

Over drinks and lobster salad Laura said, "Like I told you on the phone, I've been assigned to do a piece on Felix and I need your help for background. If there's anything you don't feel comfortable talking about, don't answer it. Okay?"

"Okay."

"What was it like being married to him?"

"You never knew what was going to happen. One day we'd be rich, rolling in money, the next day he'd sink it into another deal and lose it all. It was kind of like living with a compulsive gambler."

"And you wanted more security?"

Before Cynthia could answer they were interrupted by the

117

appearance . . . that was the word for it . . . of Carl Laredo,
wearing a light sportscoat, a black bandana tied around his neck
and a dark green T-shirt advertising Rolling Rock beer.

But there was something different about him. It took Laura a
moment to realize what it was. Carl had shaved off his beard.

"Well, if it isn't my two favorite ladies. Mind if I join you?"

"Sure, join us," Cynthia said before Laura could demure,
"Laura's interviewing me about Felix."

As Carl took the stool on the other side of her, Cynthia said
what Laura was thinking, "Carl, what happened to your beard?"

"I just got tired of it," he said with a shrug.

Lobster Bob came over, and Carl gave him an order for oysters
on the half-shell and smoked trout.

"No, really, why'd you do it? There's always more to it than
that when a man shaves off his beard," pressed Cynthia.

"Actually, I did it for my show in New York. A new image,
you know. Beards aren't in anymore, at least not in the art
world. They've become a cliché." He looked toward Laura.
"Those pieces you've been writing about that South Philly girl
were marvelous, really insightful and quite moving."

"I must agree," said Cynthia. "If you make it a series I
wouldn't be surprised to see you win some sort of award, maybe
even the Pulitzer. When I read about that girl I cried."

"Me, too," said Carl, "but what got me was that eyewitness
account. Where did you come up with that?"

"Please, guys, flattery will get you everywhere, but if I want to
keep my job I have to finish this piece on Felix. Now, Cynthia,
you were saying about Felix. What was it like when you weren't
up financially?"

"Felix could be two different people. When he was broke he
never gave up, but he would get withdrawn, silent, moody."

"That's not so unusual," Carl put in. "A lot of people get like
that when they feel pressure. What was it that broke you up?
I've never heard you say."

Laura was begining to feel like a supernumerary.

Cynthia hesitated, then said, "I guess you could say it was
mostly on account of his wanting children and my resisting. I
feel differently now . . ."

"The old biological clock?" Laura asked.

"I suppose . . ."

Carl, looking bored, said, "Enough of this biological clock stuff . . . Laura, what I want to hear about is that eyewitness of yours. You don't even say whether it's a he or a she."

As she looked at Carl, Laura thought how unhelpful even specific descriptions could be. From what Marie had said, Carl seemed to fit the description of Terri's killer, minus a beard, but then no doubt so did plenty of other men in the city.

"How about a three-way deal," said Cynthia. "If Laura tells you about the eyewitness, you have to tell us what it was like to date Missy Wakefield."

"Why?"

"Well, I saw her with Felix last night at the opera. They left before the first act was over, very noticeably and very rude . . . I was just wondering what she was like—"

"You mean what Felix sees in her?" Clearly Cynthia was not over her ex.

"If you want to put it that way."

"Fine with me. Laura?"

"Yes, Laura, if you don't go along I won't help anymore about Felix," said Cynthia.

Strange, Laura thought, how her two assignments kept being linked. Still, she'd play along, see where it took her.

"What do you want to know?"

"About the eyewitness," Carl said. "The stuff you people leave out is what's tantalizing. I understand that until the killer is caught you have to be careful, but let me try a couple of questions. Was jealousy involved? I mean, was the eyewitness jealous of either Terri or the boyfriend?"

"A good question," Laura said, thinking maybe Carl should be the reporter. He was good at asking good questions. "I suppose you could say jealousy played some part with the witness, but if you're asking whether that could be the motive for the killing, that the eyewitness got jealous of one or the other, then killed Terri and now is trying to frame the missing boyfriend, I'd say that's impossible. And that's also all I can tell you, in addition to what's in the article."

"That's fine, you just answered all my questions with one word," Carl said.

"What word was *that*?"

"I'm a painter. When I use colors I use them precisely. I don't use blue. I use sky blue, or medium blue, or navy blue, never just *blue*. I know you, Laura. We're friends, and I know you try to use words the way I use colors. The way you said that it was *impossible* for the eyewitness to be the killer can mean only one thing—the eyewitness was a female. But what was she doing hanging around outside? Don't tell me . . . she was a friend of the boyfriend or a friend of Terri's. It's not likely she was a friend of the boy; he'd hardly *tell* her about taking someone out to kill. So she's probably a friend of Terri's. Most likely her best friend. Who else would she tell?"

Laura was upset, she'd said too much and now needed to recover. "What if it was another boyfriend of Terri's?" she said.

"Not likely. You said in your article that the witness didn't actually see the killing. If it was a boy, and he thought there was sex going on inside, don't tell me that he wouldn't be peeping in the window and so would have seen the whole thing."

"That's just speculation," Laura said, again realizing she'd let out more than she should have, especially for Marie's sake . . .

"*Okay*, you've shown off, Mr. Detective, now let's hear about Missy," said Cynthia.

"Well," he said, "she's one interesting woman . . ."

"That earns you nothing. Come on, Carl."

"It's hard to put into words. She's beautiful and rich, and a loner. She knows everyone but has no friends. Not one, except maybe me—"

"Look, we all know she's not a *nice* person, but what we want—"

"What you want to know," he said half smiling, "is what she is like in bed."

Laura, who had been only half-listening, still worrying if she'd endangered Marie, was pulled back by that question and was surprised to hear herself saying, "Yes, Carl . . . let's hear it in one word."

"Touché," he said, hesitated a moment and came up with:

"Creative." He looked at them. "And that's all you'll get from me. After all, a gentleman doesn't kiss and tell." When they started to protest he held up his hands. "No, enough . . . it's your turn, Cynthia. You're on about Felix."

Turning to Laura, Cynthia said, "Are you going to see him personally for this piece?"

"Tonight, we're having dinner."

"Whose idea was that?" she said, an edge in her voice.

"His."

He didn't mention it when she saw him at the opera, she thought. "Well, what else do you want to know?"

"Tell me about his prison conviction," Laura said.

"How did you find out about *that*?"

"Someone in New Orleans told me."

"There's not much I can tell you," she said. "It happened after we were divorced. All I know is he took in a partner for a development deal. Normally Felix makes all the decisions on a project himself, but this time they split the duties between them. Something went wrong on the project and a couple of workmen were killed. Felix and his partner were charged with manslaughter or criminal negligence or something like that—and they went to prison," she said, and hastily added, "*but* he was pardoned later."

That corresponded to the information Laura had gotten from the New Orleans reporter: the charge had been manslaughter, they had both been sentenced to prison, and Felix had later been pardoned.

"Anything else?"

"I understand in prison his partner decided to change his story and took all the blame, and the governor himself pardoned Felix."

"So you're convinced he was innocent?" said Carl.

"Of course. Felix isn't the kind of man to do something like that. He's too much of a man to go around cutting corners and doing shoddy workmanship. That's just not him."

After the lunch Laura considered going back to the office but since her calendar was clear for the afternoon and she was bushed she decided against it. A nap would be good, plus she needed a little extra time to get ready for the evening with Felix. She turned onto Race Street and drove through Chinatown down to Delaware Avenue, then headed for home.

All the talk about Felix during lunch had, face it, more than intrigued her. From the moment they had met at Lagniappe she had found him extremely attractive. There was something just a bit dangerous, distinctly exciting about those finely etched features and dark beard. More than once since then she had found herself thinking about what it would be like to be kissed by him, to feel his beard and his lips against her . . . Obviously from the lunch exchanges she wasn't the only one with such thoughts. His ex, Cynthia, and Missy Wakefield were, it seemed, only a face slap short of pistols at dawn over him. However, for tonight, even though it was strictly for business, Laura had the inside track and she had to admit it made her feel good. Dinner and drinks seemed like a real date. It had been a long time since she'd been out with a man who wasn't just a friend, and she was looking forward to it . . .

She was in a good mood as she easily found a parking place on Front Street and walked the short distance down Emily to her house. Inside, she proceeded to the refrigerator, where she chose a beer instead of a white wine or seltzer. A small indulgence, but at least a beginning . . . Upstairs, she started the water for her bath, then went down the hall to her bedroom, where she took her time undressing, hanging up or consigning to her laundry bag as she went.

When she was down to bra and panties she went to her bureau to lay our fresh ones. She chose a matching set in light blue, all lace and shine, and laid them on the bed. Then on impulse she took out a matching garter belt and hooked it behind her. Even without stockings, just the feel of it around her waist and the straps hanging down made her feel more feminine—no, sexy.

She crossed the room and closed the door. On the back of the door was a long mirror, and she stood there, studying her reflection. For a moment she thought about Felix seeing her like this.

She crossed her arms in front of her and began to run her

fingers up and down her arms, causing goose pimples wherever she touched. Her fingers strayed to the lightly freckled flesh below her collarbone. As she watched herself in the mirror, her hands moved down, pausing momentarily to touch her breasts. She arched her back, running her hands over her ribs and flat stomach and back up again, but stopping short of her breasts. A slight shudder passed through her body, and then her expression abruptly changed as she forced herself to reach behind and unclasp her bra. Crossing her arms again in front of her, she slid first one strap down and then the other, still holding the bra in place as she watched herself in the mirror, as though some magic transformation had taken place since the last time. But of course it hadn't.

Slowly she lowered the bra. On her right side was a breast with a full pink nipple, with no more sag or stretch marks than on the breast of any other normal woman in her thirties. On the other side there was no breast. Just a series of crisscrossing scars she had wryly dubbed "Forty Miles of Bad Road," from the Duane Eddy song of her younger days.

A simple mastectomy was what her doctor had called it. The cause, a small lump, painless to the touch, whose only outward sign was a slight dimpling of the skin over it. But under the skin it was a malignancy.

Her mother had said it happened because she had angered God, that she had turned her back on her destiny as a woman to chase after a career and He had punished her for it. Her mother was Texas Gothic, but she had to admit there were a lot of womanly things she wished she'd done with her body before that day when it betrayed her . . . things she had put aside for her career and, like discarded toys, had never come back to again.

She turned away from the mirror. There had been a moment after the operation when she had bravely tried to have sex with Phil, a pipe-smoking professor who was her occasional lover. He tried bravely, too, but in the end the sight of her made him impotent, and the look on his face told her more than she needed to know. When she still tried to talk about it he said the thought of her operation made *him* feel old and too mortal. She hated him for that, for his weepy pseudo-sensitivity, but worse, she hated him for being the one to tell her that now she was no-man's land . . .

She started for the bathroom, the blue garter belt now lying on the floor like another of those discarded toys.

CHAPTER 13

T HE MEMBERS of Seven Squad were beginning to look the worse for wear. One set of bags under the eyes now appeared to be two. Sloan was no exception. Even though he seemed to be over his flu, exhaustion had set in.

Not so with Detective Mary Kane. The late hours she'd been keeping with Detective Spivak didn't seem to be bothering her.

"Kane, is there some sort of magic vitamin you've been taking?" Sloan said.

"I'm sorry, lieutenant?"

"Look around you. Everybody in this room looks like they're running on fumes. And then there's you. What gives?"

"I cannot tell a lie, sir. It doesn't take too much out of a girl to spend evenings having dinner in a swanky restaurant with a handsome man."

To jeers and catcalls her partner Spivak said, "Eat your heart out, peasants."

A good bunch, the veterans of Seven Squad, thought Sloan. Evans, Rafferty, Spivak, Kane. None except himself were handpicked, but what a luck of the draw to get them. They worked together as a tight, happy unit.

"All right, comedians, let's get to it. What did you turn up about Peter from the families and friends of the other missing girls?"

Silence, then Rafferty took the floor. "Not a goddamn thing, lieutenant. Not a word, not a whisper."

"Suggestions," said Sloan.

"Maybe it's not the same guy. Maybe he was only connected with Terri DiFranco and the other two missing girls and there's some other explanation for the rest of the disappearances," said Spivak.

"Don't you believe it," growled Rafferty. "It's the same guy."

Sloan had to agree with Rafferty. Although the solution Spivak posed was theoretically plausible, he didn't believe it, didn't feel it. Experience told him the unknown Peter was responsible for all of them. He'd been to the well too often to doubt it seriously.

"If it was him in each case, why'd he change his method?" asked Spivak.

Kane spoke up. "Maybe it's a progression. For some reason the increased risk of getting to know the girl first, getting her to care about him, and all the time knowing he was going to kill her, gives him a bigger thrill. I mean, that's what I think we're talking about here . . . a rocks-off thrill killer. A little more individual style than most, but that's what he is."

"What about the early girls?" said Sloan.

"He was nervous then," said Kane. "In a hurry. He'd just pick them up, get them in the car, and wham-bam. But as he went along he began to need more. The quickie wasn't enough for him anymore. He needed more danger, more involvement, more build-up."

"You turning into a shrink, partner?"

"Quiet, let her talk," said Sloan.

"Well, of course I'm speculating, but what I think is that he *feels* nothing, and what passes for emotion with him is some sort of warmth he gets from having these young girls fall for him. Kind of like a snake. Cold-blooded, you know. Picks up on the heat of his surroundings instead of generating it himself."

"Well," said Spivak, "if he gets off having these girls fall for him, why kill them? Why not keep them around? Enjoy them?"

"Kane?" said Sloan.

"Maybe he's impotent. When push comes to shove, you gentlemen should forgive the expression, he isn't there. He's humiliated, figures they're laughing at him, and then he goes into a rage and kills. We all know this is a common sort of pattern with rapists."

"Any other comments," said Sloan.

"The cold-blooded part sounds right," said Evans.

"We'll reserve judgment," said Sloan. "What do you have to report on your evening at Lagniappe?"

"Zero," said Kane.

"Nothing?"

"Nothing. We've kept our eye on Justin Fortier, the owner,

and chatted with other customers. Fortier still seems clean, nothing against him except the waitress' vindictive accusations. Everyone else, even his wife, seems to think the world of him."

"Okay," Sloan said wearily, give it another miss for a few days at Lagniappe. Maybe somebody is on to you and staying under wraps. Meanwhile, hit the streets. Theory's grand, but so far Peter is having his way with us. Not to mention these girls. Let's get the bastard."

CHAPTER 14

M ARIE ONLY made it as far as the park on Fourth between Morris and Tasker before she had second thoughts about going to Costello's to see the gang.

The coolness of the night had driven the younger kids out of the park, and she had it to herself. Climbing on top of the large stone turtle, she sat there for a long while, smoking one cigarette after another.

With Terri's death constantly on her mind, the world had changed for her. Excitement and pleasure were gone, replaced by a sleepy sort of sadness that kept her moving zombielike through the days. Days had passed since she had talked with that Laura from the newspaper, and everything she had been promised was true. Her name wasn't in the paper, but people found out and no one hated her for coming forward with her story about Terri's death. In fact, people had treated her like she was a hero.

The police had questioned her, had shown her mug shots of criminals and pictures of cars in hopes that she could identify one or the other. The car was easy, but Peter . . . when she couldn't find him in the pictures they brought in an artist. But no matter how many times they worked on it he could not capture Peter on paper. Still, in spite of her failure to identify him, the police had always gone out of their way to make her feel appreciated and safe.

At home, her parents had been kinder than she had ever thought possible. Her mother had bought her a new Phil Collins album from the K-Mart, and her father had gone so far as to take the whole family out to dinner at the Triangle Tavern during the week and had even stayed sober enough on Saturday night to go to Mass with them on Sunday.

Likewise, during the week she had enjoyed a special, unaccustomed popularity with the kids at school. Before, she had been the dumpy kid with the glasses who was friends with Terri. No more. But it couldn't make up for losing Terri. Her best friend. And when you came down to it, she had deserted Terri when it counted most. Even though no one had said it, she knew Terri must have screamed, must have struggled, and if she hadn't left because of a little rain she could have saved her best friend's life.

She thought of going to confession but gave it up because she had never liked the old priest who was sure to be on the other side of the booth. The dandruff that was always on his shoulders put her off, and she knew that a penance of Hail Marys, even if it was in the hundreds, could never bring absolution for the way she'd deserted Terri. She had tried praying, too, but it hadn't helped. Maybe if she could confess to one of the sisters it would be different. They could be so strong; they would know which punishment was right. But she couldn't do it so it was all just blowing smoke, as her father would say.

The only thing that made sense to her was a story on the six o'clock news about two sets of New Jersey teenagers who had joined together in a suicide pact leaving behind a videotape of the whole thing. She'd run out to buy a paper to get the full story and now carried the clipping everywhere she went.

Now sitting there on the stone turtle in the darkness, she took it out of her pocket but couldn't make out the headline. Still, just holding it somehow made her feel better . . . It was true, to kill yourself was a mortal sin and you went to hell for it, but that was all she could expect anyway. There was no forgiveness for deserting Terri. Maybe if God was the merciful God she'd always been taught about he'd let her spend time in purgatory with Terri. It didn't seem like too much to ask.

During the week her thinking had got beyond whether she deserved to die or not. She knew the answer to that one. The question was whether she would have the nerve to take her own life when the time came.

She fumbled for a cigarette and realized she was fresh out. She always did her best thinking with a smoke, and if she was going to figure things out she needed a fresh pack. Costello's was the closest place. She climbed off the turtle and walked through the park to the Moyamensing side and down Morris—and saw the silver car with the Springsteen bumper sticker, as it slowly drove past her and stopped in the middle of the block.

She stopped dead, strained her eyes to get a glimpse of him, couldn't, but it didn't matter. She knew he was there, she could *feel* him in the air. The night had turned evil. It was as if she was no longer on friendly Morris Street but had stumbled into some terrible place. The trees on either side of the street seemed menacing, their branches and trunks now hideously gnarled creatures reaching to claw at her and hold her for Peter, the shadows of every stoop and bush hiding handful upon handful of crawling, slithering nightmares, lying in wait to bite, sting, and torment her, until death.

Every sense told her to turn and run, to go for the police—all except one that she mistook for her sense of duty, telling her that she had run off once and failed Terri, and not to make it twice . . . slowly she put one foot in front of the other and moved toward that waiting silver car.

Suddenly everything was crystal clear to her . . . this was her trial by fire. Just like they'd learned about in school. What she had to do was to walk past the car. If she got by it without Peter knowing her, she was innocent and forgiven. If he recognized her, she was guilty and deserved to pay for it. She never considered who had arranged this imagined trial . . .

Step by step, she continued down the block, feeling Terri's presence now, giving her the courage to do the right thing, what she should have done right from the first.

Don't look around, just keep walking, she told herself.

As she neared the car, she began to pray. "Dear God, please bless and keep my family from all evil"—She was even with the rear fender now, only a few more steps—"and guide them in the way of the truth and the light"—Out of the corner of her eye she could see the door, the open window, and the darkness beyond—"Especially, Lord, please bless my father and keep him from—"

"Hello Marie," said a gentle voice from inside the car, shattering the nervous aura around her like a thunderclap.

The rest of her prayer went unsaid as she stopped in her tracks.

She was afraid to turn and look, to see her judge, but when he softly called out, "Come here, I want to talk to you," she obeyed because this was her punishment.

When she came close to the window the voice from the darkness said, "It was you, wasn't it? You're the one I read about in the newspaper. You're the one who saw us and told the police, aren't you, Marie?"

She didn't answer. There was no need to, she'd already been judged and found guilty.

"Answer me."

"Yes," Marie whispered.

"Look at me when I talk to you."

Marie raised her eyes to see this evil, but there was no horned devil . . . only a handsome, bearded man with tinted aviators, a leather jacket, white scarf, and driving gloves with holes over the knuckles.

"Was it really like you told the newspapers, you were hiding outside?" he asked.

"Yes."

"But why, Marie? Why would you do that?"

"Because I wanted to see you," she said, cooperating in her punishment. She had done the right thing not to walk past the car. Finally she was being called to account for her sins, she felt the burden of guilt at long last lifting.

Neither spoke for a moment, they just stared at one another. And then he said, "It's been hard for you with Terri gone, hasn't it?"

Marie nodded.

"I miss her, too," he said. "She was a wonderful girl."

Before Marie could give in and submit herself to him she still had to know the answer to one question.

"She loved you. Why did you have to do it?"

"Because it was her time."

It was the right answer for Marie. It was the same for her. She and Terri . . . it was the right time for both of them . . .

"You know it's a part of life. When the time comes it must happen to all of us. You understand that, don't you?"

"Yes."

"Understand that I loved her, too, and that when I did it there was no pain. I led her through pleasure after pleasure until she was ready . . . Now I'm back because I cannot leave you here alone and so unhappy, not when there's so much pleasure . . . So come around here and get in. It's time, Marie." The voice was quiet, almost a whisper. Yet for Marie it had all the force of a divine command.

She looked past him into the darkness of the passenger seat, and for a moment imagined she saw Terri there, sitting, smiling, waiting.

Marie did not hestitate. She walked around to the passenger side and got in, no longer alone or afraid.

CHAPTER 15

LAURA FINALLY found a parking place on Spruce Street near Twentieth. A young man dressed in leather jacket, red plaid flannel shirt and skin-tight faded Levis was leaning against her parking meter. Up and down the street other men either lolled in similar insouciant attitudes, chatted in small groups or walked little yappy dogs. Like many single women she had once lived in this neighborhood, finding it safe and clean, if a bit raffish and loud in the early hours of the morning.

She walked to the corner and turned north on Twentieth, her destination Clarisse's, an intimate, elegant restaurant in a storefront that had been, in sequence, a pharmacy, a waterbed store and a used-clothing store specializing in the Joan Crawford look.

The maitre d' saw her almost immediately and came hurrying over. When he confirmed that Felix had not yet arrived he led her to a small, four-seat bar in an alcove where she was the only customer. When the bartender asked for her drink order she considered a ladylike drink like a white wine or a kir, but decided on a beer. Whereupon the bartender gave her a look that said the old maxim was true: you could dress them up but you couldn't always take them out.

While she waited she studied a painting behind the bar—the portrait of a young, dark-haired girl. From the way the girl was dressed Laura guessed it had been painted sometime in the 1870s and had probably cost the owner of Clarisse's a pretty penny at auction at either Freeman's or the Fine Arts Company, but the cost or age of the picture was not what intrigued her. It was the portrait's subject. Allowing for changes in fashion, her dark-haired, stormy teenaged Juliet looks reminded her with a start of the picture of Terri on the handbill she still carried in her purse, the same combination of sensuality and innocence . . .

"Penny for your thoughts." Thoughts so deep she hadn't noticed Felix's arrival.

Before she could respond, the bartender appeared to take Felix's order. Noting Laura's beer, he said, "That looks really good,

I'll have the same." The bartender did not give Felix the same down-the-nose treatment he'd given Laura. "I get tired of all this white wine and overpriced champagne people seem determined to pour down your throat. Beer is really my favorite."

"Mine, too," she said.

"Now, about your thoughts . . ."

She told him how the girl in the painting reminded her so much of the teenager she'd been writing about in her paper.

"Oh, yes, you mean . . . Terri DiFranco."

"Well, I'm surprised but I confess rather pleased that you knew about that."

"Not just knew about it, Laura, but I read it carefully, as well as the promo for a follow-up. I was surprised at first, I admit it, to see your byline . . . putting it together with the way I met you with Carl and my impression that your beat was the art world and assorted celebrities. Surprised, but also pleased. Would it embarrass you to hear that I was moved by the piece? You made that girl and her life very real, real enough to make her death something meaningful. I have an idea that you've gotten pretty involved in it yourself. Or am I being presumptuous?"

"Well, no, you certainly aren't, and I'm certainly not embarrassed to hear you responded to my work. Believe me, it's a relief to get out of the features department where my boss wants to keep me on for the rest of my natural life. I guess I can tell you that the story on you was his idea, and at first I resisted. I wanted to concentrate all my time on Terri's story . . . I hope I'm not offending you?"

"Not at all, and frankly I wish you had had your way. I'm not much for being interviewed. Besides, Terri and girls like her are more important than a carpetbagger in reverse from New Orleans."

Better and better, she thought. The man was truly charming and even self-effacing. And he seemed genuine enough in his praise.

"One thing does bother me some," he was saying. "The last thing I want to do is alarm you, and you've probably thought of this yourself, but I doubt that this killer hardly shares my appreciation of your writing about him."

A chilling thought, and the truth was she really hadn't considered it. Thanks to him, though, she now would. "I appreciate your concern," she said, "but I think I'm safe. I have a friend, or at least am friendly with the detective in charge of the case. And criminals don't usually bother newspaper people or cops. They'd rather use the former, if they can, and avoid the latter. But like I said, it's nice of you to worry." *Take it easy with the personal stuff before the interview, Laura. Your professional persona is slipping badly.*

"If you don't mind," he said, "before we get to me, I am curious about the car . . ."

Thank God he didn't ask about the unidentified eyewitness; she wouldn't have to dance around that again. "The car, as I said in the article, is a Datsun 300ZX. The police are checking that out but they don't expect to come up with anything. They say there are several thousand of them in Philadelphia." She smiled. "It seems they call it the sportscar for accountants."

"Yes, of course, you're right, I did read about it in the article. I should have remembered . . . Well, so much for gloomy subjects. How about dinner? I'm starved."

As soon as they were seated, Laura pushed aside how attractive he was, and how good he made her feel, and got down to business. "W.C. Fields supposedly wanted his epitaph to read: 'On the whole I'd rather be in Philadelphia.' And comedians are always making the joke about the first prize being one week in Philadelphia, and the second prize being two weeks in our fair city. Question: why would a man like you, a man who could go anywhere, decide to involve himself in a major real estate project here?"

"Ah, back to work, right?"

"Right. Did you think this was just a social evening?"

"No, but I admit that's what I hoped."

And then she began to blow it again . . . "If you wanted that, why didn't you call me?" *God, how subtle.*

"Because"—and his face reddened slightly—"when I met you, you were with Carl. I don't make a habit of poaching on other men's women."

"So you wait for the woman to make the first move?" Which,

of course, she realized as soon as the unfortunate words were out of her mouth, was precisely what *she* was doing. "I'm sorry, we're getting off the track . . . you were, I think, getting ready to tell my why Philadelphia."

"Well, there's property going begging here, there's old money and banking to back sizable projects, and over the past twenty-five years the city has made a transition from blue collar to white collar, which means now there are people who can afford this middle-income project when it's finished."

"I thought you did your own financing?"

He looked at her. "You've done some homework. I understand you had some background from Cyn . . . Cynthia . . . at a lunch. Anyway, you're right, that's the way it was in the beginning, but it was very risky and my ego was a few times bigger than it is now. I even had poetic concepts to describe the way I operated . . . war and art. The war was capturing the property, the art was trying to make is aesthetically pleasing. I still try to do that, but a little differently . . . look, don't you think we should order?" And so saying he waved over the maitre d' and ordered such delicacies as sweetbreads and salmon garnished with caviar.

Laura waited until they'd finished their meal to get back to the interview. "You said you do things a little differently now. What did you mean?"

Felix sighed. "Okay, what I meant was that now I use local partners. They know the lay of the land, no pun intended, and can get local community support. It works better for all concerned."

And now Laura understood why Will Stuart was so strong for the article on Felix. The *Globe* had a quiet but steady policy of supporting commercial development in the city on the theory that it worked out by way of taxes to benefit the whole city. Entrepreneurs like Felix Ducroit were common in New York City but still fairly rare birds in the City of Brotherly Love. She took a deep breath and got ready to launch into what she knew would be a touchy subject . . . "I'm sort of surprised that you would use any partners, local or otherwise, after what happened with you and your partner in New Orleans."

Felix stiffened. "Meaning, I suppose, when I went to prison."

She waited, realizing that she'd already gone too far perhaps.

"I think you can get all you need there from the writeup in the *Times-Picayune* . . . Look, let's skip the coffee and dessert and get out of here."

"To where?"

"To a far far better place . . . forgive the feeble try at lightness, but I do think things are getting a little heavy here. We've done business, now I propose a nightcap . . ."

Should she go along? She knew what he probably had in mind, and truth to tell she was tempted. Very. She *liked* this man. He had sides to him, was intelligent and in spite of his one fall seemed honorable and decent. He also treated her the way few women were treated anymore these days. Nothing special, just good manners and reasonable attention to what she had to say. Plus he genuinely was easy on the eyes. Still . . . there was a risk that she'd never been able to be easy with, not since that damned operation . . .

"Well, shall we go? You look like you've gone off into some other time zone," he said. "Am I boring you?"

"What? Oh, no . . . Well, all right, but just for one and then I really have to get back home and get some sleep . . ." *Weak, Laura, weak all around—"just for one," and "I really have to get some sleep" . . . God, after all the practice you've had you ought to be able to do better than that.* He didn't seem to react, though, as he took her arm and proceeded to walk her the two blocks to the Excelsior, Rittenhouse Square's newest and most posh high-rise.

Along the way he opened up even more, and without any prodding. "You know, I always wanted to make a project of Angola. I could really do something there."

"Angola?"

"Sorry, I dont' mean the third world country. I mean the Louisiana State Prison. I had an on-the-scene chance to observe, as you know."

She looked at him, surprised that he was voluntarily talking about the prison thing. "Maybe you ought to try to do it right here, I mean with the Fairmount Prison."

"I don't think so. It doesn't have the same fond memories for me."

She appreciated that he was trying to keep it light for both their sakes, probably hers more than his, but she decided to pursue it, for herself as much as for the article . . . "Felix, why did your ex-partner change his story while he was in prison and exonerate you?"

"Who knows for sure . . . but he chalks it up to religion, to seeing the light. From Watergate to White House officials to a New Orleans real estate operator . . . born-again seems a common phenomenon. I'm not going to challenge it or necessarily believe in it. I'm just glad he did tell the truth and it sprung me, as they say."

"No grudges against him?"

"At first, you bet. But no more, or at least I don't let it overwhelm me like I once did. The trick is to keep going, not to waste time or energy on the past."

There was something endearing in the way he talked straight out, no dissembling or excuses. On the other hand, how long did she know him? People had been known to put on an act before . . . *There you go again,* she thought to herself as they entered the lobby and took the elevator to his apartment. *Take Felix's advice and put the past behind. Sure, do it. Well, for God's sake at least try. This was, so far, a man worth taking a chance with. And what makes you so damn precious? Ease up and enjoy it. The evening is going well; you've managed to combine business and pleasure. So far . . .*

His apartment, high-tech and located on the twenty-first floor, had a wonderful view of the Square, but seemed too *moderne* to be cozy or even very livable. She was relieved to know it was a sublet from some woman Justin had put him on to at Lagniappe who was in Europe for several months, and to know that it wasn't necessarily to his tastes either.

He made drinks, and when he brought them she was still at the window looking down at the square. "It's quite a view," she said.

"Yes, it is."

Come on, Laura, you can do better than this. It's beginning to sound like an old Dorothy Parker story ... He: Well, here we are ... She: Yes, here we are ... and so forth.

She let herself feel his closeness, even though they weren't touching. There was a tingling sensation, a brief chill, and she crossed her arms, for a change not to protect herself from her feelings but to hold onto this special sense of closeness for as long as possible, to keep it from slipping away.

And just as it was about to fade, when they were in danger of losing it, he touched her and she turned to him. They came into each other's arms and held each other, at first just standing there, their bodies touching, and then, without coaxing or question, she raised her face to be kissed, and the darkness of his shadow crossed her face as he lowered his lips to hers. Whiskers and mustache, strange lips and whiskey added to the swirl of her emotions.

And then reality, her reality, abruptly stopped her from what she wanted most. To go on would mean the old nightmare she still couldn't cope with. The further they went, the closer he would be to discovering her secret. And when he found it out, even with a man like Felix, there would be the same look of pity that had been on Phil's face when he, too had touched her ... She pushed him away, not looking at him, not seeing the surprised look on his face.

Her breath was ragged. "I can't. I'm sorry, I want to, but I just can't ..."

And she had gathered up her things from the sofa and was out the door, never once daring to look at him.

CHAPTER 16

MISSY HAD had enough. Only moments earlier she had learned that her credit had run out at Le Club, the exclusive Olde City health club on Arch near Second. And it was not just the bounced checks. No, it was because the word was out—her father had left her nothing. She no longer was the right sort, no longer had the right stuff . . . a matter of genes and an inadequate inheritance. Nothing for it but to call in a major chit.

She drove down Second Street to Walnut and circled the block to reach Chestnut, where she parked at a meter in front of the Philly Fish Company, then walked up Chestnut Street toward Third and entered a loft building near the corner. She rang for the elevator, tapping her foot impatiently while she waited for it to arrive.

Long ago the five-story building had served the garment industry, and the elevator was a serviceable but old-fashioned freight elevator. When it at last arrived Missy pulled down and pushed up the heavy doors that opened horizontally rather than vertically as on passenger elevators. Once on board she closed them, pulled down the picket-fence safety gate and pressed the button for the fifth floor. When she got there she repeated the laborious process with the doors, this time not bothering to close them when she exited the old elevator.

The front part of the floor, the studio of Klaus Knopfler the sculptor, was filled with half-finished statues in stone, wood or welded metal, along with enough tools to stock an auto repair shop.

She moved past the sculptures without seeing any of them and began to pound on a plain door set in what looked like a temporary wall dividing the floor into halves, the rear half being the loft that served as Carl Laredo's living quarters. She could have used her key, but after the way Carl had behaved at Lagniappe, and with that Laura, he could damn well wake up with a bang . . . although not the sort of bang he'd prefer. That would come later, depending on his being a good boy . . .

143

After a few minutes a grumpy Carl, still half-asleep and wearing nothing but a maroon satin-and-brocade robe, opened the door. Clearly, she thought, he would have preferred to see someone else. Laura, no doubt.

Without being invited, she moved in past him and proceeded to the kitchen area, where she sat down at the large round table, lit a cigarette, settled back in her chair and looked at Carl, who was still standing.

"I finished my workout early this morning, thought I'd have breakfast with you before the lab. How about some coffee?"

"Sure . . . Look, about that night at Lagniappe and Laura, well, there's nothing between us. We were just friends out celebrating . . ."

Missy smiled. "Yes, how is Laura? Have you seen her recently?"

Measuring coffee into the filter, he said, "Actually I have— yesterday at lunch. She was having lunch with Cynthia Ducroit at the Reading Terminal Market, I happened to be there and Cynthia invited me to join them."

Missy's interest perked up at the mention of two of the women she despised most in Philadelphia being so chummy.

"And Laura? Did she invite you, too?"

"No, she was interviewing Cynthia for an article on Felix."

Getting better and better. "The coffee's ready, Carl." When he brought it she patted the place next to her at the table and asked him to tell all about his lunch with the ladies. "You *know* how fascinated I am when girls get together to dish someone . . . Did they mention me?"

"Yes, or at least Cynthia did."

"Why was that?"

"Jealousy, what else? I suspect Cynthia wants to get back together with Felix, only you seem to be in the way."

Missy took a drag on her cigarette. "Does she really think she can get Felix back?" she said, looking at him over the rim of her cup as she took a sip.

"I don't think she knows but I'm pretty sure she's going to try." Seeing her obvious discomfort at that piece of intelligence, Carl was secretly pleased. Missy deserved a little back, always so demanding, making him feel less than he was, so dependent on her when it was his art and talent that really opened the way for him. All his life, though, if he were to be honest with himself, it had been that way ... domineering, controlling older women, or women who acted as though he were something to be manipulated. Beginning with his darling sister, six years older, who always lorded it over him, beat him up even, whenever she caught him doing something no more venal than sneaking a cigarette in the bathroom or behind the shrubbery that surrounded their house. One time she'd gotten so mad at him she'd knocked him unconscious with her hairbrush, and just for looking, for God's sake, at her and some of her girl friends in a girls-only session in her bedroom. He was only ten at the time; you'd have thought he was some kind of most-wanted criminal. He never forgot that beating, and when she died a couple of years ago, he had to admit the tears wouldn't come, even though he tried to fake them for the sake of family and friends ...

"Well, Carl, wherever you just went, come on back. Now tell me how the ex-Mrs. Ducroit thinks she's going to get Felix back."

"Probably by giving him what he wanted when they were married."

"And that is ... ?" Although she knew the answer too well.

"A baby."

She forced herself to sound calm. "What makes you think that?"

Warming to it now, Carl gave a full exposition of the lunch with Cynthia and Laura, told how Cynthia had admitted her career-oriented head at the time wouldn't allow for children but that she felt different now and if she got another chance she wouldn't make the same mistake twice.

Missy felt her throat tightening, could hardly breathe. And there was the flare-up of the pain around that scar, that twelve-year-old scar ... Since the last attack at the opera with Felix, brought on by the same thing, the talk about pregnancy, she had done her best to keep even the notion of that unwanted state out of her mind. She had also bought a simple gold tie-clip and sent it to Felix with a note of apology and the inscription,

"Please forgive this impetuous lady. Until next time . . ." But now, with Carl confirming what she had worried about herself, she knew she would have to go into action, give up the demure and passive Miss Missy to get Felix. The little lady Cynthia with her cutsie La Charcuterie on Pine Street was going to be sorry she ever showed up in this town. The grand opening of her store was one thing . . . the grand opening of her legs to win back the prodigal ex was too much . . .

She took a deep breath and reminded herself of the reason she'd come to see Carl this morning. "Carl," she said, moving close to him, putting her hand on his thigh, "believe it or not, I've missed you. Sure, I was annoyed that evening at Lagniappe, but friends should stick together, right? We have so much in common, we've shared such pleasure . . ." And now her hand had moved upward, massaging him, squeezing, causing pain and then releasing him for pleasure . . . a cycle that she knew he couldn't stand and couldn't resist.

"Missy, for God's sake, stop it. It's too early for that sort of thing. I've got to go to work, lots to do before the opening in New York—"

Which earned him a most painful tightening around his scrotum. "I'm glad you mentioned the move to New York, Carl. I want to be able to be with you, share some of it with you. I assure you Laura isn't the only one who knows people in that art world. We'll have such fun sharing things, like before, and I won't even interfere with your little teenie-boppers. After all, a man needs variety, I understand all that . . . but, Carl, for me to be with you, to help you, I'm going to need your help." All the while her hand being busy, busy, busy.

"Missy, what? Please . . ."

"*What*, Carl dear, is that I need you right now this minute to write me a check for fifteen thousand dollars. It will help me clear up some nonsense that's happened since my father died and free me to be close to you when you need me. And you're going to need me, Carl . . ."

He tired to pull away. "Missy, my cash is tied up. And I'm not as rich as you think I am anyway. There's a limit—"

But there was no limit to Missy's not so tender ministrations, and finally, he had no choice but to write her a check and beg her to bring him relief, which, smiling, she proceeded to do.

"You and your little winkie," she said. "All better now, lover."

And then she was saying, under her breath, "We're two of a kind," but she did not mean herself and Carl, she meant herself and Cynthia Ducroit. Two going for one—Felix. And only one would be left standing when the final round ended.

CHAPTER 17

WHEN LAURA looked at herself in the bathroom mirror, the gray morning light showed a face filled with exhaustion. The night had been a long and bad one, the two sides of her battling over the way she'd run out of Felix's apartment.

She was brushing her teeth, the bathroom radio tuned to WMMR's "Morning Zoo," when she heard someone downstairs knocking forcefully on her front door. She tried to ignore it, but the banging wouldn't stop. Probably the meter man. But why so early? Holding her robe around her, she went barefoot downstairs to let him in.

Her front door was a blue-and-gray farmhouse door, the top half panes of glass, but the curtain over them kept her from seeing who was outside. When she opened it, she got a shock. Waiting on the steps was a darkly bearded man with aviator-style sunglasses and wearing a leather jacket. Momentarily . . . it was more than enough for her already frazzled nerves . . . she thought Terri DiFranco's killer had come to call. Then she shook off the image and took in the most welcome if unexpected sight of Felix.

"Good God, I thought you were the meter man . . . well, uh, come in . . ." She thought she'd never see him again after the way she'd run out of his place like some hysterical virgin.

"Sorry to disappoint you," he said. "No meter, but breakfast. Okay?" He jokingly turned it aside.

Laura nodded vigorously. "Yes . . . sure, but how did you find me? I didn't give you my address—"

"Oh, I did a little detective work. I looked in the phone book. By the way, keeping your number listed isn't such a good idea for someone in your line of work, is it?"

"I only used initials," she said lamely.

"Well, I've got coffee and fried eggs and bacon sandwiches on whole wheat with mayo, horseradish and Louisiana hot sauce."

She looked at him. "Thank you, Felix, I'm really glad to see you, but I can't eat that stuff. I start off my day with coffee and a cigarette, never eat before noon—"

He marched to her small kitchen table where he began opening bags. "I figured as much. That's why I'm here. Someone has to save you from yourself, and breakfast is as good a place to start as any." He waved some newspapers at her. "I brought the papers but forgot the orange juice. You *do* have orange juice, don't you?"

"Yes, of course."

"Good. Now, I think you better put on something a little less interesting or there's no telling what might happen . . ."

Was he making fun of her? Giving her a bit of needling for last night? Whatever, she hurried upstairs to her bedroom and proceeded to fix things as though Felix were right behind her . . . She picked up her clothes from last night and separated them into the laundry or dry cleaning bags, straightened the teetering stack of books on the old steamer trunk that still served as her bedside table, emptied the ashtray and put last night's beer can into the wastebasket.

She took her time dressing, staying nude longer than necessary, knowing that she was half-daring, half-afraid Felix would open the door. That way she could get it *over* with, see the look on his face when he realized that she had only one breast, and she could finally stop kidding herself . . .

Glancing at the door, she began to dress: first, panties, silky soft, trimmed with lace. As she slipped them on she thought that even if her relationship with Felix couldn't go all the way, there was also no reason why she shouldn't *feel* as womanly as possible while she was with him . . . She chose a matching bra, also lace trimmed, and put it on, fitting her rubber prosthesis— she privately called it the thing—into it. Before she pulled on her pantyhose she checked herself in the mirror. Not so bad.

She finished off with a pleated, gray wool skirt, white blouse with a bulky sweater vest and boots.

He was at the table, steaming coffee in a styrofoam cup in front of him, reading the paper.

"You were gone so long I was beginning to think you'd tied the sheets together and made good your escape."

She started to apologize with the cliché about women taking a long time to dress, but she stopped herself before it came out. She smiled sweetly and sat down. "I see the *Globe* here by my place, thanks. But what are you reading?"

"The *National Enquirer*, what else?"

"I don't believe it. Let's see," she said, reaching across the table for it. "Okay, your tastes are noted," but she still took the time to flip through it, feeling his gaze on her as she did.

"While you were upstairs I read the *Globe*. That was a moving piece you wrote about Flora, the old woman, and the relationship she had with this Terri girl. Like I said at dinner, I admire the way you think, your involvement, the way things affect you."

His soft, quiet voice touched her, and in spite of the tight rein she kept on herself she also felt herself beginning to relax, open up. She wanted more.

"Keep on doing what you're doing," he said seriously, looking directly at her, "and I'll be behind you a hundred percent." He reached across the table to cover her hand with his own.

"Thank you." It was what she wanted to hear, but still wasn't able to look at him.

Instead she looked at their hands, liked the feeling of his on hers, covering, protecting. His palm felt so soft. This was a hand meant to touch, to stroke, to bring pleasure, and she almost shivered at the thought of it. But it was not a weak hand. Soft as the palm was, that was how scarred and broken the back was. Two of the knuckles had been broken and were misshapen. In the valleys between them were angry red weals where the skin had been ripped open and sewn back together. She lightly traced the scars with her finger. "What happened?"

"Prison," he said. Nothing more.

And now she felt an overwhelming desire to protect *him*, to cover the broken part of his hand with the softness of her own. Then, just as at his apartment, when the feeling between them was created and began to fade, he moved, this time gradually pulling away, leaving her wishing for more.

When he said, "Should we go?" she decided he was as uncertain of them as she was.

"Yes," she said, hoping her tone would convey more than the simple word, that he would press her, take away her initiative, force her to see him again. She went to him and touched him, her hand moving lightly down his arm until they were holding hands again.

"I'm very glad you came," she said. "I mean it."

"Today is Halloween. What are you doing tonight?"

"I have to go to Henri David's ball at the Warwick, for the paper. And you?"

"I have to meet Cyn."

"So we couldn't have been together anyway," jealous at the idea of him spending time with his ex-wife, and even at his nickname for her.

"No, no, it's just for a drink. She called up, there's something she wants to talk about. I agreed to meet her but after that I'm free."

"What about Missy? I would have thought she might figure in your Halloween plans." *Wonderful, Laura, play the jealous shrew. Just what he needed to hear. Cut it out . . .*

Felix stopped, took her by the shoulders and turned her to face him.

"Laura, enough. I don't need you to remind me about my ex-wife or Missy. I already know what I'm going to do about them, and I'd appreciate it if you'd keep a button on those very pretty lips of yours. Anyway, jealousy doesn't become you, never mind that it doesn't apply so far as I'm concerned."

"I'm sorry . . . of course you're right . . ."

"Good. Now, it seems tonight is out. So dinner tomorrow." It was not put as a question.

She quickly agreed and they sealed it with a kiss, one that took something for the moment and left more for the future.

At the door they kissed lightly again, almost like old lovers parting, and she stood on the steps watching until he was out of sight.

Before she could go back inside, Jean, her heavyset next-door neighbor, came out all red-faced and upset.

"What's wrong?" Laura said.

"I just got a call from one of the girls over on Mifflin. A cop making his rounds cruised by the old depot and noticed a window was open. He checked it out. There was another body inside. They think it's Terri's girl friend. Marie . . ."

Laura felt sick. Not Marie. *No.* She turned and began to run toward the depot, hoping against hope that this time the neighborhood grapevine was wrong, but in her gut afraid they were right—and that her articles had caused it.

CHAPTER 18

W HEN THINGS were under control at the depot Sloan left the cleanup work to Rafferty and the rest of the squad and headed back to headquarters. He felt lousy, and from more than his cold. The case was falling apart in his hands, and he was responsible for at least some of it.

Up to now he hadn't admitted it to himself, but, face it, he'd brought Laura in on it not just because he liked her—which he did—but also as a bit of grandstand play. It looked simple and harmless enough at the time. Take over the missing-persons files, canvas the neighborhood for information about Peter and make the arrest. All to the tune of some very positive headlines for Seven Squad and the department, and himself. He never imagined that no one in a tight-knit neighborhood like South Philly would have seen this character. The guy was linked with three separate girls. But, it seemed, no one had. No one except one teenage girl, and now she was dead, too.

He'd also lost his cool at the depot. Laura had shown up again, and he had all but accused her of causing Marie's death with her stories, which she was already blaming herself for. But it wasn't her fault. It was his—for not nailing this Peter by now. Kane let him know how off-base he was with Laura, and that was when he decided to leave the cleanup to the squad and get away from it for a while.

A nightmare. They'd had no substantive breaks since the La- gniappe matchbook. The costumers check gave them nothing. For a moment there he'd thought Justin Fortier looked good for it, but that went down the tubes when the accusing ex-employee, Spivak reported, turned out to be a thief and her own friend the victim. And Fortier didn't own a Datsun 300ZX. Evans and Rafferty had actually come up with the two sex offenders who owned 300ZX's. Likewise a dead-end—one was the wrong color, black, and the other was dead from a heart attack.

Now he was back to square one, only this time he had a second body. Marie—his only eyewitness.

He parked in the lot and had started for the Roundhouse when he heard someone call to him, the voice coming from a black Corvette parked across the street.

"Hey sailor . . ."

He wasn't in the mood for games, but walked across the street to find at the wheel of the Corvette Delores Inverso, the daughter of mobster Nicholas Inverso. She was looking punk as ever, but somehow even with the streaked red hair and fingerless gloves she seemed somehow easier to take than at their last meeting. He shook his head. Too much down time. He'd been without a woman too long if he found a mob leader's daughter a prospect.

Next to her in the passenger seat was a Catholic priest. Sloan couldn't see him too well, but well enough to make him out as Oriental. Sort of strange.

"How goes it, Delores?"

His hand was resting on her windowsill, and she covered it with hers. Her fingers felt warm. "I'm good, you look terrible." She didn't move her hand from his. "Today's Father Nguyen's market day. You know Father Nguyen, don't you? He's from Sacred Heart."

"Hello, Father."

"Bless you, my son," which somehow sounded odd coming from this face and accent. He had grown up on priests that sounded like Barry Fitzgerald. He almost smiled. Years ago Bob Dylan had said a mouthful: "The times they are a-changin'."

"I bring him down here every week so he can shop in Chinatown. He says you can't get good rice in South Philly."

"Makes sense, I guess. Pasta, yes. Rice, no."

"Anyway, Sloan, Dad heard about the second body and he wasn't too thrilled. People know he asked you to wrap this up in a hurry, and he's starting to look bad. Especially with the second body."

"Well, goddamn it, tell Dad we're trying—"

"So this time," she continued smoothly, "he's going to make an exception. You know what I gave you the last time . . . well, that same guy—the one who's interested in the young girls—is going to be at the corner of Eleventh and Washington at four this P.M. A friend arranged for him to meet some girls there. Dad thinks it might be a good idea if you dropped around." She patted his hand, then squeezed it. "Now we've got to be running. Father's saying Mass tonight. Call me sometime. Let's have a drink. *Ciao*," she said, as she put the black Corvette in gear and pulled away from the curb.

Sloan looked at his watch. It was after two. Hardly enough time to collect the squad and get set up on Washington before four.

He hurried to his car and put in the radio call to the squad at the depot, then headed for Eleventh and Washington.

Rafferty and Evans, Kane and Spivak met him there.

About three o'clock the players started showing up. A brown Mercedes sedan stopped alongside the trolley stop and several females got out of the backseat. All were dressed like teenagers, but Sloan recognized a couple of them from prostitute round-ups. They were anything but teenagers. As the Mercedes drove by, the driver waved at Sloan. Sloan recognized him, too—at the wheel was Sylvester "Slick" Gianni, the man in charge of prostitution at the docks.

At four on the nose an old white Cadillac convertible pulled alongside the tracks and stopped. The ladies at first appeared coy, and then gradually one by one they began to approach the car. When they had all gathered around the passenger side, one of them gave a little wave.

"That's it, move in," Sloan said into the radio.

As he pulled out so did Rafferty and Evans in their car, and Kane and Spivak in theirs. Rafferty and Evans were the closest and immediately blocked his escape. Kane and Spivak did the same on the other side.

Sloan got out, gun and badge in hand. The ladies around the car scattered. Sloan called out: "Don't move, police."

The driver of the car didn't try to move. Rafferty jerked open the door on the driver's side and pulled the suspect out.

Sloan read him his rights. Then: "What's your full name?"

"Carl Laredo, but what's all this—?"

They handcuffed him and put him in the back of Sloan's car.

Rafferty rode with Sloan to police headquarters while Spivak followed in the Cadillac. Carl kept asking what this was about. Nobody answered him.

Once at the Roundhouse they immediately gave him a saliva test. If his ABH factors didn't match the killer's or didn't show up at all, meaning he was a non-secretor, he was in the clear. Otherwise . . .

While they were waiting for the results of the saliva test Sloan began the interrogation, with Rafferty the only other cop in the room. It was good cop-bad cop time. He, good. Rafferty, bad.

"Soliciting sex is a crime. You know that . . ."

"I wasn't soliciting or propositioning. I'm an artist," Carl said nervously. "I was trying to commission them to model for me—"

"What will they think of next?" said Rafferty.

Sure, far-fetched, but the word "artist" rang a bell with Sloan. Kane said she'd met an artist at Lagniappe . . . He went outside. "Kane, is this the guy you met at Lagniappe?"

"Yes, lieutenant." She sounded unhappy.

"He says he was trying to hire those girls as models. Know anything about it?"

"Not a thing."

Sloan went back inside. Evidently in his absence Rafferty had begun to apply some pressure, because Carl Laredo looked at him like some kind of savior.

"I'm just *trying* to tell this man that I was *not* soliciting those girls for sex. Nobody in their right mind would mess with a street girl. Not with AIDS and all. I'm an *artist*—"

"We know that, Mr. Laredo," Sloan said. "Now calm down and tell us what you were doing there."

"Same thing I've been doing there for the last several months. Like I said, I'm an artist. I lived in France for several years. You know about Paris street scenes; artists always paint them. While I was there I got interested in the Apache dancers of the Fifties. You know, the guy in the beret and the woman in the split skirt. I thought of combining them with a conventional street scene to make what would be sort of mean streets Paris-style. When I came back here I decided to do the same with Philly street scenes, and the best-looking girls for it are in South Philly. So every few weeks I hire a couple of the hookers, take them back to my place and take some Polaroids to work from. That's all. No sex. No nudity even. The way they're dressed with the high heels and the tight jeans, that's what I want to paint—"

Kane stuck her head in. "Lieutenant, can I see you?" Her voice sounded better.

He went outside.

"The lab report is in."

"And?"

There was a hint of a smile. "He's not our man. He's a secretor, all right, but with blood type A, *not* O."

Her smile told him that she liked Carl Laredo more than she was saying.

Sloan sighed. Even the mob was wrong once in a while.

CHAPTER 19

Missy held the double old-fashioned glass filled with ice at eye-level as though it was a chemist's beaker and poured into it from the frosty Stolichnaya bottle. Her hands were rock steady. Up, up, up, rose the level of the clear liquid, thickened by the cold of the refrigerator, until she stopped just short of the rim.

She carefully put the bottle down on the kitchen counter as though it was filled with nitroglycerin. Spread out next to it on the counter's black ceramic tile surface was a single-edged razor blade, a small pile of white powder, and a tiny silver coke spoon.

The sounds of Bryan Adams singing "Heaven" filled the room, and outside on the Delaware River, through her kitchen window, she could see a tug muscling into its berth a white tanker showing rust streaks through its paint job and flying the Panamanian flag of convenience in the fading twilight. But if she noticed either she gave no sign of it.

Holding the glass with both hands in a peculiarly little-girl fashion, she brought it to her lips, looked over the rim of the glass as she tilted it upward and drank, her eyes bright and staring, but at a point that only her mind could see, her pupils portals to the darkness beyond.

A drop of moisture fell from the glass onto her bare chest and trickled down between her breasts. She paid it no mind. Seemed unaware of it.

She drank again, taking in the icy sterile bite of the alcohol; the level in the glass dropping noticeably, its frigid coldness seeming to bring her back to the here and now.

Since that night at the opera her hatred of Cynthia had been building. Her scheming was obvious. There was her play for Felix at the opera. Her lunch with Carl and that Ramsey woman when she all but said she would even get pregnant to get Felix back. And now today she'd called him for a date and he'd accepted. Out of obligation, of course, but nevertheless it had spoiled tonight's Halloween plans Missy had made for them.

She'd called him with fabulous plans. A great costume party. Special turn-on lingerie she was going to wear for him. Tonight was going to be the night when they finally went to bed together. But now it was all off, and it was all because of Cynthia.

Twice after she'd heard about their date she had had blinding attacks of the pain, trying again to come to terms with the idea of getting pregnant, giving Felix the child he wanted. Cynthia had provoked all that, and there was no reason in the world for Missy to put up with it. Like she'd told herself when she left Carl that morning, only one of them was going to be left standing when this thing was over. And it wasn't going to be the ex-Mrs. Ducroit.

Putting her glass down beside the bottle she leaned over the counter and scooped up powder with the tiny spoon. She sniffed it up each nostril, twice, three times, and daintily wiped away any excess with the tip of her middle finger.

Cynthia was like a Barbie doll she'd had as a child. When Barbie thought no one was around she would torment Ken, her male doll, and make him do horrible things. Missy tried everything to get her to stop. She lectured her, scolded her, even separated the dolls, but it did no good. As soon as Missy's back was turned Barbie would begin to torment Ken again. Missy had no choice except to punish her. Each night when she was alone in her room with the dolls she would take off all of Barbie's clothes, then press her against a hot lightbulb, softly talking to her all the while, trying to get her to see the error of her ways. Barbie was stubborn, parts of her would blacken from the pain and the heat, but even that didn't help. She was still bad. Finally Missy had no choice except to do away with her.

She hid Barbie's remains beneath a bush near the swimming pool, and that night when the Ken doll asked her where Barbie was, she told him that Barbie had gone away and wouldn't be back. The Ken doll knew what had happened, but he wasn't sad. He knew Barbie was bad, too . . .

She picked up her glass and padded barefoot across the kitchen, her bare body caught and reflected in fragments around the room like strewn parts in the aftermath of destruction—her face reflected in the shiny ceramic tile, her hand and forearm in the surface of the toaster, her leg and buttock in the window of the oven door.

Felix . . . he was gentle like the Ken doll. He didn't understand how women could be. They were deceitful creatures like her mother. They took from men and gave nothing in return. Laughed at them. Committed adultery with their best friends. Made fools of them. Even drove them to an early grave, like her father. Well, she would not let that happen with Felix. She would protect him . . .

In her bedroom, laid out on her king-size bed with almost military fashion, were a dark leather jacket, a white aviator's scarf, leather driving gloves with holes over the knuckles, trousers, shoes and socks, a shoulder holster with an automatic in it, jockey shorts, a Latex set of cyclist's shorts, two rolls of wide elastic bandage, a pair of handcuffs, a small pile of stainless steel chains, a plastic bag filled with what looked like human hair, and a flesh-colored dildo with a head at each end.

She picked up the elastic bandage from the bed and turned to face the wall of mirrors that concealed her closets. As she began to bind her chest, the elastic flattening her breasts, forcing them into a square shape like a man's pectorals, she felt a familiar surge of pleasure and almost purred at the thought of her own wetness.

When she finished her binding she stopped to admire herself in the mirrors. What stared back at her had no gender identity. Her face, while still attractive, without makeup seemed curiously angular and almost boyish. Her bandaged breasts were squared off, showing no nipples, not even tiny male ones. And below, on her mons veneris where a brunette would normally have a triangle of rich, dark hair, she was shaved clean, the lips of her labia invisible from across the room, as though she had no genitals at all. This was the moment she always savored most—presto, chango, alakazam, gone was the woman, born was the man.

But today the vision was marred, and it took a moment to

figure out why. Her scar, no matter the pain, was normally flesh-colored and invisible, but tonight it seemed angry and red. She looked down at the twelve-year-old scar. It wasn't red at all, but when she looked in the mirror it again seemed so.

She turned away, afraid that if she looked any longer at herself the scary, truncated memories would start again, and so would the pain.

Twice in one day was more than enough. She'd had all she could take. Twice she'd seen herself standing in the doorway of her father's study, waiting to tell him. Twice he'd looked up from his desk. And twice the pain had come as strong as if she'd stuck her finger in a light socket. She didn't want to know what happened afterward. Not anymore. She just wanted to get on with her life with Felix. There was so much for them to have together . . .

She crossed the room and took a long pull on her drink, her hands no longer rock steady, now shaking as if she were cold.

The alcohol helped. It always did. The very clinical nature of the vodka was soothing, gave the illusion that she was sterilizing, purifying herself deep inside.

From the bed she picked up a thin stainless steel chain that she fastened snugly around her waist, leaving one end free and dangling down behind. The dangling end, resting in the cleft of her buttocks, felt cold against her skin.

She picked up the two-headed dildo. It was made of flesh-colored rubber, giving it the approximate rigidity of a real penis but also a certain overall flexibility. Near the midpoint was a small hole in the shaft. Reaching between her legs with her free hand she grasped the end of the chain and pulled it to her.

The hole in the shaft accommodated the chain perfectly, and she threaded it through like it was the eye of a needle. Opening her legs slightly, she worked one head of the dildo into her vagina, pushing it in, in, in until several inches were lodged inside her. Holding it with one hand, she used the other to pull the chain through the hole until it was taut. The friction of the chain against the rubber made a sound like a zipper. She adjusted it carefully, forcing the chain into her labia until it was almost painful and cutting, finally clipping it in front to the length around her waist. Viewed now, the chain was not entirely unlike a sanitary napkin of the old belt-and-pad days, and unrefined as it was it still served its purpose, firmly anchoring the dildo in place and giving the remaining shaft and head very nearly the angle of a real penis.

Next came the white jockey shorts that she pulled on with brisk familiarity, taking a moment to work the dildo through the fly as if she was preparing to urinate . . .

When she was ten, she remembered, her father had taken her to Jacob Reed's and bought her her first jockey shorts for her, telling her that she should wear them when she rode horseback to keep down the chafing. The intimacy of what he had done didn't embarrass her, it made her feel good, so good, to know that he thought of her as one of the boys. That night at home she managed to get him alone for a few moments and took down her pants to show him that she was wearing them. At her age it wasn't sexual or even flirtatious. She just wanted to please him. He looked at her oddly as she stood there with her jeans pushed down to her knees and her shirt pulled up. It wasn't a look of disapproval. It was a look that made her tingle, a look she wanted to see again . . .

Over the jockey shorts she pulled on the latex cyclist's shorts, again pausing to work the dildo through a hole in the front of the shorts before she pulled them all the way up. Turning sideways so she could see her behind in the wall of mirrors, she kneaded and prodded her buttocks until they, too, like her breasts, were flattened into a more square, masculine shape, kept that way by the elastic restraint of the tight, girdle-like shorts.

Satisfied, she tugged on the dildo a couple of times to be certain it was still firmly in place and was rewarded with delicious sensations from its friction. There was no doubt about it, she would be able to have an orgasm later with Cynthia. Just because Cynthia was going to die was no reason they shouldn't enjoy themselves beforehand. That's the way it had been with all the South Philly girls. She could see no reason to change it.

Originally her intention had only been the seduction. Nothing more. But the very first one, long before Terri and Marie, had seen through her disguise. That was before she had perfected Peter's look. And that little tramp had tried to blackmail her right on the spot. Either give the money or she would tell her parents. They wouldn't have any trouble tracing the license number; her uncle was a cop, she'd said. A real tough one. She'd left no choice. Couldn't have her father find out something like that. So she'd killed her out of necessity. But she'd also found a tremendous, unexpected release. A release she'd sought over and over ever since then.

Outside her bedroom window the river was shining darkly. That was where all the bodies had gone. One by one, weighted down and sent to their watery grave in the river channel. All she had done was ferry them out from her condo dock in her little runabout and shove them overboard.

All except Terri and Marie. They were special. She was closer to Terri than to any of the others, and through her, to Marie. And when it was over she couldn't leave the parents watching the door, waiting for the phone to ring, wondering what had happened to them. It wouldn't be fair. So she had left their bodies behind. As a favor.

With a rather wistful smile on her lips, Missy picked up the plastic bag filled with hair and went into the bathroom. She darkened her skin slightly with makeup and added the illusion of fullness to her brows with an eyebrow pencil. Then after daubing spirit gum on her cheeks, chin, upper lip, and jawline, she took the false beard and mustache purchased from a Center City theatrical costumer and carefully pressed it into place. The transformation was complete. Missy was gone, and staring back at her from the mirror was Peter . . .

She walked back to the bedroom and pulled on the shoulder holster with the automatic in it. Her phony badge, purchased along with the handcuffs from a Market Street junk shop catering to the switchblade crowd, and the gun, a present from her father, were insurance against something going wrong. With most of the teenagers no insurance was necessary.

It would be with Cynthia. She was too prim, too uptight to let herself go and enjoy herself. She would finally see through Peter, and only with the help of the gun would Missy be able to make her relax.

And afterward, when they were both physically satisfied, Cynthia would die, and Felix would belong to Missy.

She pulled on the leather jacket and draped the white aviator's scarf around her neck. From the inside pocket of the jacket she produced the dark glasses that Peter always wore. The stereo was booming with Tina Turner's "Private Dancer" as she looked in the mirror and ran her fingers through her hair one last time, then went into the kitchen, where she took a clean syringe with a small vial from a pot of warm water near the sink. The vial contained sperm. A sample she had taken from the office. As always, it was from a man who was a secretor with blood type O. She always used this type for two reasons. It was by far the most common type, so it was easy to get. Most men were secretors with blood type O. Her father had been. So was Felix. She recalled how cleverly she'd asked him what otherwise would have seemed a peculiar question: "Most people exchange zodiac signs when they meet. But I work in a lab, so for me it's blood type. I hope you don't mind . . ." He had looked at her a little strangely, but then had laughed and told her it was type O. She couldn't have been more pleased . . . one more thing in common with her father.

Her other reason for using sperm from a secretor with type O was her knowledge of police procedure, gained from the lab work her office did for the department. One of the first things they did in a rape case was to check the rapist's sperm for the presence of the water-soluble ABH factors to see if the man was a secretor and if so, to use them to determine what his blood type was. Then they would try to match it with any suspects they brought in. A secretor with type O was the most common and so the most difficult to identify. They'd need a very wide net indeed to catch Peter. Who, of course, didn't even exist. It was really quite delicious . . .

She put the syringe into the inside jacket pocket she had

taken the glasses from. Taking the vial in her hand, she unzipped her pants and reached deep inside, pulling out the leg of the tight Latex cyclist's shorts and shoving it up inside, as high on her thigh as possible to keep it warm in a natural way. After she finished with Cynthia, she would inseminate her. She pulled on the driving gloves with the holes over the knuckles and left by the door that led directly to her downstairs garage.

Inside her car she checked one last time. The automatic was loaded, she had the neck chain and handcuffs, she had the sperm, and she had cigarettes and a silver flask filled with brandy for the wait. Satisfied there was nothing left to chance, she punched the "Open" button on her remote control and the garage door quietly began to swing up.

As she backed her car out she happened to glance at her front steps. There, clutching Strawbridge & Clothier shopping bags, were two little girls in their Halloween costumes. One was dressed as Snow White, the other as a cowboy. Missy saw them turn to look and hurriedly pulled the sun visor across the open window on the driver's side to keep them from seeing her face. The tinted glass on the other sides kept anyone from seeing inside.

At the end of the driveway she spun the wheel and stopped long enough to get a good look at the trick-or-treaters, who were no longer looking at the car but were busy peeking into each other's shopping bag as they trudged down the steps and headed for the next house. Missy did not recognize them, which didn't signify: they still probably lived in the Delaware River townhouse complex; she just hadn't noticed them. She watched them walk away, certain they offered no threat, put the car into gear and pulled out into the Delaware Avenue traffic.

The area around Second and Chestnut was still quiet even though it was Halloween, and Missy easily found a parking place with a clear view of Lagniappe. As she settled down to wait behind her tinted windows, she looked at the clock. It said five-fifty. Good, she was early. Felix wasn't due to meet Cynthia until six.

She lit a cigarette and made herself comfortable. She would

wait until they left, then follow. Sooner or later the date would be over, Cynthia would be alone, and she would move in.

At two minutes past six a red and white United cab pulled up in front of Lagniappe. Cynthia got out. Felix was nowhere in sight. Missy guessed he'd been inside all the while having a quiet drink before the fireworks began.

As Cynthia paid the driver and went inside, Missy in a low, soft voice, the voice of Peter, said, "Don't worry, darling. It won't be long now." She could have been talking to Felix, to Cynthia, or to herself.

The time dragged slowly. The twilight turned to full darkness. Twice, Missy thought about the little trick-or-treaters at her front door. The first time she thought how they had been so cute, especially the one in the cowboy outfit. But at seven or eight they shouldn't have been out without an adult. There were too many bad things that could happen to them. The second time she wondered what it would be like to be the mother of one of them, how much fun it must be now that they were old enough to do things for themselves. Maybe soon she would find out . . . The kit she had purchased to predict her cycle of ovulation showed more blue today than yesterday when she tested her morning's urine, indicating her fertile period couldn't be more than a day or two away. She had to get a grip on herself. Perhaps if she loaded up on Valium and smoked some dope she could close her mind to what was happening, get through it without screaming. Ideally she would prefer a Quaalude with a little Southern Comfort to go along with her dope, but she didn't think Felix would be turned on by a limp rag doll . . .

She was brought back with a start when a young man dressed like a chimney sweep in top hat and high-top Converse sneakers smacked the hood of her car with the flat of his hand before going into the Khyber Pass. She reached for the door handle to get out and give him a piece of her mind, remembered how she was dressed and dropped the idea.

It was seven-twenty-four by her watch when Felix and Cynthia emerged from Lagniappe. She watched them walk north toward Market Street and past Rib-It, Los Amigos, and Brownie's Pub. At Nick's Roast Beef she began to lose sight of them in the costumed crowd now beginning to fill the street. Knowing that Felix habitually parked on Market Street, she started her engine and pulled out of her parking place, retracing much the same route she had used earlier in the day to Carl's, down Second past Waldo's to Walnut, up to Third, only this time she continued past Chestnut and on to Market. Felix did not take Cynthia to his car but hailed a cab. As he opened the door she put her arms around him and gave him a kiss that confirmed Missy's worse suspicions. After a moment he gently pushed her away and helped her into the cab. As it pulled out into traffic he watched for a moment, then turned and headed back in the direction he had come from.

It was what Missy had been waiting for. Half a block down she did a U-turn in traffic and started to follow the cab, the sound of Warren Zevon's "Sentimental Hygiene" filling her car.

Following them on Market Street through the tangle of construction was tricky but she stayed on their tail, not concerned about discovery, just about losing them.

As she maneuvered the car through the sights and sounds of jackhammers, backhoes, and bulldozers she thought about her plans for Cynthia's funeral. Naturally Felix would want to make all the arrangements. He was that sort of kind and considerate person. And she would help him, like the good wife she was going to be.

At Twelfth a cop was parked at the corner, so Cynthia's cabdriver turned off his blinker for the illegal left turn he had intended to make and continued up on Market Street and around City Hall. Missy did the same.

Around the west side of City Hall the cab veered off and headed south on Fifteenth. Missy followed, barely making the light at Chestnut as a stream of people from B. Dalton crowded the intersection. At Locust she was prepared to turn, since she remembered Lois saying that Cynthia lived in the nearby Locust Towers, but they continued on to Fifteenth and Pine and took a left. Missy stayed with them across Broad Street and down Pine to Twelfth, where the cab dropped Cynthia in front of her business, the Pine Street Charcuterie. Missy passed them and pulled into a vacant parking place further down the block.

The moment she had hoped for had arrived. Taking the automatic from the shoulder holster she waited until the cab pulled away and Cynthia was busy opening the door of her darkened store before she got out and approached her.

Cynthia didn't look up until Missy was beside her, and even then there was no recognition on her face. It was the confirmation Missy needed. She jammed the gun into Cynthia's ribs and shoved her inside before she could scream or cry out.

Without taking her eyes off her prey, Missy closed the door.

Cynthia wheeled around and backed deeper into the darkness. "What . . . ?" She was staring at the gun, not at Missy.

Missy took two steps forward and swung the gun hard, catching Cynthia near the temple. Cynthia let out a little cry as the force of the blow dropped her, taking with her a display of crab pots and Old Bay Seasoning.

As she lay dazed in the straw and litter of the display, her skirt up over her thighs, her nightmare began.

Missy grabbed her hair and pulled her to her knees, forcing her into a kneeling position, where Missy slipped the choker chain with the medallion over her head. Taking hold of her hair again, she slowly brought the gun up. Even in the darkness of the store it seemed to gleam and shine, holding Cynthia's attention as though it was a poisonous snake as it came closer and closer.

Gently Missy brought the muzzle to Cynthia's lips. Cynthia pulled back, tried to turn her head away, her lips pressed together. Missy tightened her hold on Cynthia's hair and brought her face back close to the muzzle, taking care to be sure that Cynthia could not raise her eyes.

Even in this providential darkness she was taking no chances on Cynthia getting a long enough look to maybe see through her disguise. That was a surprise to come later.

Talking gently, Missy said, "Don't be that way," her voice

barely above a whisper, as she increased the pressure of the muzzle against Cynthia's lips, not enough to hurt or bruise them but enough to provide a note of insistence.

Cynthia wouldn't keep still.

"Please, you don't want me to hurt you. Just cooperate and I'll be out of here in a few minutes," Missy said.

It was a voice whose tone, as much as its words, told Cynthia to be reasonable, not to force an escalation of the situation, that this was nothing more than a simple robbery if she didn't make it so.

She felt the pressure of the muzzle increase against her lips, listened to that voice, opened her mouth.

Missy slid the gun barrel inside a couple of inches, but not enough to make her gag.

"Now close your lips around it like it's your lover," she said.

Cynthia obeyed.

"Good, now we can talk without you getting hysterical on me. I want you to put both hands behind you. Do you understand?"

Cynthia nodded slightly and did it. When the handcuffs were in place Missy breathed easier. Now there was no chance that Cynthia could resist anything she'd planned for her. Cynthia, too, seemed to realize this . . . she made one last show of resistance after the cuffs were on, but Missy simply held her head with one hand and pressed the barrel deeper into her throat until she either had to stop moving or gag.

In a scolding whisper Missy said, "Please, don't move around like that again, not yet anyway. This gun has very sharp sights. It could do a lot of damage to your mouth if you get too carried away. I wouldn't want that, would you?"

Cynthia shook her head slightly.

"You're wondering why this is happening to you, aren't you?" With her free hand Missy flashed her badge in front of Cynthia's eyes, keeping it there only long enough for her to get a glimpse . . . but in the darkness she couldn't see what kind of a badge it was.

"I'm going to tell you. I'm a private investigator. I've been following you for the last couple of days. You see, your ex-husband—you know, the real estate tycoon—hired me to do that. And he hired me to do something else as well." She paused for effect, then: "He hired me to kill you."

Cynthia started as if she'd been hit with a jolt of electricity. Missy smiled.

"I know, you can't believe it. But it's true. There's apparently some beautiful, rich bitch here in town—the daughter of a doctor, I think he said—that he wants to marry, but everywhere he goes *you* keep popping up and spoiling things."

Even with the gun in her mouth Cynthia tried to deny it.

"I told him yesterday that I thought it was too extreme a solution, that you seemed like a reasonable person. Maybe if I talked to you we could work things out. Well, he wouldn't hear of it. He wants you dead, and in the worst way." She stretched the word "dead" for a full effect.

She felt Cynthia begin to tremble, kneeling there before Missy in the darkened store. With her free hand, the one not holding the gun, she began to stroke Cynthia's hair. The trembling continued, and Missy felt cold chills at the thought of the wonderful excitement Cynthia was feeling. She forced Cynthia's head over, all the while still stroking her hair with her gloved hand, until her cheek rested against Missy's trouser front and she felt the press and hardness of the dildo inside the trousers like a real penis.

"May I tell you something else? Following you like I have the last couple of days, I've become real fond of you. You're a special person, and I don't think you should die. Do you understand what I'm saying to you?"

Cynthia nodded as best she could from her awkward position.

"I don't know how it happened, but damned if I didn't find myself thinking about you all the time. I just can't handle the idea of killing you. But if I let you go, you've got to help me—"

Missy paused to let the faint ray of hope sink in. She looked around the store to see where she could take her for their moment of truth. In the rear was a kitchen used for cooking demonstrations and classes that opened onto a small courtyard and herb garden behind. Perfect.

"You've got to do two things," she went on. "Neither should be too difficult. I want you to promise me that if I let you go, you'll disappear for a few weeks. Go down to the islands, go to Europe, Florida, California, anywhere—just go away so everything has a chance to cool down. While you're gone I'll give your husband his money back, and when he sees you're not causing him any trouble I think I can convince him to forget about the whole thing. Then everyone can live happily ever after. Will you do that?"

Cynthia tried to nod furiously.

"Now I'm going to take the gun out of your mouth because I need to hear you say it, to tell me that you'll go away, but first you must understand something else. I haven't hurt you yet, except for the little bump on the noggin, but if you try to scream, yell or do anything except be the proper lady you are, you'll be hurting me. Our deal will be off, and I'll finish your husband's contract and kill you."

Missy slowly, sensually removed the gunbarrel from Cynthia's mouth. Cynthia obediently kept her lips around it, like it was a rare treat, until the sight touched her lips and she had to open her mouth wider.

"I'll do it," she said. "I'll go away, I promise, tonight as soon as you let me go. Only please don't—" she couldn't even say "kill me"—"don't hurt me."

"Remember, I said there were two things," Missy said in a stern, half-whisper. "The other thing is that you must let me make love to you. Seeing you like I have the last couple of days, it's all I've thought about. I know it's wrong but this one time I've got to have you. After that we can never see each other again. Will you do it?"

"Here?"

Missy took her arm and helped her to her feet. As she guided her through the darkened store toward the kitchen she realized she had never wanted anyone so badly in her life as she did Cynthia at that moment. She hadn't been lying about that. It seemed that Cynthia was feeling it too. Missy heard it in her voice as she stopped inside the kitchen and said breathily, "Where?"

She led her to the kitchen table in the center, and Cynthia, with her hands still cuffed behind her, obediently bent forward from the waist and rested her cheek and upper body against the tabletop.

"It's so dark in here. Please turn on the light over the stove. It's only a little light. No one outside can see it, honest."

Missy smiled. Better and better. The lady really wanted to enjoy it.

The soft light brought everything into sharp relief for Missy's cocaine-sharpened senses. Moving behind her, Missy raised Cynthia's skirt and gently lowered her pantyhose and panties. She really was very pretty, waiting like that, so *open* to Missy's desire. It was easy to see why Felix could fall under her spell, because she felt it, too.

As she unzipped her trousers and brought out the dildo she looked around the room. Someone had left the window over the sink cracked, and a slight breeze rustled the brown-and-white cafe curtains decorated with old-fashioned coffee grinders and weathervanes. Watching them stir gave her a sense of peace. The tableau was sort of like a Norman Rockwell painting. What a nice setting.

NOVEMBER

PINE STREET was sleepy in the chilly morning air. Two gays still in Halloween costume made their way home arm in arm, the last celebrants from the last party. Near Thirteenth the swampers for Dirty Franks and the Pine Street Beverage Room wrestled out to the street huge garbage cans filled with empties and swabbed down their places with pine-smelling mop water.

In the ten hundred block a couple of early-bird antique dealers cast a weather-eye about whether to entrust their valuables to the sidewalk or to keep him inside for the day. One chose to take them out; one chose not to. The one who chose to soon had his sidewalk cluttered with a wooden Indian, a rocker, two trunks, and a mirror decorated with deer antlers. The one who chose not to watched all this activity and quietly wondered how his competitor could make a living selling such junk.

Near Twelfth the ice cream place was making waffles and coffee for its breakfast crowd, and across the street, in front of the Pine Street Charcuterie, an old Buick 225, known in some circles as a "deuce-and-a-quarter," pulled up and stopped.

At the wheel of the Buick was Claude Washington, a black man some sixty years of age who made his living cleaning offices and stores. He had been working since long before dawn, and the Pine Street Charcuterie was his fifth job of the morning. His back was bothering him some as he opened the trunk for his cleaning supplies. Forty years of industrial cleaning could do that, but Claude was not complaining. His had been a good life. He had lost one son to a rocket attack in Vietnam, but he still had a loving wife and two other sons, one a lawyer, the other a dentist. The sons were always after him to retire, take it easy, let them support him, but outside of a little high blood pressure Claude was in good health and intended to stay that way by continuing to get up early and work hard, as he had done all his life.

He carried the first load of cleaning supplies to the door and put them down. Going back for another he too cast a weather-eye and, without knowing, agreed with the second antique dealer: rain was on the way. He only hoped it would hold off until lunch when he was home with his wife, resting his back and watching "All My Children."

With this load he slammed the trunk lid and fished in his pocket for the keys to the store, but when he used them, to his surprise, he found the door was unlocked. That had never happened before, not here anyway, but he guessed that whoever had closed the night before was a little too eager to get to a Halloween party and had forgotten. Still, he would have to leave a note, just in case. He didn't want there to be any possibility that Miss Cynthia would think he had stolen something.

He opened the door and set his brooms and mops inside. Before he could go back for the bucket filled with rags and cleaners he saw the debris on the floor from the smashed display of crab pots and Old Bay Seasoning. That wasn't right. None of Miss Cynthia's sales people would go off and leave a mess like that, and the idea of a burglar came immediately to mind.

The idea held no fear for him. If it was a burglar he would be long gone by now. More likely, some kid high on dope, but still sixty years of living told him to be a bit more cautious than usual.

He brought in the bucket, set it next to the brooms and mops and proceeded to look around the room. Only the one display seemed to have been disturbed. Everything else looked all right. If it was a burglary, at least it wasn't by a bunch of vandals.

Moving toward the center of the room, he was careful not to touch anything. He had no illusions about the police fingerprinting the place over a simple burglary; they would not do it, but that was their business. His was not to get in the way.

Deeper in the room, the only sign of an intruder was still the smashed display. The stereo hadn't been touched and everything else in the place was either food or cooking utensils. Not even a dopehead would be stupid enough to try to sell a set of pots and pans on the street.

All that was left was the counter and the cash register. He walked behind the counter. Everything seemed normal there, too. Like most stores, the Pine Street Charcuterie left the drawer of the cash register partially open at night as an incentive to keep a burglar from smashing a machine worth more than what was inside it. Using a cleaning rag, he pulled the drawer out a little more. The change inside, about twenty-five dollars from the look of it, seemed intact, and he decided that he had been wrong about the burglar and right in the first place about the careless employee and the Halloween party.

Muttering to himself about the quality of help today, he crossed the room and began his cleaning. He did not go into the kitchen. First he cleaned up the broken display and put things into order as best he could. The rest of it would have to be done by Miss Cynthia and her troops because he didn't know how they would want it. Then he wiped down all the shelves and counters as he did each day. It was only when he neared the end of his sweeping that he rounded the small partition separating the kitchen area from the store.

There, still draped across the table, was Cynthia Ducroit. Her dress had been pulled down in the front to expose her breasts and pushed high over her buttocks in the back. Her hands were cuffed behind her back, and her pantyhose and panties had been pulled down.

"Oh, my Lord . . ."

When he saw her face he could barely recognize her. The collected blood had turned it to a vivid dark purple. Her eyeballs were bulging, the veins in them broken from the pressure of apparent strangulation. Her mouth was open, her tongue partially out. There was a trail of blood across her cheek from her nose.

His hands shaking, Claude fumbled with the chain deeply embedded in the flesh around her neck. "Don't die on me, please, don't die on me," he said over and over as he pulled and tugged until the chain finally came free.

Gently as possible he turned her on her back and pulled up the front of her dress to cover her breasts. "Just rest easy.

Claude's got you. Everything's going to be all right." He couldn't absorb, or accept, that she was already dead.

He began to administer the CPR he had learned at the Mount Zion Baptist Church auxiliary. As he worked her chest to get her heart going as he'd been taught, he could hear his wife's voice telling him, "Claude, you better take that course. You don't know when someday that stuff might come in handy." He had been a good student and he did everything right. Not a move was wasted. He held her nose closed with one hand, put his lips over hers and began to blow air into her mouth. Some of the blood from the nosebleed had congealed on her lips and was sticky, but he ignored it.

Cynthia's chest rose and fell in time to his efforts, and he settled into a rhythm. Breathe, blow; breathe, blow . . .

Unaccustomed to such effort, he soon was lightheaded, even dizzy, but he refused to stop for a second. After about ten minutes he looked at her face between breaths, and felt rewarded. By loosening the chain around her neck, the blood collected in her face had begun to drain, and the vivid purple color was gone. Her skin had a more natural tone. Encouraged by this change, Claude doubled his efforts, trying his best to save a life that was already lost.

The pain in his back grew worse from the strain of being bent over the table so long, but he would not give in to it. *Old man, you can rest in that easy chair of yours all you want later. Right now, take care of business . . .*

Around nine, an early arriving employee found him still at it. When she saw him bent over Cynthia she screamed and ran out. He knew he was in trouble now, a black man in the room with an unconscious white woman, he would have a lot of explaining to do, but that would come later. Right now he was needed here, and he kept on—breathe, blow; breathe, blow . . .

Some five minutes later the hysterical clerk returned with two burly policemen. They took in the situation at a glance, and one of them relieved him while the other called for help.

Claude sank down in a chair, tears on his face. He had been at it for over an hour.

The rescue squad arrived and took over. They worked on her for at least fifteen minutes more, but it was no use.

Cynthia Ducroit was gone.

CHAPTER 21

I T WAS late when Missy padded barefoot into her bathroom, groggy from the Valium and alcohol she had used to slow the cocaine and help her sleep after the excitement. She had missed work again without calling in sick, but with the way things were going for her there, she no longer cared.

Her bladder was filled to bursting but she did not attend to it right away. Instead, making a game of the sharp pains from holding back, she inspected her face in the mirror for bags and circles, then slowly brushed her teeth, relaxing her muscles several times until her water almost forced its way out but stopping it at the last moment each time.

Near the sink on the counter was a small test tube holder and a plastic tray containing what appeared to be lab paraphernalia. On the tray was a decal showing a spray of flowers followed by the word "Essence," the name of a popular ovulation predictor kit, and a color chart that went from white to light blue to medium blue. She picked up from the tray a small plastic cup a little smaller than an old-fashioned glass and carried it with her to the toilet.

She raised the hem of her floor-length black nightgown until it was past her waist, then straddled the toilet. Holding the cup between her legs, she relaxed and let her urine flow. Its warmth, seeping through the thin plastic sides of the specimen cup, felt good to her fingers.

She dropped the hem of her nightgown and carried the specimen cup to the counter. Even though she had been doing this for several days, she first consulted a blue-and-white instruction booklet provided with the ovulation predictor kit before she began the test for luteinizing hormone.

Satisfied now that she remembered the proper steps she took an eyedropper of urine and squeezed it into one of the small tubes, then filled a second tube with the developer, set the timer for fifteen minutes and took a shower.

While the water beat down on her she thought about how it had been with Cynthia. The gun, the terror from the attack *and* the idea that her beloved Felix wanted her dead made her wonderfully passive, not resisting anything she was ordered to do. She had kept her eyes closed almost the whole time, even though at first she'd asked that the small light over the stove be turned on.

The couple of times she did open her eyes they had a faraway, glazed look in them, like she was trying to retreat into a never-never land where none of this was happening.

It hadn't done her any good, not one damn bit . . .

Missy turned off the water and dried herself. The timer had gone off while she was showering. She returned to the counter, where she rinsed the test stick in cold water, then inserted it into the second tube filled with developer. Five minutes to kill. She went to the kitchen to make herself a Bloody Mary. This waiting was the worst part, but it also gave her some time to come to grips with what she was doing—getting ready to get pregnant. No one was forcing her to do it. And she was doing it of her own free will as a present to Felix. Something that would cement their love and eventual marriage.

The sound of the timer going off made her grab her drink and hurry back to the bathroom. The developer in the second tube had turned a deep blue that she compared to the color chart. No doubt about it. This was the fourth stage. Today she was fertile. And *she* was the one who would decide what would happen. No more terrible look from her father that made tears stop. Her father . . . she was shocked to realize she was glad he was gone. He didn't deserve to share in this, in her child, not after what he had made her do . . . *What?* She still couldn't remember.

She looked at one of the pictures on the bathroom wall. It was a small framed photograph of her and her father and her first horse. He was much younger then, his hair was still dark . . . which helped make him look so much like Felix . . .

She took a ten-milligram Valium to keep her rising excitement in check and began to dress, stopping only long enough to telephone Felix and ask that he stop by immediately after work.

When he claimed a previous engagement she pressed until he agreed to stop by "for just a few minutes." She smiled, knowing that for the rest of his life he would thank her for those "just a few minutes."

She drove into town. Choosing the exit off Delaware by the Sheraton, she took a left and a right on the cobblestone street around Society Hill Towers and in an effort to avoid the heavy traffic on Walnut went west on Spruce past block upon block of restored townhouses. Near Tenth the neighborhood changed to brownstones with apartments inhabited by singles, especially art students. At Fifteenth it turned into a male hustler's paradise.

As she drove on she thought about how the evening would go. It would be their first time in bed together. She decided she'd been too willing, too forward. Felix wasn't Carl, not yet anyway. He was a romantic Southerner. Well, he would be pleased. He would arrive to find her dressed in something simple with a full skirt. They would have champagne, caviar and oysters . . . Louisiana men always liked oysters, she'd heard somewhere. They would sit close and talk. She would carefully lead him into talking about his feelings for her. They would kiss. She would allow him liberties, and when he saw how bare she was under her skirt he would *have* to have her. Who could resist it?

But then she would resist, exciting him even more, until they would go to her bedroom where a small fire would be burning in the fireplace. She would lie back and offer him the missionary position. And when it was over, there would be no doubt about them being together. Thinking on it, she was at Eighteenth Street and her turn almost before she knew it.

She parked in a garage on Sansom and set out on foot. Her first stop was Treadwell & Company, a men's furnishings store in the same block on Walnut with Nan Duskin. During his lifetime her father had often raved about their superior selection. What better way to recognize her bond with Felix than with a present: something simple in gold, something to mark her territory. What she really wanted was to give him a wedding band. Later. Too bad men don't wear engagement rings.

At Treadwell & Company she was waited on by a tall, cadaverous man who, except for his discreetly striped suit, could have been the male half of "American Gothic." She told him she was looking for a chain. Something in gold. He led her down the aisles past umbrellas and scarves, past wallets and briefcases, past bowlers and skimmers to the jewelry section. Once behind the counter and leaning on it with both hands like a preacher in a pulpit, he said, "A watch chain?"

"No, a waist chain."

"I beg your pardon," he said giving her precisely the same look he would give a hostess who tried to serve him saltwater taffy for dessert after a full meal.

"A waist chain. I want a simple gold chain to go around my"—she hesitated, and then used the word—"husband's waist."

"Madam, I'm afraid we do not carry such an item."

Normally if a salesperson—man or woman—dared to speak to her like this she would have had his guts for garters, as her old roommate used to say, but today she felt so at peace with the whole world she took no notice of it.

"Hmm, I see. Well, show me something nice in an ankle bracelet."

The salesman's knuckles whitened as he squeezed the edge of the counter. "I'm afraid you've found the wrong shop. Perhaps you should try one of those on Market Street"—and to himself added, "One with an Italian name"—"I'm sure they would be able to help you better—"

"No, I want it to be from *here* . . ."

In the end she settled on a gold bracelet with no ornamentation, over the salesman's suggestion of a set of gold-and-diamond cufflinks, feeling that the bracelet was more personal and therefore more symbolic of their future.

She had two more stops to make before returning home to wait for Felix: the first at Kaleidoscope, her hairstylist, on Nineteenth Street, and the second at Bonwit Teller, whose bridal department was her first stop in the intricate process of choosing a wedding gown.

She arrived at Kaleidoscope unannounced, but with the aid of a fifty dollar bill passed with a hand squeeze she was able to get the receptionist to juggle the appointments around and take her right in. As she entered the private cubicle a look of surprise crossed the face of Kelly, her stylist, a striking blonde in her early twenties whose *Vanity Fair* looks made her seem more like she belonged on a tennis court at the Germantown Cricket Club than working for a living.

Kelly recovered quickly, straightening her clothes slightly and running her fingers through her streaked hair. "Missy, I didn't know you were coming in today. We only did you last week. You're not due for at least two more weeks."

Missy closed the door and crossed the small space to kiss Kelly lightly on the cheek. "I know, but I woke up this morning sadly in need of you."

The intimacy of the remark did not seem to fluster Kelly. "How sweet. But I want you to know you're throwing off my whole schedule."

To appease her, Missy reached into her purse and pulled out a small vial filled with white powder and a coke spoon.

"That's why I brought this. After a couple of toots you'll race through everyone else."

"Oh, all right. Get undressed," she said, taking the vial and spoon from Missy's outstretched hand.

While Kelly lit the small burner and put the wax in a pan to melt, Missy quickly undressed, shedding shoes, slacks and panties but leaving on her blouse.

She climbed into the chair. The stereo system throughout the salon was playing the Beatles' "Strawberry Fields Forever," and the music seemed caressing as she made herself comfortable, gazing at the somber black-and-white photos that decorated the walls of the cubicle.

"What's so important that would make you get waxed twice in such a short time?" Kelly asked.

Missy smiled. How different her reasons were this time. The

waxing, not her legs, she'd always had that done, but her pubes, had begun when Peter began to prowl. Knowing police lab work as she did, she also knew that a stray pubic hair of hers found at the scene could, in the hands of an inquisitive lab technician, prove incriminating. But this time she was doing it for Felix, to be smooth, clean and ready for him.

"It's because I'm getting married."

Kelly looked at her with surprise, said nothing as she piled a couple of handfuls of strips of white cloth near at hand and tilted the chair back so Missy was almost horizontal. Working methodically and efficiently from the feet up, she began to spatula on the hot wax over a small area, press a strip of cloth onto it and immediately rip it off like a Band-aid, taking the embedded hair with it.

As she worked Kelly said, "Tell me all about him. Is he gorgeous?"

"Oh, yes, also rich."

"Good, you'll still be able to afford to come to me and you'll still be able to bring your little gifts. What does he do?"

"He's a real estate developer from New Orleans who's doing a project here in town. But that's all I can tell you. We want to keep it a secret until we see if I'm pregnant."

"Are you?"

"No, not yet, but I expect I will be after tonight."

"So that's why you're here."

"That's right. I didn't want him to find any five o'clock shadow."

"How did you figure out your time? Did you take your temperature?" Kelly asked, still spreading on wax, pressing cloth into it and ripping it off as she worked her way up Missy's legs.

"No, I used one of those kits. 'Essence,' it's called."

"I've seen them in the drugstore. Do they really work?"

"Oh, yes, they measue the amount of luteinizing hormone in your morning urine. That's one way to tell when you're fertile."

"That's right, you're in the lab business. You'd know that sort of thing . . . What does your fiancé think of all this. I mean, these days men don't seem to like the idea of a woman getting pregnant—"

"He *wants* me to get pregnant."

"Does that mean if you don't he won't marry you?"

"No, he's old-fashioned. He wants to marry me either way, but unless I'm pregnant we might as well live together. Don't you agree?"

Kelly nodded, finishing with Missy's legs. As she bent to apply the hot wax to Missy's mons veneris, she abruptly stopped, and stared.

"What in the world *happened* to you? You're all bruised down here," she said.

Missy, of course, knew that the bruises were from the chain between her legs, securing the dildo and rubbing against her labia, and she smiled as her thoughts drifted to her final moments with Cynthia . . . how she had managed to break through Cynthia's reserve and bring her along . . . how as Cynthia's time came near, in her own voice she had said aloud, "Cynthia, darling, you should see the lovely dress I've picked for your funeral." The shock had been complete. Cynthia's eyes had opened wide at the sound of her voice and she had desperately tried to turn and look. Missy had allowed her one long look, and then had pulled the chain tight around Cynthia's neck . . .

"They were from my lover," she said now in a soft voice, and Kelly did not notice that she had used the past tense.

CHAPTER 22

THE NEWSROOM was busy. Telephones were ringing, keyboards clattering. Laura took no notice of them. Her whole attention seemed focused on the bottom of her styrofoam coffee cup as if whatever dregs remained were tea leaves that could predict her future.

Wearing jeans, she leaned back in the chair, feet on the desk. In the hand holding the cup was a freshly lit cigarette, and the ashtray nearby was already starting to fill with butts. She knew it was bad for her but right now she was too frazzled to care.

Yesterday had begun on a high note, filled with a bit of promise when she'd discovered Felix on her doorstep with breakfast. All that had ended abruptly with the news of Marie's death.

The run, the neighbors, the depot were all the grisly déjà vu very bad dreams are made of. Only this time it was real, Marie was the victim, and as soon as Laura saw the body she was convinced that somehow she was to blame, that if she hadn't written the articles Marie would still be alive. It was as if the killer had left a personal message on the wind, a laughing, nasty whisper only she could hear, absolving himself of the guilt and putting it on her.

Sloan had been cool and distant and accusing, apparently sharing her own feelings that she was responsible for Marie's death. The certainty that her actions had caused this awful thing hit her harder than anything since the dark days of her operation.

The rest of the day she'd moved zombielike through her chores, staying at Henri David's Halloween ball only long enough to gather the necessary information for the article, then returning to the paper to write it. Later at home, though exhausted, sleep was out of the question. Several times she almost picked up the phone to call Felix and ask if he would talk to her for a while, but she didn't . . .

Now her funk was interrupted by Gene, another features

reporter, waving the phone receiver at her from his desk. "Laura, Lieutenant Sloan on line five for you."

Sitting up a bit straighter in her chair, she reached for the phone. "George?"

What she heard was not good news. Sloan was all business on his end, and Laura's only response was, "Yes, I know Cynthia Ducroit," before he broke the news. When she heard about Cynthia's death her expression changed to unbelieving shock.

To say that she and Cynthia were close friends would have been wrong, but as she sat there trying to absorb the news, images of lunches and walks, of talks and trivial confidences bombarded her. And echoing over it all were Sloan's words about her death.

Gene, the other features reporter, noted the change in Laura's face and came over to her desk. "What's wrong?" he said, putting a hand on her shoulder.

She looked up at him. "Cynthia Ducroit has just been found, raped and murdered by the same creep who killed Terri and Marie in South Philly . . ." Her words sounded faraway, like someone else was saying them.

"Can I help?"

"No, they want to see me, but thanks."

On the drive to Pine Street she tried to will herself not to cry, knowing she would be doing it as much for herself as for Terri or Marie or Cynthia. This was not the time for tears. This was the time to be counted. She *owed* them—especially Marie. She'd be damned if she'd dissolve in self-pity.

Police cars and vans jammed up the street, and she had to park near Eleventh and walk back. There were uniformed officers securing the premises outside, but unlike South Philly there were no crowds of spectators.

She gave her name to one of the officers, and waited. In a few moments Sloan came to the door. "Come on in," offering his hand as he said it. It was more the gesture of a funeral director.

She stopped just inside the door, not sure that she could take seeing Cynthia's body.

The store was buzzing with policemen. Lab men were dusting for prints. In the rear of the store behind the counter detectives were talking to a young woman with curly blonde hair. Although Laura could not hear what was being said, the young woman, dressed in a long white shirt belted at the waist, an oversized vest, and tights, seemed quite shaken. On the other side of the store, another team of detectives was talking to an elderly black man who also was obviously upset.

Sloan waited for Laura to talk, and when she didn't he started. "You said on the phone that you knew her—"

"Yes . . . what happened?"

When he said, "For publication?" she winced slightly at the unspoken reference to her article on Marie. Sloan didn't belabor it and filled her in on the cleaning man finding the body and keeping up CPR for over an hour until the clerk arrived.

Laura said, "CPR for over an hour on a dead person? My God, that must have been awful—"

"Yeah, it was, I'm sure. He has a bad back to boot, but if there'd been a spark left in her he would have saved her."

"Are you sure it's the same one that killed Terri and Marie?"

"Yes. The body was in a kneeling position—well, not actually kneeling but the old fellow tells us she was bent over the table with her skirt up and her panties down, positioned for a rear entry like the other two—the hands were cuffed behind the back with the same type of handcuffs, and she was strangled with the same type of chain. Plus, like the others, the blood type of the sperm matches, there were no extra public hairs found and the victim's vagina was not brutalized. It's the same guy, all right, only now he's decided to work Center City as well as South Philly."

"Why? Why the move to Center City?"

When Sloan hesitated, Laura understood there was still a strain between them.

"George," she said, "I know I was wrong when I wrote the article about Marie. It's all I've been thinking about since her body was found, and I know you hate me for it. I wish you would yell at me, call me names. Do something, anything if it will make things better between us. But we need to work together. Maybe my help isn't the most important in the world but I need to give it, and it just might be worth something down the line. Tell me to drop dead, but don't shut me out, please. I owe them."

Sloan didn't acknowledge it, instead said, "Fill me in on the lunch you had with Cynthia Ducroit."

"What do you want to know? It was just two people, well, three, having lunch."

"Who was the third?"

"Carl Laredo, an artist. We were having lunch in the Reading Terminal Market. He was there doing some shopping and saw us and joined us."

At her mention of Carl's name Sloan did a mild double take, quickly said, "Was it a friendly lunch?"

Laura was trying to think what there could be about the lunch that interested Sloan. Could he suspect Carl? Hardly seemed likely. If he did, wouldn't he have had him under surveillance and know about the lunch?

"Yes, it was very friendly," she said. "I hadn't seen Cynthia for some time, and Carl is always . . . pleasant."

"Who set up the lunch?"

"I called her. I was doing an article on her ex-husband, Felix, and I wanted to interview her about him."

"I don't remember seeing it. And why a piece on him?"

"He's a real estate developer doing a big project here in town. He's not from here, so the paper thought it would be a good feature piece with a business slant."

"Why an interview with the ex-wife before you do a piece on him? You're not *People* magazine."

Laura was beginning to feel annoyed and a little intimidated. "I had met him before and found him very reserved. I thought if I had a chat with Cynthia she could at least give me some background that would make the actual interview go easier."

"What did she have to say about him?"

And Laura suddenly had the distinctly uneasy feeling where Sloan's questioning was leading. "Wait a minute, you don't think Felix had anything to do with this . . . ?"

Sloan was looking at her more closely, and Laura realized that her tone had revealed more than professional feelings for Felix. She covered it as best she could. "I mean, earlier you said it had to be the same one who killed Terri and Marie—"

He didn't respond to that, instead said, "You were starting to tell me about what his ex said at lunch."

"Damn little," Laura said, trying now to appease him with the minimum. "Mainly, she talked about their divorce. They split up over children. He wanted them and she didn't. She also talked about the ups and downs of being married to a wheeler-dealer, what it was like to be rich one day and broke the next."

She didn't feel guilty skipping details because she was sure Sloan was on the wrong track. Felix couldn't have had anything to do with it. He hadn't even seen—and then suddenly she remembered his date with Cynthia for cocktails. Was that only yesterday? But so what? What possible motive could he have? And besides, he was new in town and—

"I thought you wanted to help."

"I do. What makes you think I don't?"

"You're not exactly a poker-face. You look like someone just stepped on your grave."

He was right, why was she acting defensive? Felix was innocent and like they said, an innocent man had nothing to fear. She had no reason to hold anything back. Her obligation was to help find the real killer. Still, it just made no sense to suspect Felix. "He's only been in town some three months. Girls have been disappearing a lot longer than that . . ."

"True, but we still have nothing to tie in the earlier disappearances to these deaths. The fact that we found the bodies indicates a different pattern." Sloan purposely did not mention the two missing girls whose bodies had not been found but who had also been linked with Peter "So . . . ?"

"Well, yesterday morning I had breakfast with Felix and he told me he had a date with Cynthia for cocktails early in the evening—"

"We know about that. Did he intend to keep the date?"

"Yes, as far as I know . . . how did you know about it?"

"The same way we knew about your lunch—from her datebook. It was in her purse. The entry for you read, 'Lunch with Laura Ramsey at the Reading Terminal Market to discuss Felix,' and it had a question mark after it. Any idea why?"

"I don't know. Maybe to indicate it was an interview," said Laura. "Like she wasn't sure about it."

He nodded. "Makes some sense. The way she wrote her entries—last names included—she was very complete, almost like she was keeping a record rather than a reminder to be someplace at a certain time."

"Oh, well, I wouldn't know about that . . . What did the entry for yesterday say?"

"'Drinks with Felix at Lagniappe.'"

"Was there a question mark after that, too?"

"No, just exclamation points. Going by her other entries she seemed to think this one was important. Why?"

"I don't know. She made the date, not Felix, and he didn't seem to know much about it either."

"How were things between them?"

"There was a certain distance, like with any divorced couple, but on the whole they seemed on better terms than most."

"Was there any chance of a reconciliation?" he said, watching her closely.

It was an unpleasant question for Laura to answer. By admitting earlier that she had seen Felix socially, and by saying that she was Cynthia's friend, no matter what she said now her answer would make it seem as if the three of them were some sort of tacky love triangle. A damned-if-you-do, damned-if-you-don't situation.

She looked at Sloan. "She wanted to think so."

"But you don't agree—"

"Look, I don't know Felix well enough to agree or disagree. I've seen him three times . . . once in a group at Lagniappe, once at dinner to interview him for the article, and once for breakfast . . . "

Even as she disclaimed their relationship she knew that by mentioning breakfast she made it sound like she'd spent the night with Felix, but she didn't care. Let him think what he wanted, as long as it didn't hurt Felix or jeopardize the case.

"At Lagniappe? That's twice it's come up. You were introduced to him there, and Cynthia was supposed to meet him there. Sounds like he hangs out there."

"Well, he's new in town, but Justin Fortier, he's the owner of Lagniappe, is his friend so I believe he does go there quite a bit."

"You said he'd only been here about three months . . ."

"Since late July, I believe. At least that's when his project actually started. He may have been here a little earlier . . . George, come on, why do you keep questioning me about Felix? He couldn't have done it—"

"At the moment it seems he was the last one to have had contact with the deceased, and he is her ex-husband, and there was bad feeling between them at one time . . . Plus we ran a quick check on him this morning. He's been in prison, for manslaughter. That's not like running a traffic light. It's for killing someone. We sure as hell have to check him out and consider him at least a suspect."

"But he was pardoned. It was an industrial accident that turned out to be his partner's fault. His partner confessed to the whole thing and Felix was pardoned."

"But his partner got his religion in prison after an unknown assailant damn near beat him almost to death. *That's* when he changed his story about Ducroit's involvement."

As he talked, Laura remembered the scars on the back of Felix's hands where his knuckles had been broken, and how Felix wouldn't talk about them. She felt sick. Sloan was building a case against Felix, but he was wrong . . . "It could have been anybody, prisons are violent places . . ."

"Wait here a minute," Sloan said, and went across the store to the counter and returned with something he had taken from a purse on the counter.

"George," she said, "nothing you've said is evidence, but you seem all ready to convict him. You don't have one concrete thing that ties him in to Terri's and Marie's deaths—"

"We do. It's not much, but added on to the rest, it's one damn strong circumstantial case. Sure, with the right alibi it could come tumbling down, but we won't know about that until we question him."

Sloan, she knew, was not the sort of man to bluff or grandstand. If he said he had something he had it.

"What is it?" said Laura, anxiety now clear in her voice. "I swear to God it goes no further than right here. No newspapers, nobody. Not unless you say so."

He looked hard at her. "One word to anybody and I guarantee I'll charge you with obstruction. I'll make it stick, too; I know your editor. You follow?"

She nodded vehemently.

"Okay, when we found Terri's body, we also found in her purse a pack of matches from Lagniappe. We knew they sure as hell couldn't have belonged to her, not to a South Philly kid wet behind the ears. We figured they might belong to the killer; he gave them to her to light a cigarette or something, and she kept them."

"But that doesn't mean they were Felix's—"

"True, but at least it establishes a link between Society Hill and South Philly, and more important, between Lagniappe and the killings. Between the killer and someone who'd been at Lagniappe."

"It doesn't prove a thing—"

"That's right," he said. He showed her something else from the purse. It was a wallet. "This belonged to the deceased. There are some photos in it. I'd like you to look and see if you can identify anyone."

The first photo was of Felix and Cynthia. In the background she recognized Jackson Square in New Orleans, but that wasn't what held her attention. It was Felix.

His dark, bearded looks eerily matched the description of Peter.

CHAPTER 23

M ISSY DIDN'T know how she would have made it through the afternoon but for a second ten-milligram Valium.

Nothing after Kaleidoscope had gone right. Her next stop had been Bonwit Teller. She had only been there a little over an hour when her morning Valium failed her. It didn't just fade, allowing anxiety to replace calm, it evaporated, vaporized. One minute she was fine, all calm serenity, the next her pulse was racing and her body was drenched in sweat.

The sense of panic that had filled her as the anxiety dug in hard had made her want to cut and run, but she had fought it, forcing herself to stand her ground. She excused herself from the gray-haired saleslady with the perpetual glasses hanging around her neck and quietly took her second of the day, swallowing the bitter pill without water. Then she had walked out of the store and around the corner to the Commissary on Sansom Street, where she sipped her way through a double vodka while she waited for the Valium to kick in, thinking about what a nervous bride she was going to be, and for the first time in years wishing she were closer to her mother.

Once she was calm again she had walked to the State Store on Chestnut where try as she might she could find no champagne to her liking. The same happened at the one on Walnut Street, but there the manager was kind enough to call a couple of other stores and did locate a bottle of Dom Perignon *blanc de blanc* at the State Store in the Bourse, which meant she had to drive to Fifth Street.

The caviar had been difficult, too. Since the William Penn Shop had closed its Center City store, beluga was out of the question, but she did find some acceptable substitutes at the Coastal Cave Trading Company in the Reading Terminal Market. In the end she had settled on trout, a delicate, light-tasting one, as an alternative to the saltier Russian and Iranian varieties. And while she waited for the Korean fish merchant across the market to shuck her oysters, she had spent a moment or two at the hot dog stand enjoying a spicy hot chili dog and chatting with David O'Neill, the market manager, whom she had met a couple of times at Savoy Opera Company performances of Gilbert and Sullivan.

Not until she was back home did she realize how much time all her errands had taken. She rushed to lay out the caviar, champagne and oysters, and took a hurried shower. She dressed in a cream linen blouse with a high neck and a black pleated paisley dirndl by Ralph Lauren, then went back to the living room to be sure everything was right and ready.

Looking over the elegance of the spread, the understated dignity of Felix's little gift in its Treadwell & Company box, and feeling the sensuality of the dirndl as it touched her legs when she walked, she knew she was going to be perfect for Felix.

As she had done for her father and the office, she would see to it that his house was kept in good order, that all his needs were fulfilled. There would always be food, liquor and drugs. She would shop for him, always look her best for him, and be there whenever he needed her. Any affairs she might have would be discreet. She would never go to bed with anyone from Lagniappe, and she would be very selective, and more careful, as Peter. She would never embarrass her husband, the way some people did. She would be an ideal wife and mother . . .

The sound of a car in the driveway intruded on her fantasy. She went to the window. Rain was beginning to splatter against the glass. Outside was Felix's dark blue Jaguar XJ6 sedan.

The doorbell rang, she waited, taking a couple of deep breaths and forcing herself to relax. When it rang a second time she walked toward it as though going to her judgment.

She opened the door and positioned herself so that for Felix to enter the room he had no choice except to come to her.

"Darling," she said as her arms closed around him. She loved the feel of his body against hers. Their lips met, and it was all she could do to keep from pushing her tongue deep into his mouth. It would be too much too soon, she decided . . .

As it was she felt him stiffen, seem to push her away. She

waited, expecting him to say something about Cynthia's death. It was a workday, her employees would long ago have found the body. And naturally the police would have wanted him to identify it.

But he didn't. Instead he merely said, "What is it, Missy? You said it was very important when you called."

And then she understood . . . he still didn't know. He must have been en route between the site and his apartment or the office, and they had missed him. Well, she wouldn't be the one to tell him.

"Later," she said. "There'll be time for that later."

She stepped back to look at him. He was still dressed in his work clothes: the battered leather jacket, an old button-down shirt and wrinkled chinos with pleats. With his slightly tousled hair she thought he looked wonderfully boyish.

Turning slightly so he could see how the cream linen blouse fitted her breasts, she said, "I like what I see. Do you?"

". . . Yes, very attractive," with more than a touch of impatience in his voice. "Now, please, what is it that's so urgent?"

Missy smiled at his impatience. "Come in and relax, we'll have a glass of champagne first."

She led him into the living room, actually did what for all the world looked like a Loretta Young turn with one hand on her long skirt and the other making a sweep to show the spread awaiting his royal highness. A critic on the wall might have found her performance more like the lady showing off the prizes to contestants on "The Price Is Right."

Sitting on the sofa she said, "Why don't you come over here, and we'll have a drink. Then if you're a good fellow I just might give you a massage to help you relax after your hard day's work . . . come on," patting the cushions beside her.

Felix received all this with a certain wariness. "I'd still like to know what's so urgent."

"Darling, I didn't say urgent, I said important, and it's nothing bad, so relax. It's a very nice surprise, and I'll get to it in due time, but right now do come here. Shall I pour?" she said, reaching for the champagne.

"All right, all right, but first I'd like to wash up. I'm a bit rank after a day at the site."

She poured the champagne, stood up with a glass in each hand.

"You know where the bathroom is, but have a toast with me first."

He took the glass. "What shall we toast?"

She smiled. "Us?"

He raised his glass. "To us—friends . . ."

"And more, much more," she said, clicking glasses.

They drank, she more deeply than he, and while he went to wash up she sat down to wait, enjoying a rare feeling of contentment, her anxieties in the past.

A few moments later she realized that in her hurry to shower and dress she'd left him no clean towels. She went to the linen closet and followed him to the bathroom, hoping to find him at least bare-chested.

He had taken off his jacket, that was all, and was at the sink with his sleeves rolled up, washing his hands . . . And there, next to him in plain sight, was the ovulation predictor kit. In her hurry she had forgotten to move that too. The tubes, the tray, the booklet, there was no way he could miss them, and she felt embarrassed, like the first time her father had caught her smoking.

She lay the towels down carefully on the counter near the exposed kit, not looking at him but sure he was watching her in the mirror while he washed his hands.

"I see you've found my little surprise," she said, lightly stroking the edge of the test tube rack with her fingertips. "Well, it doesn't matter. I was never very good at holding out surprises anyway."

Still bent over the sink he looked at the kit, and then at her, clearly puzzled.

She smiled. "It's called an ovulation predictor kit. It measures when a woman is fertile . . ."

Straightening, he picked up the instruction booklet. "I can see that from the title," he said, holding up the blue-and-white booklet. "But what has that got to do with me?"

"Darling, really, don't be dense. It *means* that today I'm fertile.

I know how much you want a child, and being with you has made me want the same thing. *I want to have your baby.*"

Astonishment crossed his face. Replaced by uneasiness. "Missy, don't you think you're . . . rushing things a bit? We haven't even—"

"*That,* my darling, is the reason for the rushing, as you put it."

Her smile was gone. "I have a fire going in the bedroom. We can take the champagne with us—"

"Missy, back up a bit, none of this is making sense—"

"—and afterward, we'll toast each other and pick out names· for the baby, *our* baby. It will be wonderful, just like it should be . . ."

She was looking at him while she talked, but her voice sounded flat, distant, making it seem as though she was talking to a shadow or perhaps an imaginary playmate.

Felix, carefully drying his hands on one of the fresh towels, never took his eyes off her . . . "Don't you think we should at least discuss this first?" His voice had the tone of someone indulging a headstrong child, but she seemed to miss it.

"If you like," she said, standing there, waiting.

As he took her arm and they went back to the living room, she felt calm, assured. She knew Felix so well, knew what he wanted and how to be what he wanted . . . His touch on her arm felt so strong and reassuring. She wanted to be kissed by him. And she wanted to drive him crazy with what she could do for him . . . but she held back, still determined, for the moment, to remain the lady, knowing well how temporary restraint could be a catalyst, and certain that once they were together she would make herself unforgettable to him.

He led her to the sofa and they sat facing each other, their knees almost but not quite touching. "Missy, tell me, where did you get this idea about a baby? What made you think of it?" Still the indulgent father.

"I felt it that first night when you brought me home from Lagniappe . . ."

Shaking his head, "I don't think I quite understand . . ."

Missy took his hand and brought it to her knee, stroking his scarred knuckles with the other.

"I know, with you it all comes naturally—"

He took his hand away and reached for his champagne glass.

She went on. "When we were alone you made me feel wanted, even without going to bed. Which"—she smiled brightly—"I assure you I look forward to . . ."

Felix set the glass down.

"What's wrong?" she said, voice rising. "It's Dom Perignon."

"I know," he said quickly. "Sometimes champagne, even the best, doesn't especially agree with me."

She smiled. He really was sweet. "Would you like something else?"

He hesitated. "You don't happen to have any beer, do you?"

"Sure, I'll get you one—"

"No, no, I'll get it. You stay right here."

When he came back with a Beck's in his hand he didn't sit down on the sofa with her. He sat in a chair across from her.

Taking a long drink from the bottle he said, "I'm so dry after a day at that site that all I can think about is a cold beer." He was sweating.

Missy was losing patience. Here they were, one minute sitting next to each other talking about her pregnancy and going to bed, and the next he was sitting across the room talking about goddamn beer.

"That's nice, darling. Whatever makes you happy," she said, thinking to herself that after their marriage Felix's beer drinking was one habit that was going by the boards and fast. He would drink champagne and learn to love it.

"Now about this pregnancy business—"

"Darling, you don't have to talk about it like it's a construction problem. This is our *child* we're talking about, not a shipment of cement blocks or girders or whatever the hell."

She lit a cigarette, got up from the sofa, began to pace with cigarette and champagne glass in the same hand. Watching her, he couldn't help thinking of Bette Davis building to one of her cinematic tantrums.

"I mean, sometimes I don't understand you. You come over here, I have a grand spread for you, you don't drink the champagne, you don't eat the oysters—I thought all Louisiana men liked oysters—"

Felix shook his head. "Missy, do you hear yourself? *You* call me up, invite me over, and then out of the blue announce that you're fertile and want to have my baby when we hardly know each other. Then you get hysterical because I didn't appreciate the hors d'oeuvres or the champagne . . ."

It felt like a reprimand, and it stopped her short. Just like with her father . . . "I'm sorry, I didn't mean . . . what I wanted was for everything to be just right for us tonight." She tried to keep the anger she felt out of her voice.

Felix stood, walked to the window and stared out into the rain. "It's all very nice. I'm sorry I haven't been appreciative, but, Missy, it's not right, it's unreal . . ."

She didn't say a word, only kept looking at his back.

He turned to face her. "I don't know quite how to put this . . . well, this just isn't the kind of relationship we have. I want us to be friends, I don't want to be your lover, and I really don't want you to have my baby—"

"Why? Aren't I *good* enough?"

"That's not it at all. Right now I don't want anyone to have my baby."

"But the other night at the opera you said that your marriage broke up because—"

"Yes, I know, but the key word there is marriage. I was married to Cynthia; she was my wife. It's a normal thing for a man to want his wife to have a baby."

She took a deep drag on her cigarette. "What about me? What about me? I'm talking about *our* baby"—she hesitated, then said it—"our marriage . . ."

"I'm sorry, Missy. You flatter me but it's out of the question. There's just not going to be any baby, or marriage . . . or anything else between us—"

"There's someone else, isn't there?"

Her tone was not the usual accusatory one of a jealous woman . . . It was, Felix thought, deep, almost a growl, and damned unsettling. Still, she was right, there definitely was someone else, and he decided now was the time to tell her so, regardless of her temper, and stop this craziness. "Yes, there is, so you see what you're proposing just isn't possible."

The storm he was expecting didn't happen. Instead she showed him a tight smile. There was *no* competition, she thought. He just didn't know it yet. He was no doubt thinking sweet Cynthia was out there waiting for him. He hadn't heard the news, just as she'd thought earlier.

"Who is it?" she said, wanting to hear him say it, and thinking of Cynthia's pointless struggle at the close of their evening together.

"It's not important—"

"Yes, it is. To me it is important. I want you to say her name." She was savoring her triumph, as she waited.

He looked at her, shrugged. "It's Laura Ramsey."

Missy shook her head. "But what about Cynthia?"

"Cynthia? Good lord, there's nothing between Cynthia and me. We're just friends now, and not very good ones at that."

"I don't believe you."

"It's true; believe it."

"And you want *her* to have your baby?"

"Look, Missy, you've blown this baby business all out of proportion. With Cynthia I now realize I was using the notion of children to hold a shaky marriage together, to get Cynthia to give up her career. I was wrong, but that's water over the damn. I've learned, and the important thing for me now is to be with Laura. I figure the rest will take care of itself—"

"When did this *Laura* business happen? You couldn't have seen her more than a couple of times . . ."

"True, but sometimes that doesn't matter—"

"You stupid . . ." She stubbed out her cigarette. "What am I saying? *I'm* the one that's stupid. I let you *use* me. I went through hell deciding to have your goddamn precious baby."

"Missy, I said I'm sorry. I think we've both said enough. I really have to go now . . ." And so saying he moved toward the door, quickly opened it and was out in the rain.

As she watched him go she said aloud, "Yes, we have said enough. More than enough."

It was the voice she once used with her dolls, with Barbie and Ken, when they were bad and needed to be punished.

CHAPTER 24

IT WAS after eight when Laura finished her story on the rape-murder of Cynthia Ducroit. The bone-deep tiredness of the morning had returned, but this time she was at least satisfied with her work. And along with covering Cynthia's death she had done a follow-up piece on Terri, Marie and Cynthia, all tied together by the common bond of their murderer. She called it "Evil Knows No Neighborhood," a head that Stuart clearly approved.

The newsroom was empty now. The few still working were on their dinner break, and she thought how cold and impersonal it felt without colleagues around.

Hours had passed since she had heard from Sloan. She couldn't wait any longer to hear about Felix, so she called Sloan, who told her that he couldn't be located at his office, his apartment or his construction site. Clearly Sloan was burning up over the lack of results.

Not until after she hung up did she find the message, taken earlier by Gene, from Felix telling her to meet him for drinks at Lagniappe. She briefly considered calling Sloan back, telling him where he could find Felix, letting Felix clear himself, then decided against it. It would be better to see him first herself.

As she pulled on her trenchcoat and belted it against the rain she knew that no matter what George Sloan thought, Felix was not hiding from the police. Somehow they were just missing each other. She would go over to Lagniappe, meet him for the drink and get the whole thing straightened out.

The streets were empty in the rain and she even found a parking place on Market near the subway entrance. Turning up her collar, she made a dash up Second Street.

Tem, the Mongolian doorman, greeted her and helped her with her coat. When Laura asked if Felix had arrived, Tem's face darkened.

"I don't know. You'll have to ask Justin or Lois about that. They're in the back," he said coolly.

As she walked through the bar toward the dining area, his tone struck her as odd. Normally Tem was much warmer. What was wrong with him tonight?

Justin and Lois were at a table in the corner finishing their dinner. When he saw her Justin frowned but Lois smiled and invited her to sit down. Felix was nowhere to be seen.

Hesitant to intrude, especially since Justin's brief frown made her feel unwelcome, she remained standing. "I'm supposed to meet Felix here."

Lois pressed until Laura joined them. "It's cold and wet out there. How about an Irish coffee to warm you up?"

When Laura again mentioned her date with Felix, out of the corner of her eye she caught sight of Justin shaking his head slightly. Finally Lois said, "He was in earlier but he left . . ."

Justin was not being at all subtle. He obviously did not want Lois to talk about Felix, and it wasn't until Laura laid her cards on the table that Lois came over to her side.

"Look, I'm not here as a reporter. I'm here because Felix asked to meet me here. I know what's happening, I've been with the police all day and I want to help him—"

"Tell me one thing," Lois said.

"What?"

"Are you in love with him?"

Laura felt decidedly uncomfortable as Lois and Justin stared at her, waiting for her answer. Well, she thought, might as well level with them. Secrets didn't last long in this place anyway . . .

"Yes, I guess I am," she said quietly. "I know you think I'm mixing business and pleasure, but sometime before that and—"

"I'm going to tell her," Lois said. Justin, not agreeing, didn't try to stop her.

"The police came and went; there wasn't much we could do to help. We hadn't seen Felix, and the news about Cynthia—" She reached for her cigarettes, offered one to Laura and held her lighter for both of them. "After our finest had come and gone the second time, Felix did show up. I could see he was upset, and I thought it was about Cynthia. I was wrong . . . he didn't even know about Cynthia . . ."

"What *was* bothering him then?" said Laura.

Violet interrupted Lois' answer with their drinks, and Justin used the opportunity to get up and leave the table.

After Violet had gone Lois said, "When I asked him what was wrong he started telling me some weird story about having just come from Missy Wakefield's place and how he'd left her there almost hysterical because she wanted to get married and have his baby and he wouldn't go along. Can you beat *that*?"

Laura shook her head. "It sounds crazy. There's got to be some sort of explanation—"

"It is crazy." Lois agreed. "I don't care who the guy is, even if it's Felix, the day our Missy Wakefield gets pregnant will be the day Willie Penn's hat blows off the top of City Hall. Missy once said that having kids meant having someone to loathe you when you get old. Nobody's going to get her pregnant."

Laura tried to push back her own jealous feelings about all this. "What happened then?"

"That's when it got off the wall. I told him about Cynthia. Naturally, that really threw him. I mean, after all, he was married to her. And then when I told him about the police, I thought he was going to lose it entirely. He started saying things like, 'Not again, not this time,' and he had a look that made you think he was going over the edge. I talked to him, Justin talked to him, but it didn't do any good. He seemed convinced the police were going to try and railroad him again, like they did in New Orleans. Do you know that story?"

"Yes, and I know he was innocent. But I can see how he'd feel like he does about the police. Do you know where he is?"

Lois hesitated.

"Come *on*, he needs me."

"All right, he's at our house in Cape May. On Washington Street." She wrote out the address.

Laura stood, and leaned over the table to kiss Lois on the cheek. "Thanks, I'll keep you posted," she said as she turned to go.

Outside the rain was coming down harder as Laura hurried to her car. She took Front Street past La Familia and Raymond

Haldeman's to the Delaware Avenue exit. She tuned the radio to WFLN, where the announcer said she was listening to Mozart. She didn't recognize it. Her thoughts were all on Felix, what she'd just heard, the scary resemblance to the picture of Peter . . . At Oregon Avenue she turned right and headed for the Walt Whitman Bridge and New Jersey.

She understood that what Lois was not saying, but was afraid of, was that Felix might be guilty. Fortunately Lois didn't yet know about the tie-in to Terri's and Marie's deaths. As for herself, she still had no doubt about Felix's innocence; how could she? But he needed her help; running away like this was making things look worse. She had to convince him to come back with her.

Traffic was light on the bridge. She paid the ninety-cent toll and started for the Atlantic City Expressway. As she drove through the rain and the New Jersey night she thought how she would like to be holding Felix in her arms right now, helping him put all this awfulness in the past . . . Between Philadelphia and Atlantic City she stopped at a rest stop for coffee and cigarettes—her stomach was too knotted up to eat anything . . . About ten miles out of Atlantic City she took the Garden State Parkway south, and when her radio station began to fade and she couldn't find one that suited her she turned it off and drove on in silence . . . The weather, the time of night and the off season made the road almost solely hers as she passed Ocean City, Avalon, Stone Harbor, working her way south. Twice she stopped to pay tolls; once in Atlantic County, once in Cape May County.

Finally, about an hour and a half into her trip, through the rain she saw the sign for the end of the Garden State Parkway and crossed the bridge into Cape May. Even though it was late autumn the marina was still filled with pleasure boats, motor and sail, all shapes and sizes, and the lights at both the Anchorage and the Lobster House showed they were still doing a lively business in spite of the late hour.

She took Lafayette Street until she could make a left, then turned and went the one block to Washington Street. Normally the tree-lined street with its brightly colored old Victorian houses trimmed in the intricate gingerbread woodwork of a bygone era made her feel as though she had stepped back into a time of innocence. But tonight it was different. With the leaves gone from the trees and many of the grand houses closed and empty for the winter, she somehow felt unwelcome.

The street lights were widely spaced, leaving long patches of darkness between, and she drove slowly, trying to make out the house numbers through her windshield wipers. Squinting through the rain, she at last found the number she was looking for on a brown, cedar-shingle house with white trim, and there, as far back as possible in the drive, almost hidden from view, was Felix's Jaguar.

She pulled to the curb and stopped, suddenly exhausted and shaking from the strain of the day. Taking a couple of deep breaths, she forced herself to move on, the sea wind blowing the rain hard against her back as she went up the walk and mounted the steps to the house.

She pounded hard on the door to the glass-paned, year-round porch. No response. Inside the house, through the lace curtains, she could see a hint of light. She pounded again. No response. She rapped once again.

This time she saw a shadow move inside the house, and then Felix was at the door, astonishment on his face as he pushed it open. "Laura, what are you doing here?"

"Aren't you going to ask me in?"

He stood aside for her to enter. The living room was ice-cold, the furniture was covered with sheets.

"They're remodeling. The only place there's any heat is in the den. Come on."

It was also the only place where there appeared to be any light. Laura followed him through the darkened dining room and kitchen, her arms crossed to keep down her chills and shakes.

The den was a shambles. Most of the furniture had been pushed to one side with the exception of a recliner and a sofa that was covered in sheets like the living room furniture. The recliner wasn't. A lighted table lamp was beside it and there was a bottle of Jack Daniels, a glass and an open bottle of beer on the table.

The non-working fireplace was covered by stacks of lumber and tools being used in the remodeling. Heat came from a kerosene heater sitting on the plywood subflooring.

Felix poured a generous dollop of Jack Daniels and handed the glass to Laura. "Drink this, it'll help warm you up."

He pulled the sofa nearer the kerosene heater and took off the sheets. Laura shed her wet trenchcoat and sat down. The warmth of the heater felt good.

Without looking at him, she said, "Felix, I know that you've heard about Cynthia's death. Lois and Justin told me about seeing you. I'm very sorry. And I know how she died; well, I can understand how you feel. But you can't stay down here, no matter how upset you are, or afraid of another unjust arrest. The police are looking for you. They need to talk to you. You were one of the last people to see her alive. They think maybe you can tell them something to help find her killer . . ."

Felix stayed outside the small circle of light and began to pace. When he finally spoke there was a deep sadness in his voice. "We hadn't even been friends in a long time, but I wished her well, I wanted her to get on with her life, to find some new happiness. It didn't seem to work out that way. After our divorce, except for her store, she seemed to live in some sort of limbo, not even trying to rebuild her life. And now this . . ."

"You'll come back then?"

"I can't help them. We had a drink, I put her in a cab, that's it. We didn't even have dinner."

"Felix . . . are you saying you *won't* come back?"

"Laura, believe me, I have nothing to contribute—"

"Let them be the judge of that. You may know something you're not even aware of. Let's go back right now, talk to them—"

"It's out of the question."

"Felix, you've got to put the past out of your mind. You don't know this, but they're sure Cynthia's killer is the same man who killed Terri and Marie. That should eliminate you. Please, come back with me, face them and at least clear yourself . . ."

"You forget something—the past doesn't go away, I'm an ex-convict, already convicted of a killing. Times like this, the fact I was innocent and pardoned gets forgotten. It's not my help the police are interested in; it's my hide—"

"That's not so. You're innocent—"

"I was *innocent* before but I still went to prison."

Laura got up from the sofa. "I can't believe what I'm hearing. All right, I understand how you'd be bitter, but you can't go through life being paranoid, running—"

"You're a great one to talk. Everytime someone gets close to you, you run like a scalded dog."

"That's a different—"

"Why is it different? I don't know what your problem is, but I sure as hell know mine. Those cops came by Lagniappe *twice* today looking for me. Think about it. I don't own Lagniappe, I don't work there and I don't live there. Which means that if they wanted me badly enough to come twice to a place I just happen to go to, then they were at my apartment and the job site who knows how many times. I'm no material witness, I'm the number-one suspect, innocent or not. I've got a damn good reason to run—"

Laura tried to interrupt but he wouldn't let her. "You, on the other hand, you seem to run from shadows, from phantoms. Who knows from what. So please, don't talk to me about running—or *do* talk to me about running. You're an expert. Maybe I can learn something."

His words stung. Especially since she knew he was right. Right about her, but wrong about himself. She had to make him see it, and there was only one way, even though taking it would probably ruin what was between them . . .

She turned her back to him, and there in that small circle of light slowly pulled her sweater over her head, dropped it on the sofa. The air felt cool to her bare skin, bringing goosebumps with it. She felt him behind her, his eyes on her every move, but he said nothing. Her heart was beating like a triphammer as she reached behind to unclasp her bra, slid it slowly down her arms, laid it aside, being sure the prosthesis was with it.

Dear God, please don't let him say anything. And then she turned to face him, her eyes on the floor, not wanting to see the look on his face.

He was quiet for what seemed like hours. She wouldn't look at his face, but she could *feel* him looking at her, his gaze searing her flesh as he stood there in the darkness outside the circle of light.

And then, finally, he said, "I understand." He said it quietly, without pity, with acceptance. And she began to cry.

Now, just as she'd fantasized it, she was in his arms, and he was kissing her—lips, hair, her eyes, everywhere.

She opened her eyes and looked at him. What she saw, or rather didn't see, brought a huge relief. Pity, sympathy, none of them was there. What she saw was desire. Good God, he *wanted* her—even with . . . he *wanted* her. She closed her eyes and returned his kisses.

"I love you, Laura. Believe it. I love you . . ."

The coarse wool of his shirt made her skin tingle as she moved against him. His hands were on her, touching her, even on her breast and scars . . .

"You're beautiful," he whispered. "I'm going to make you believe that . . ."

He wasn't afraid of her body, wasn't revolted by the sight of her. That was enough. She felt his need, his hardness pressing against her.

"I can't wait, I want you now," he was saying.

She let him lead her to the sofa, undress her and make her lie back. Good, he understood she wasn't fragile, wouldn't break.

He knelt between her legs. When she saw the eager redness of his erection, she wanted to hold it, fondle it. She wanted to feel the smoothness of its head against her cheek, her lips, her belly . . . her breast.

"You're breathtaking," he was saying, looking down at her.

She felt tears. Opening her arms to him, she said, "Come to me, baby. Come to me. I want you, too, and I've waited so long, so long . . ."

When he entered her she suddenly found herself in sync with him . . . moving, squeezing, brazenly urging him onward with word and movement, the desire for the wetness of his come inside her, a need such as she had never experienced before.

He felt it, too, and he never faltered, never hesitated, giving as he was getting.

In the cold of the room, sweat covered their bodies . . . slick belly to slick belly. It was marvelous, she wanted it to go on for hours, but soon he was rasping in her ear, "I'm going to come . . ."

She held him tighter and whispered back, "Now, now," and melted with him as he pushed into her with one last shuddering thrust.

Afterward they lay together, drained. No bridal suite this, the room cold beyond the circle of warmth and light, the covered furniture, the stacked lumber, the waiting tools the only witnesses to their lovemaking.

Laura, resting under him, his head nestled against her, had to wonder now that the moment was past, what future, if any, there would be. Was this the end? A few minutes from start to finish?

Felix stirred slightly, and as if he had read her mind he said, "I can't risk losing *you*, lady. We'll go back together and I'll talk to the police. First thing in the morning." And to himself, "Even if it turns sour, she is worth it . . ."

CHAPTER 25

I T WAS after ten when the first police car answered Missy's call for help. He waited for a backup that arrived no more than a minute later, and together they approached the slightly ajar front door of her townhouse.

The first policeman, an Irishman named—what else—O'Malley, formerly of Kensington but now living in the northeast section of the city, cautiously pushed open the door with his flashlight and called out.

What they heard were a woman's sobs from inside the darkened living room. They called out again, then went in with guns drawn.

The flashlight beam of the second policeman, a black man named Perkins from West Philly, picked up the figure of a woman on her knees, her head resting against the seat of a leather-covered chair. "Holy shit!"

It wasn't until they turned on the lights that they saw she was nude. O'Malley went to the bedroom and came back with a blanket while Perkins quickly removed the stainless steel chain from around her neck and used his master key to open the cheap handcuffs imprisoning her wrists.

As O'Malley put the blanket around her, Missy peeked between sobs to be sure he was the white one, then threw herself into his arms. He did his best to comfort her while Perkins asked what had happened.

Missy shifted her position slightly against O'Malley to make it easier to keep her legs together so that the sperm sample from the office that she'd inseminated herself with wouldn't leak out. Sobbing louder than ever, she said in a broken voice, "He raped me."

When they asked who, she told them in near-hysteria, "*Felix Ducroit.* He raped me and tried to kill me . . ."

The officers looked at one another. Both understood from the handcuffs and chain what they'd stumbled onto—the identity of

219

the rapist-killer who'd been keeping a whole section of detectives working overtime.

Perkins went to the phone to call in, and Missy snuggled a little closer to O'Malley, pleased with her performance so far and their response to it. Nice guys, good little cops, who would help her make Felix Ducroit pay and pay for the way he'd treated her.

Sloan told Perkins and O'Malley to sit tight until he arrived with a policewoman to be on hand during the questioning and to help during the trip to the hospital.

In less than fifteen minutes Missy's townhouse was a hive of activity. She watched in silence while the team from the mobile crime lab went over everything, pleased that she had had the foresight to remove all of Peter's things and put them in the trunk of her car.

When Sloan and the policewoman, Detective Kane, arrived, she went into the bedroom with Missy and helped her dress. When they came back to the living room one of the lab men was talking to Sloan. Missy couldn't hear what was being said, only saw Sloan nod a couple of times.

The policewoman kept her back until the conversation was finished, then brought her over to Sloan, who asked if she felt up to a few questions before they left for the hospital, and when she agreed the three of them went into the kitchen and sat around the table.

She let him coax her before she began to tell her story. "Two, or was it three, months ago I was introduced to a man named Felix Ducroit, a businessman from New Orleans. After that he began calling me. He was charming, so I went out with him a few times—nothing serious, just friendly. The opera, places like that. As time went on he got more serious about me, calling late at night and telling me how much he loved me. It was flattering but I knew it couldn't work out. I just wasn't attracted to him. That was why I invited him over tonight for drinks—to break it off. I wanted to be decent to him—champagne, caviar, the works—and let him down as easy as possible. Thinking about it more, I realize he must have known what was coming, because when I told him I couldn't see him anymore, he slapped me hard, and then took out a set of handcuffs . . . You know the rest . . ."

She paused to cry. It probably wasn't the right place for it, but if she'd stopped in the middle of her story she might have lost track and left out something important.

Sloan and Kane exchanged looks, and when Missy saw it she stopped crying. Never mind, let them be suspicious. She had the proof inside her—sperm from a blood type O secretor. Precisely the same as was found in Terri and Marie and Cynthia. *Felix's* type. No disputing *that*.

Sloan warned her about the personal nature of his questions and advised her of her rights about answering or not answering. She said she understood, and he then asked if she had ever before had sexual relations with Felix Ducroit.

Only moments before she'd told them that she and Felix had just been friends, but obviously her answer hadn't satisfied. For a moment she thought of changing her story, giving them something more juicy to bring them over to her side, but in the end she decided to stick to her original story.

"No, not until what he did to me tonight," she said, not sure whether to sound pitiful or angry.

Sloan went over her story from different angles, questioning her on each point until he seemed satisfied. Finally, to her relief, he moved on to a new topic. "Are you presently involved in a sexual relationship, having sex, even casual sex, with anyone else?"

"No, no one at all. Really . . ."

"I warned you the questions would be personal. Now, are you sure?"

"Yes, it's not exactly the sort of thing one forgets."

"Then could you explain why you have a kit in your bathroom to predict your ovulation cycle?"

Goddamn, she'd forgotten to throw that damn kit away. Nothing for it now but to go on the offense.

"I wasn't aware, officer, that *I* was the one on trial. In case you've forgotten, *I'm* the victim here." She was stalling to come up with some explanation.

"That's true," Sloan said. "Please don't be offended, but that's one of the standard moves for the defense—to try to discredit the victim. I was just testing you as an attorney would. We're on the same side here."

And now she had her explanation. "I see, I'm sorry I snapped at you. The reason I have that kit is that I have a hormone imbalance and have to keep track of my cycle."

Her answer seemed to satisfy them. And when Sloan mentioned Cynthia, it was all Missy could do to keep from smiling. They had made the connection.

"During your evenings with Mr. Ducroit did he ever talk about his ex-wife?"

"Yes, occasionally. I know that they weren't on very good terms. He seemed to have bad feelings over the break-up of their marriage. But why would you ask?"

He ignored her question. "Do you know if he saw her recently?"

"Well, yes. We both saw her at the opera. She made a small scene there and he was terribly embarrassed, so much so that we left after the first act. Later he said he was unhappy about some conversations she'd had with a local newspaper reporter . . . but I don't see what all this has to do with what he did to me? The man *raped* me, and then tried to kill me. I'm not really very concerned about his ex-wife," she said, hoping she wasn't overdoing it.

Neither Sloan nor the policewoman gave any clue about what they expected from her. Both just sat there watching her.

Missy tried a new tack. "God, I could use a cigarette," she said, turning to look for some. When she saw a pack on the kitchen counter and moved to get up, the policewoman stopped her with a firm hand on her forearm.

"Stay put," she said, "you've been through a lot. I'll get them."

The policewoman returned with her cigarettes and sat down again. Missy took one and tightened her bicep to make her hand shake as she brought it to her lips. Before she could light it, she felt the policewoman's warm hand taking the matches from her.

"Let me," she said softly, and lit it for her.

"You're right to be concerned about the things we're asking you," said Sloan. "But please understand, while it might not seem so to you these things have a bearing. We're not here to annoy or ask off-the-wall questions. We're trying to see that every base is covered."

"I don't know anything more about his ex-wife than what I told you," she said flatly.

"All right, let's get back to Mr. Ducroit. For us to nail him, we need your help. We need to do three things," he said, ticking them off on his fingers as he spoke. "You must press charges, you must identify him from the lineup and you must testify and be cross-examined in open court. Will you do these things?"

Missy took an angry drag on her cigarette. A vision of her earlier scene with Felix flashed across her mind. She *had* been raped, in a way. He'd violated her by his terrible rejection . . . "He deserves to be punished for what he did to me," she said. "And I'll do *anything* to see that it's done. He took everything, my self-respect. He violated me and when he was finished he left me for dead."

This time when she raised her cigarette to her lips she didn't have to tighten her bicep to make her hand shake. She was trembling with anger.

Sloan smiled. "Good. Now we can get on it and put this guy away."

"Believe me, we'll do it, too," said the policewoman. "All we need is your cooperation."

Missy looked from one to the other. "What did you think— that I wouldn't press charges?"

The policewoman said, "You'd be surprised. After something like this most women just want to put the whole experience behind them. It's wrong, and we have to do our best to convince them that if they don't do their part there's nothing we can do and the scum who did it to them will walk away free to repeat. But sometimes, too many times, it doesn't do any damn good."

"Well, you can count on me. I'll do my part," said Missy, a part of the team.

"If you feel up to it, there are just a couple more points I'd like to go over with you and then we'll get you over to the hospital for the night," Sloan said.

"I'm okay, go ahead and ask."

"From the look of your neck, the bruises and the chafing, it looks like he seriously tried to kill you. What did you do to stop him? I mean, why didn't he succeed?"

Missy's hand went to her throat, which was red and raw in places and darkening in others from where she'd pulled the chain tight and sawed back and forth on herself.

"What did I *do*? I didn't *do* anything. I didn't struggle; I didn't scream. What I did was try to appease him and stay alive. When he choked me I passed out. That's the last thing I remember until I woke up, knocked the phone over and somehow managed to punch out nine-eleven with my hands cuffed and call for help."

The policewoman nodded. "You're very lucky to be alive."

Missy was getting to like this woman. If she wore her hair differently she would be quite pretty. Maybe after all this was over . . .

"I second what she says," Sloan added, paused for a moment and then said, "We're also fortunate here because not only are you able to identify your assailant, you *know* him. From the things he did to you, we have reason to believe he may be involved in other crimes we're currently investigating. Do you know of any interests he might have had in South Philly?"

"Interests? You mean like the Mafia," she said, pretending not to know where this line of questioning was heading.

"Business, social, whatever."

"No, not really. I mean, nothing unusual. A few times he wanted to go down there for Italian food. Afterward we would ride around for a while. That's all I know about Felix and South Philly."

"Where did you ride?"

"Oh, I don't know. Everywhere, I guess." She paused for a moment, as if thinking it over. "That's not right, either," she said. "Most of the time we stayed near the river. It would be after dinner. We'd ride a bit, then take Delaware Avenue up to Society Hill for a nightcap at Lagniappe or one of the other places. Sorry if I can't be of more help to you." And then, as if it had just occurred to her, she added, "Does this have anything to do with those teenagers I read about in the paper?"

"Could be," Sloan said.

"Oh, my God," said Missy, putting her hands to her face. Sloan turned to Kane. "I think we've got enough from Miss Wakefield for now. One of the officers will take the two of you to the hospital for her examination. Stay with her tonight after it's finished."

Kane got up and went around the table to where Missy was sitting with her hands still partially covering her face. Missy let Kane help her up . . . the woman's strength was comforting. As they walked to the door, Sloan said, "When you're at the hospital, be sure to have them do a pregnancy test."

His words startled Missy. "Why?" she said, pulling away slightly from the policewoman.

There was sympathy in Sloan's voice. "Because the lab man tells me if that ovulation test is accurate you're fertile today, and there's a good chance this attack may result in your getting pregnant—"

Missy screamed. And this time it was no act.

CHAPTER 26

PHILADELPHIA IN the morning had never so glistened or sparkled for Laura as it did when she and Felix drove across the Walt Whitman Bridge together.

The rain was gone, the day was new and she was in love. For her, nothing could be better, and not even the heavy rush-hour traffic streaming in from South Jersey could dampen her feelings.

Several times during the trip from Cape May she had reached over just to touch him, to reassure herself that he was there, that it was real, what had happened, and each time he had rewarded her with a smile that seemed to light the depths of her. She was thinking how good it had felt when he had awakened her in the middle of the night and made love to her again. She didn't just welcome his desire, it was like feeling reborn. A man saying she was a woman in the way that really counted . . .

When they had gotten up near dawn to return to Philly, she had gladly agreed when he insisted that she leave her car behind and go back with him. She had only half-listened when he said that he would have her car picked up and brought back later in the day. Who cared? What was important was that they spend as much time together as possible. On the ride back they had stopped for coffee at a rest stop on the Garden State Parkway, and she watched as though he was performing magic as he tore "trucker's holes" in the plastic lids of the cups so they could sip without slopping. It was delicious; his every move pleased her . . . But after a while she couldn't resist asking him about Missy and what in the world had happened. He wasn't too anxious to talk about it, not, he said, because anything had happened between him and Missy . . . it had *not* . . . but because it had all been so unexpected and, in a way, sad. She was so set on this pregnancy business, but it really didn't seem to have anything to do with him—or rather he was just, he felt, a sort of object in her plan . . . as though he was a substitute for somebody else. But when she had gotten abusive, he had decided enough was enough and he had gotten out of there.

"And you know," he said, "the whole business of Cynthia and me breaking up over not having children was really only part of the story. Eventually I'd probably have gone along, if we'd stayed together. But what really tore it was prison . . . She just couldn't handle that, not that I blame her . . . Anyway, children aren't my top priority right now; the right woman is, and I've found her."

As they approached the toll booth on the Walt Whitman she settled back, smiling to herself, feeling almost guilty about how happy she was, even willing to forgive Missy for all her little tricks . . . Once through the toll booth she noticed he had ignored the exit for her house and was going on toward Center City.

"Hey, mister, what are you doing—kidnapping me?"

"That's right, I'm taking you to my apartment where I plan to do unspeakable things to you, providing I don't do them before we get there."

"Whatever you say, I can hardly wait." She meant it.

"Well, once we get to my place I'm going to change out of these work clothes and call my lawyer, and then I'm going to drop you off and try to take care of this business about Cyn . . . Meanwhile I want you to take a hot bath and get a few hours of sack time. You must be bushed. It also won't kill you to take a day off. That's one of the reasons I wanted you to leave your car behind. I figure without it you'll maybe listen to me."

Laura protested but Felix wouldn't budge.

"I don't have to be a doctor to see how tired your eyes look. I'm not going to have you killing yourself with exhaustion— especially now that I've got a lifetime investment in you."

How nice to have someone care, Laura thought. "All right, you win, I'll do it, but on one condition. As soon as it's over you'll come to my place and tell me *everything* that happened."

He hesitated. "Is that because of us, or because you're a reporter?"

She answered truthfully. "For both reasons."

"Good," he said. "It's a deal."

They took the Thirtieth Street exit from the Expressway, made a right on Chestnut. Across Market, Laura could see the imposing columns of the entrance to the train station. Mostly in the past she had just hurried past them to catch a train to New York or Washington to interview someone. Now she *saw* them. Being with Felix made all her senses come more alive . . .

At Nineteenth they made a right and drove the short distance to Rittenhouse Square, where a fair with brightly colored booths was going on for the benefit of Graduate Hospital, and with the break in the weather business seemed brisk.

Felix stopped in front of the Excelsior, his apartment building, and left the motor running as he got out and went around to open the door for Laura. At her unspoken question he told her the doorman would put it in the garage—

But suddenly two men had come up to them, men with red tough faces. Angry faces, the kind you saw in brawls in the upper decks at Eagles games. Each wore a sport coat and a tie, and neither looked comfortable in his get-up. They quickly closed in.

Laura looked at Felix. His face was very white.

"You Felix Ducroit?"

When Felix nodded, one of them showed a badge. "You're under arrest."

They handcuffed him, and one of the officers read him his rights. Laura was shocked . . . she knew that Sloan suspected Felix but this was too much . . .

"What are you arresting him for? He hasn't done anything."

At first everyone, including Felix, ignored her. Then Felix turned to her, his eyes cold, questioning, but not saying a word. He didn't have to. She could read in that look what he was thinking, and it terrified her.

"Darling, believe me, I didn't know . . . I'll get your attorney. Just tell me who it is, we'll get you out—"

"I'll take care of it myself. You've done enough." He turned and went with the detectives to their car parked at the corner.

Laura watched them go, then realized that she had no car. Hers was still in Cape May.

Throughout all this, the Excelsior's usually omnipresent

doorman had stayed inside the building. Now that the police were gone he was coming out to move Felix's car. Laura stopped him with an upraised hand. "Never *mind*. I'll take care of it," she said as she went around to the driver's side of the Jaguar.

The car responded unlike anything she had ever driven, but as she sped across town toward the Roundhouse at Eighth she barely noticed, she was so furious at Sloan for ordering Felix's arrest.

At police headquarters Sloan kept her waiting for a good half hour. When she finally did see him, he had a big smile on his face and before she could say any of the things on her mind he was saying, "We've got him," and smacking his fist into his palm. "We've got him dead to rights."

"What do you *mean*, we've got him?"

"I *mean* Felix Ducroit. Last night he raped another Center City woman, only this time she lived to tell the tale *and* she just identified him from the lineup. He's our man, all right. I wanted to tell you before we started the interrogation. He already has some high-priced legal talent in there with him but it's not going to do any good . . ."

Laura shook her head. "No, he couldn't have. He was with me last night—*all* night."

Now Sloan was paying attention to her, and his voice had become very quiet. "What do you mean?"

"I *mean*, last night Felix Ducroit and I were together—spent the night together in Cape May. So it couldn't have been him . . . Your victim is wrong. What's her name? We've got to convince her that she's made a mistake. People do that all the time, right?"

The news obviously did not set well with Sloan. "I'm not allowed to release the name of a rape victim . . . but you say *all* night. From what time to what time?"

She told him and his face relaxed. "Laura, it happened *earlier* in the evening. *Before* you were together."

"You're wrong, it's not possible—"

"Why not?"

Laura felt herself blush but looked at him squarely. *"Because* he made love to me—twice—last night."

"Laura, don't be naive," Sloan said and left her standing there alone . . .

The next hour seemed like twenty-four as Laura paced and smoked in the hallway. Finally two men emerged from the interrogation room. Laura recognized one of them from charity functions they had both attended—Coleman Green, the city's top criminal lawyer. Obviously the high-priced legal talent Sloan had mentioned.

When he turned to her she could see the weariness in his eyes.

"How . . . how is it going in there?"

"Laura, this isn't the time to talk about it. We'll issue a statement later, and I promise we won't leave out the *Globe* when we do."

Decision time. She could either be a reporter, or she could be Felix's . . . woman, girl friend, lover, whatever . . . She didn't hesitate.

"Coleman, wait," she said, hurried after him, and told him everything about her relationship with Felix.

"Whoa, whoa," he said. "Slow down. I hear what you're saying. Join us for coffee."

"Coffee? Why the delay?"

"His bail hearing."

"Explain that exactly," she said, hurrying to keep up.

"It means that the district attorney thinks he has enough evidence to prosecute." As they walked through the corridors of the round building he would not say any more, except to introduce the man with him as Felix's corporate attorney. But once they were having coffee at a table safely out of earshot of any eavesdropper, he began to explain in a low voice the true seriousness of the situation.

"The charges he's been brought up on right now are rape and attempted murder. He's accused of handcuffing a Center City woman last night—Society Hill, in fact—raping her and then trying to choke her to death—"

"I know all that, George Sloan already told me, and I know the implications—that they're also going to try to prosecute him for the rape and murder of two South Philly teenagers and his ex-wife. A one-man crime wave. What I want to know is *who* is this woman, and *why* is she accusing Felix of something he hasn't done?"

"The one part I can tell you, but not the other. Her name is Missy Wakefield."

Laura's face froze.

"Do you know her?"

"Yes, I know her." And then she proceeded to tell them the story of Felix's scene with Missy over her sudden overwhelming desire to get pregnant.

Coleman Green listened without interruption until she finished, then said, "Yes, I heard the story. Felix has already given it to us, and normally it would go a long way toward knocking the rape charge out, if it was of and by itself. But not this time. What they've got is a three-point case. They've got the testimony of the officers who answered the call. Listen to what they found . . . Miss Wakefield nude, her hands handcuffed behind her back, a thin steel chain around her neck. She tells them she's been raped by Felix Ducroit. When he's brought in and shown to her in a lineup she immediately picks him out and identifies him. Next, the method used in the attack is identical to the one used in three other attacks, including the murder of Cynthia Ducroit, Felix's ex-wife, only a day earlier. The handcuffs, the chain—all identical, and none of these details were released to the press. You know that. You wrote the story. Only the killer could know these details, and they tie Felix in to the other cases. Even if Wakefield came forward now and said it wasn't rape, that they were just playing around and it got out of hand, Felix would *still* be tied in to the other deaths by the unique method."

"Oh God . . ."

"It gets worse. At the hospital they found bruises on Miss Wakefield's neck from the chain, consistent with the kind of bruises that would result from someone trying to strangle her. Just as she said. And now the third point. Sperm found in her vagina was immediately tested for the ABH factors that determine a person's blood type. About eighty percent secrete these factors into all their bodily fluids—"

"Yes, yes, I know about that. Lieutenant Sloan told me about it, secretors and non-secretors. What did they find?"

"They found a secretor with blood type O. The same as in the other three cases."

"And Felix?" said Laura, afraid to hear it.

"When they brought him in they gave him a saliva test. Felix is a secretor with blood type O. If he'd been a nonsecretor or had a different blood type he'd be a free man right now. But his ABH factors match the killer's. They have positive identification by a victim, identical method and scientific evidence." He shook his head. "I hate to say it, but there's no sense kidding ourselves. Right now it looks like an airtight case."

"No, it's *not*. Almost everybody has type O blood, and almost everybody is a secretor, for God's sake. That's no conclusive evidence."

"True," said Coleman. "By itself it doesn't mean all that much. But with all the rest of it—"

"And Missy Wakefield . . . I've already told you what she's like, what she did or tried to do with Felix and he turned her down . . ."

"Yes, and by itself we could make something of that. But the *method* is what ties it all together. As I said, only the killer could know that, and remember, one of the victims was Felix's ex-wife, another his ex-girl friend—"

"She was *not* his ex-girl friend."

"Whatever," said Coleman. "But they do have a case that's going to be mighty persuasive to a jury."

His words infuriated Laura. "You sound like you *believe* he did it."

"I didn't say that."

"But you do—"

"I'll give him my not inconsiderable talent and the best defense money can buy, but Laura, *listen* to me. Most, almost all, of the people I defend *are* guilty. The police don't routinely go around arresting innocent people, contrary to some people's prejudices. I fight on procedural grounds, not guilt or innocence."

"What the hell kind of a lawyer are you—?"

"The best," he said."And I think you know it."

Laura turned and looked out at the almost empty cafeteria. "He did not have sex with that woman," she said.

"Prove it to me, and maybe we have ourselves a case," Coleman Green said. "I'd like to defend an innocent client for a change."

"Well, here's your chance, Mr. Green. Felix Ducroit is innocent. It's *your* job to defend him and get evidence to clear him."

"Yes, it is, but this is a rape case, and the victim's rights are special, different from other cases. I can't apply any pressure, in fact I'm not even going to see her until court just so there's no possibility of jeopardizing what very little we have in our favor."

Laura looked at him. "But I can. I can see her."

"I didn't say that or hear it," said Coleman Green as he and the other attorney stood up and gathered their briefcases.

CHAPTER 27

T HE TWENTY millgrams of Valium and her second Bloody Mary had only just begun to steady Missy's nerves when the doorbell rang.

Last night's examination at the hospital had been a nightmare. Strange eyes looking, strange hands touching her private parts. Twice she'd seen images of her father, his hawklike face showing the same angry scowl as when she told him about her pregnancy. Under the lights of the examining room she had forced herself to stay quiet, holding the policewoman's hand.

The pregnancy test had been negative, but that meant nothing. One couldn't expect it to be reliable within hours of conception. She was pregnant; she knew it, *felt* it. The first thing she'd done when she got back home was to shower, to scrub away the dirt of those strange hospital hands that had touched her and then to douche, although she was sure the douche was pointless. Too little, too late. It was already inside her, growing.

She heard the doorbell ring again and went to answer it, muttering to herself.

To her surprise, it was Laura Ramsey. Missy narrowed her eyes and smiled a tight little smile.

"Well, if you don't look like something the cat drug in," she said to Laura.

"May I come in?"

"Are you housebroken?" Still blocking her entrance.

"I need to talk to you."

"I can't imagine what for."

"Yes, I think you can."

"If you must . . ." Missy stepped aside to let her enter, preceded her into the living room and sat down on the couch. She patted the cushion next to her. "Why don't you sit here, my dear? If we're going to have girl talk, it's so much more intimate, don't you think?"

Laura did, and Missy thought how much fun the next few minutes were going to be. She picked up her drink. "I'm having a Bloody. Would you like one?"

"No thanks."

"Suit yourself." Missy took a sip of her drink and set it down on the table, never taking her eyes off of Laura. What Felix could see in this washed-up piece of dogshit was beyond her. Lagniappe had better-looking women going begging at closing time.

As Laura fumbled in her purse Missy said, "How did you get my address? I'm not in the book."

Laura brought out a small tape recorder and laid it on the cushion between them.

"Carl told me."

"How convenient for you. I'll have to speak to him about that."

Something in Missy's voice made Laura look up from winding and rewinding the tape.

Laura's gaze was steady and knowing, as if Missy had just let something important slip, and it made Missy feel uneasy. She was not accustomed to such open defiance from anybody, especially other women. Now she was the first to look away and glance at the small tape recorder. "Are you here as a reporter or as dear Felix's little whore?"

The intended shock value didn't seem to faze Laura, who said quietly, "Take your pick."

Missy reached for her drink, took a gulp. "It really doesn't matter to me which, since you obviously are a bust at both of them."

Laura decided to play it cool. It seemed she was getting to her. "Look, I understand that you don't like me and I don't blame you. In your place I'd feel the same way but—"

Missy thought she saw her opening and went for it.

"What do you mean in *my* place you'd feel the same way?"

"I mean that you're an intelligent—"

"Don't patronize me, damn you. You're an intelligent woman," she mimicked. "Where the hell do you get off coming in here, to my house, and starting up with this shit? I don't have to take this—"

It worked. Before Missy could get to her feet Laura said, "You're right. I'm sorry." Her tone was softer and, to Missy's ear, more contrite. She sank back into the cushions and cocked her head slightly. *Better,* she thought. *Shows a little humility.*

Reaching for her cigarettes, Missy said, "All right, let's try it again from the beginning. What are you doing here?"

"I'm here, as I think you know, because of Felix."

"So you've heard what he did to me. News travels fast."

"I've just come from the police headquarters—"

"Then you *are* here as a reporter. You're here to interview me—"

"No, I'm *not* here as a reporter."

"Then why the tape recorder, dear? Are you going to play D.A.?"

"Just habit, I guess," Laura said, feeling she'd been one-upped, and pushed aside.

Missy took a drag of her cigarette. She wanted to press the point, to make Laura say if she wasn't there as a reporter, then she *was* there as Felix's whore. But she tabled the ploy, at least for the moment. "Go on," she said.

Laura looked her directly in the eye. With, she hoped, an air of the supplicant. Put her off guard . . . "The reason I'm here is to appeal to you—"

Missy laughed. "*Appeal* to me? Dear, you don't appeal to me at all. Not when you show up on my doorstep looking like a fashion ad for Lad 'n Dad. I mean dykie is one thing, but this," she said with a gesture that carried with it all the disdain of a queen tossing out handfuls of goat turds to the rabble, "this is something *else.*"

Laura had seen Missy in action before, but she was topping any previous ugliness. Stay calm, she ordered herself. Don't take her bait. Don't blow it.

"We both know Felix is innocent," Laura said evenly, still looking directly at her.

"*Innocent?* Darling, I don't know who you're talking about. It's *not* the Felix Ducroit I know. Look at these," she said, pulling down the neck of the black turtleneck.

Laura saw the bruises. They were ugly and dark. *Someone* had hurt Missy, that much was obvious. But she was not exactly acting like a victim. More like a winner. Admittedly she was no expert on rape victims, she'd only known two, but after the experience both had been emotionally devastated. Missy decidedly was not acting that way. Damn curious. Whatever, Laura decided, she had to provoke her out of this unreality, to bother her if she was ever going to make her cooperate . . .

"Just for the moment, at least, let's put Felix aside and say he didn't do it—"

"But we know he did," Missy said, reaching for her drink.

"Just pretend. And let's explore something completely off the wall. Let's think about . . . what if you had sex with someone—a person you know—things started out okay but they got out of hand. We've all had that happen before—"

"Maybe you have—"

"Oh, I'm sure you have, too. Let's say that's how you got the bruises. What does this mean?" She leaned forward slightly as she said it.

Missy pulled back slightly at the narrowing distance between them, then cursed herself for giving ground so easily. She set her drink back on the table, using the movement to cover her combat faux pas. "Look, can we get to the punchline?"

"Sure. It goes like this. Whoever did this to you, the police are sure, is the same person who killed the two South Philly teenagers I've been writing about, as well as Felix's ex-wife."

"I don't know about South Philly teenagers, for God's sake. I never read the papers."

"Missy, you're the only person who can identify the man, and he *knows* it. He *doesn't* know about Felix. He has no choice; he has to come back and kill you before it's too late. Your only hope is to tell the police everything. It won't get you into trouble; it'll save your life."

"That's what I did. I have nothing to worry about."

Laura lost her cool. "Damn you, Missy, what you did is frame an innocent man. What you did is act like the spoiled brat you are, always have been—"

"You listen to me—"

"No, you listen to me," said Laura, shouting her down now, letting it all out. "Felix told me everything. He told me about how you got him over here, about the champagne, the caviar, the oysters. He told me about the pregnancy test, and how you just *decided* to have his baby—even though you'd never even been to bed with him. He told me about the whole sick thing. After he left I'm betting that you picked up someone, called up someone, or someone called you. *That* someone is the one the police are interested in, and if you know what's good for you, my *dear*, you'll tell them the truth."

Missy had to force herself not to laugh. After all, the "someone" was herself. But she played it out. "Are you threatening me?"

"No, I'm telling you that your life is in danger."

"Let me tell you something. Let me tell you about the whole sick thing. I'm only going to say it once, so listen up. I need to go back a bit . . . you were there at Lagniappe, sticking your nose in where you weren't wanted the night I met Felix. You saw him; he couldn't keep his hands off me . . ."

She paused to stub out her barely smoked cigarette and lit another. Now she was genuinely angry, losing her superior position.

"After you left with Carl *I* wanted to come to the party. *He* was the one who insisted we come over here. Once we were here he did everything he could to get me to go to bed with him but I wouldn't. After that night he wined me, he dined me, we went to the opera, everything he could do to get me into bed. *I* wasn't interested. That's no doubt what did it, pushed him to do what he did. Men, my dear, are like that. They like difficult women, women they can't have. Not like you, not like an old shoe."

Laura said nothing.

"It was the excitement," Missy went on. "It drove him nuts. Anyway, I invited him over to tell him I wasn't going to see him again. *That's* when it happened. I fought like hell, but it did no good. He handcuffed me and did what he wanted. And then he tried to kill me." Feeling in control now, she said, "That's the reason I called the police. If he hadn't tried to kill me, hadn't left me for dead, handcuffed and naked, I could have lived with it. Men get carried away like that. But this was way over the edge. He's dangerous. If what you say about the teenagers and, did you say his ex-wife," adding astonishment to her voice, "are true, then I didn't realize how really dangerous he is, and I thank God he's behind bars where he can't hurt anyone except the other boys in the shower." *Very nice, Missy*, she said to herself, critiquing her act.

Laura leaned forward to touch Missy's hand. It was all Missy could do to keep from burning her with her cigarette but she sat still.

"Look, Missy, I understand your hurt, but it's not fair to ruin a man's life over a bad love affair."

Missy only looked at her, then said, "If you know how he talked about you. I knew he was going to bed with you. I made him always be open with me. He said your body was old before its time, that you'd let yourself go, your tits were ugly and sagging. I felt so sorry for you, that you didn't know how he felt. It was me he was in love with, me he wanted to marry. It's all so ironic . . ."

Laura couldn't resist. "I've never heard my body described with such knowing detail." She even allowed herself a slight smile.

Missy noted the smile, and it bothered her. What did Laura have to smile about? There was no way she could know what Felix had said about her.

Laura was talking again. "Irony is not a word I'd have used to describe this situation. What are you saying?"

"That pregnancy test you mentioned earlier, it was to check my cycle. The ironic part is that I was fertile when he raped me. So there's a good chance I *am* pregnant with his baby."

Laura, nervous, clapped her hands. "How wonderful for you. In fact the whole story is wonderful. It belongs in a novel, but in real life it doesn't work—"

"What are *you* talking about?" Missy said, now definitely fearful that she had said too much but without a clue as to what.

"The caviar, the oysters, the champagne. No one buys Dom Perignon to tell a man to kiss off. You might convince the police of it but we know better, don't we, dear?"

"No, *dear*, the reason for the Dom Perignon was a matter of style. Something I have. Something you could do with a lot more of."

"Style? Is it style that makes you frame an innocent man just because he has the good taste *not* to go to bed with you?"

Missy had had enough. "This interview," she said grandly, "is terminated. You print any of it that you like, but be prepared to hear from my lawyers." Getting to her feet so that she loomed over the still-seated Laura, she said, "Now I want you out of my house, and out of my sight. You upset my stomach."

For all her scored points, Laura felt, she hadn't gotten what she came for. Still, she felt she had rattled Missy some. But it wasn't enough, damn it . . . She noticed her tape recorder on the coffee table and decided to leave it behind. It would give her an excuse to come back and try again . . .

She got up and crossed the living room. At the door she stopped and took out one of her cards. On the back she wrote her number and handed it to Missy. "This is my home number. If you see the light and change your mind and want to talk, call me. I'm not going to print anything we've said." Then added, "In fact we're not going to print a word about *any* of this—your rape, Felix's arrest, *nothing*. And neither are any of the other papers in town. I'll see to that. After all, you're a rape victim and we all have to protect your rights. Of course, what that will do is leave you out in the open, since the man who really did it to you won't know what's happened. Which means he'll have no choice except to come for you."

She paused, and coldly added, "In the long run, when that happens, at least the police will know Felix is innocent. The only bad thing about it is with you gone we'll lose the only lead that can bring the real killer to justice and maybe he'll never be found. Your epitaph can read: She proved you *can* take it with you. Should look good on a tombstone. Lots of style."

As Laura went out and quietly closed the door behind her, Missy wadded up the card and threw it on the rug. "You simple, stupid bitch. You think you're *so* smart. You haven't even got the imagination of a sadass bag woman. If you did . . ." The truth disappeared down her throat in a growl.

Turning back to the table to retrieve her drink for a refill, she saw the tape recorder. She picked it up, along with her glass. Passing through the kitchen, she set the glass on the counter and took the recorder out the back door and into her garage. As she hit the button to open the automatic door, she was muttering, "So you think you'll leave this and come back later. Well, it won't fucking work."

The door opened, and she saw Laura at her car, about to get in. She took two steps and threw the recorder at her. "Take this, dear, and shove it up your sad ass."

The throw was wide of the mark, but it wasn't the throw, or Missy's outburst, that startled Laura. It was what she saw in the garage.

There, behind Missy, was a silver sportscar with a Bruce Springsteen bumper sticker.

Missy saw the change in expression on Laura's face. She did not know what had caused it, not at the moment, but there was little doubt in her mind that in that instant Laura *knew*.

And Missy knew what she had to do.

She began to shiver with anticipation . . .

CHAPTER 28

A S LAURA drove away, the image of what she had just seen
sharpened and refused to be denied: the car in Missy's garage *had* to be Peter's. The Bruce Springsteen bumper sticker
clinched it, there was no other explanation. What it was doing
there, what Missy had to do with the killings she couldn't even
guess—*that* was something between Missy and Sloan. But to be
involved in *any* way . . . it made her shudder. It also, she realized, gave her new evidence that should help Felix. Now Sloan
would have to listen to her.

An accident on Arch Street had traffic bottled up, but she was
so deep into her thoughts that she didn't notice it until it was
too late either to turn or back up. She waited patiently, honking
her horn like the other drivers around her. Up ahead she could
see the mishap, a minor collision between a taxi and a truck
with Oriental characters on the side, probably a delivery truck
bound for Chinatown. Both drivers were out and arguing as the
crowd around them grew, and not a cop in sight.

She knew she had to hurry. Sloan was her only police contact,
and he had already been on duty all night. If she didn't get there
soon she would probably miss him. The minutes ticked by; the
traffic got worse; more cars jammed the streets.

She pounded the horn with her hand, holding it down. The
driver in front of her looked in his rearview mirror and gave her
an extended finger. To hell with him. And then, the small distance from him was just enough to allow her to pull the Jaguar
to the curb and park beside a fire hydrant. She got out, locked
the car and hurried off, her walk breaking into a run.

She was soon badly winded but she kept on running, covering the blocks to the Roundhouse. She caught an elevator and
headed up. Sloan was not in his office. One of the men, said,
"You just missed him. He headed home to get some sleep—"

"When?" she was gasping, totally winded.

"A couple of minutes ago."

"Then I can still catch him—"

"Yeah, maybe, if you hurry."

She got aboard a down elevator and ran out when it hit bottom, hoping Sloan had been tired enough to be taking it slow.

Success . . . she caught sight of his balding head just as he was ready to get into a car.

"George, *wait*."

He looked around and saw her waving.

She rushed up to him. "George, I've got some news—"

Sloan seemed nearly out on his feet but told her wearily to get in and tell him about it and make it good.

"I've found it, the car you're looking for . . . the silver Datsun with the Springsteen bumper sticker. *It's Missy Wakefield's car*, or at least it's in her garage . . ."

It took a moment for it to register on Sloan. "Come on, that can't be," he said, rubbing his hand wearily across his face.

"But it *is*. I've just come from her house and I *saw* it. It's the same car Marie described to me." Tugging on his arm, she said, "Don't you *see*, this proves Felix is innocent—"

"Does it? Run it by me again, first tell me what you were doing there."

"You know damn well. I went to see her because I couldn't let her get away with framing Felix."

Sloan looked at her, shook his head. "Okay, hawkshaw, let's hear."

"I talked to her; I put it to her; I told her I knew all about her trying to get pregnant, and when Felix wouldn't do it, framing him with this rape—"

"And—?"

"And what do you think? . . . she was her usual hateful self, only more so. I tried to reason with her, even to scare her by reminding her that the real killer was still on the loose and she was in danger because she was the only person who could identify him, but she pretty much stonewalled."

"Laura, how does this tie in to the car?"

"It was when she was throwing my tape recorder at me, that's when I saw it."

"You're a hell of a reporter, you know. But *getting* a story out of you is like pulling teeth. Slow the hell down and tell me what happened. Start from the beginning."

And she did, told him everything starting with her hurry-up drive to Cape May and ending with the driveway scene at Missy's, intercutting her exchange with Missy with her talks with Felix in an effort to further demonstrate his innocence.

Sloan listened quietly until she finished, then said, "When we boil all this down, all you have is a visual of a car with a Springsteen bumper sticker in the lady's garage. Correct?"

"Yes and no. At least now we know that Missy is somehow involved in these killings—"

"Involved?" said Sloan, thinking about how Laura's feelings for Felix and hatred of Missy weren't exactly irrelevant here.

"Well, maybe not directly involved . . . we know from Marie that she wasn't *at* Terri's murder. But she *must* know who's doing it. Please, just look at the facts, Sloan. We find Terri's body, a missing South Philly teenager. I write the story without once mentioning Marie's name, but Marie is killed. Same neighborhood, best friends, and the whole pattern of missing girls down there. It fits."

Sloan said nothing, waited.

"But all of a sudden the pattern changes. The same killer murders a Center City businesswoman. There's no doubt that it's the same person, but this is a dramatic shift. Why? Then, not weeks apart like in the past but within a couple of days, he strikes again, only this time the victim lives and when I go to see her I find the killer's car in the garage."

"And therefore . . . ?"

"And therefore, how about blackmail. I mean, Missy blackmailing the killer, and he comes after her. She knows what the killer has been up to. She's even *loaned* him her car to do it. Who knows why? She's one strange lady. She's probably getting some sort of perverted charge out of it, getting off on having him tell her about it. But now *she* decides that Cynthia is a problem. Why, I'm not sure, but I *do* know Cynthia wanted to get back with Felix. Maybe she and Missy met; maybe they argued.

Anyway, Missy turns to her friend the killer and *voilà*, Cynthia is stone cold dead. But it doesn't do any good. Felix still leaves her, and as we all know, hell hath no fury, and so forth. She turns to her friend again. This time to frame Felix, the man who had the good sense, and bad luck, to reject her. How could he, after she'd gone to the trouble of relieving him of his ex-wife . . ."

"That's quite a scenario, Laura, but also full of leaps of conjecture that wouldn't stand up in court—"

"All right, damn it, but at least go check out the car. See for yourself. It is Peter's, but you convince yourself I'm wrong. You owe me—yourself—that much."

Sloan was silent for a moment.

"Please, George."

"All right. We'll check it out."

She impulsively kissed him on the cheek. Front page stuff: Reporter Kisses Cop. "Thanks, George, can I wait upstairs in your office?"

"No. This is going to take some time. Why don't you go to your office and do some of *your* work for a change, or go home or . . . just get out of my hair."

"And lovely hair it is," she said, getting out of the car.

"Jesus," he said, but a slight smile had broken through.

"I'll be at the paper."

This time she walked instead of ran. Things around Arch Street had settled down, too. Gone were the Oriental truck and the taxi, and gone was the traffic jam. Everything seemed to have more harmony, more order, until she arrived at the place where she'd parked the car, and discovered it was gone.

Her first sensation was panic. It was a Jaguar. With the way car prices were that could only mean a minimum of about thirty thousand dollars, probably more. And if some bastard stole it, she'd never get it back. Hands on hips, she looked around, maybe she was at the wrong spot, but the car was nowhere to be seen. Then she noticed the sign, which clearly marked the area near the fire hydrant as a towaway zone. Some cop had it towed while they were breaking up that damn traffic jam.

"Damn," she muttered. "Why did I let Felix talk me into leaving my car in Cape May?"

She hailed a cab and told the driver to take her to the car pound at Delaware and Spring Garden.

At the pound, sure enough the first thing she saw was the shiny Jaguar inside the high wire fence. She paid the cab driver and marched inside the old bus terminal that served as headquarters for the lot.

A uniformed policeman looked up and asked if he could help her. When she told him she wanted to pick up the car he asked for the registration. Of course she didn't have it. She tried bargaining, descended to pleading, then a mild threat of journalistic revenge, never very smart with any member of the gendarmes. No cigar.

Finally she said, "Call George Sloan in homicide. He'll straighten it out." She could only hope he was still there.

The uniform couldn't dismiss that so easily. He picked up the phone and dialed. When Sloan came on the line he talked for a moment, listened, handed her the phone.

"What the hell now?" Sloan asked impatiently.

She started to tell him, he interrupted and asked for the officer again.

The officer listened, started to hang up.

"*Wait.* I need to talk to him again."

He handed the receiver back to her.

"Any news yet, George?"

"*No.* I'll call when we know something. If we do."

She handed the phone back to the officer. "Lady, you've got friends in high places," And to one of the drivers he said, "Bring the Jaguar out."

As she turned to go he said, "That'll be seventy dollars."

Laura paid it without a word.

At her desk she went through her messages. The second one in the pile was from Sloan, in Gene's handwriting.

"Gene," she called out across the room, "when did Detective Sloan call?"

"Five, ten minutes ago at most."

The drive to the paper had taken some twenty minutes. Her hand was shaking as she returned the call, and she was barely able to keep her voice steady as she asked for Sloan.

As soon as she heard him say, "Laura," she knew it was trouble.

"Two of my men talked to her, two of my *best* men. At first she didn't want to go into it, but then she told them. You were right. She did loan the car to someone, several times. But the someone was Felix Ducroit."

She was going to be sick.

"*NO*, goddamn it. She's lying and—"

"I don't think so, Laura. There's no evidence . . . And you, Laura, have plenty of motive for wanting to nail Missy and clear Felix."

"It can't be," Laura was saying. "Terri and Marie were only the latest of that string of missing South Philly girls. He has to be innocent. My God, George, he's only been in town a few months. You know as well as I do this thing goes back. *It couldn't* have been him."

Sloan felt sorry for her, enough to lay it out gently as he could. "Laura, we don't know that Terri and Marie were the latest. Just because they were found and their names appeared on the missing persons sheet doesn't, I'm afraid, prove anything. I think you know that as well as I do. We've never found any trace of the other girls. For all we know they're still alive, and Terri and Marie were the only two killed. Could well be the rest of them are out in Hollywood trying to get in the movies—"

"You can't believe that—"

"Laura, look, I just can't talk about this anymore right now. I know how you feel, and why, and I'm sorry. But I can take this just so far. I did what you asked. Now I'm going home and get some sleep before I pass out. You have my home number, but do me a favor and don't use it."

Laura hung up, stopped the tears that had begun to form. Come on, this was no time to lose it. Felix needed her. She needed him. But what to do? So far all her moves to help had backfired, got him in even deeper trouble. Okay, she needed help, expert help. It was on the fifth floor.

Outside Will Stuart's office, Martha, his sixtyish secretary, was passing the time leafing through a copy of *Vanity Fair*, the ever-present unfiltered Camel smoking in her right hand.

"Is he in?" Laura asked.

"Yes, but very busy—"

"I've got to see him."

"Tell me about it," said Martha. When Laura finished, Martha said, "You're right. You need to see him. Wait here."

A few minutes later three men in shirtsleeves, department heads, came scurrying out with file folders tucked under their arms. A moment or two after that Martha reappeared, patted her tight, gray curls. "He'll see you now. Good luck, kid."

Will Stuart was seated behind his desk. He, too, was in shirtsleeves, but unlike the men who'd just left his office, his tie was still knotted at his throat, and he was wearing pale yellow paisley suspenders. He didn't seem too happy about the intrusion, but told her to have a seat.

"What can I do for you?"

She quickly decided from his manner it would be best to approach him on a professional basis rather than as a friend asking help. "It's about the Felix Ducroit story."

"Yes, a nice piece. We'll run it Sunday." He seemed relieved that a reporter's ego was all that was at issue here.

"I think you'd better hear what I have to say before you do," she said. And before he could stop her, she rushed to tell him everything from start to finish, leaving out nothing, including her personal feelings for Felix Ducroit. He listened without a comment, with building interest. "Laura, this is a story. A story, hell . . . maybe a major scoop . . . You're right, we'll have to kill your piece on him, at least until we get a resolution. But we need something for the next edition. What have you got?"

"Nothing, because it's not over yet. Don't worry, the other papers don't know about it yet."

"You're sure?"

"I'm sure."

"Okay, go ahead. But don't you think combining personal and professional is a bit dangerous? Let's concentrate on the facts, ma'am. It might help us both to give me the *pertinent* ones again."

She did, and Will listened without interrupting. When she was finished he said, "What you're saying is that to satisfy the police that Mr. Ducroit is not the guilty party, you either have to get Miss Wakefield to change her story, or you have to prove scientifically that it *couldn't* have been Ducroit—that it was someone else's sperm in her. Right?"

"Right." Whatever he said, even if she didn't quite understand it, was progress. He was lining up on her side . . .

"Also, from what you tell me, you've taken two shots at Miss Wakefield, and nothing. If anything, they made matters worse."

"Right, again."

"Doesn't surprise me. It sounds like maybe the lady's in a corner. To change her story now and tell the truth *could* make her look bad, going on speculation at this point, about how she's involved in these murders. If somehow she knew only about the first two—the teenagers—that's one thing, but if she used what she knows to cause the third one, well, that's something else . . . For her to come clean in that case could mean she'd go to prison, maybe worse, along with the killer. No, she's got too much at risk. If you're going to do anything, you've got to do it from the other angle."

"You mean, the sperm?" She never felt comfortable with that subject. No time to be squeamish now, though.

"Yes. What have you done about that?"

"Nothing yet."

"Figures." He picked up his phone, saying, "I'm going to get you started. After that, it's up to you. You're supposed to be the reporter."

When his party answered he said, "Let me speak to him," waited a moment or two, then said, "Charlie, it's Will. I've got a reporter here who needs a crash course in sperm, spermology, whatever the hell you call it. I'm going to send her right over."

He listened for a moment. "You're damn right, it's important." Looking at Laura he added the flourish: "Charlie, I think I can say this one really is a matter of life or death."

He hung up and scribbled something on a piece of paper that he handed to Laura. "That's the address of Charlie Christian, one of the city's top urologists. Never you mind how I know him. He's expecting you. Keep me posted."

Laura nodded and hurried out the door. In less than fifteen minutes she was in the offices of Dr. Charles Christian.

The doctor was in his early fifties and wearing a white lab coat. He shook hands with her, sat down at his desk and got to business. "Will and I are old friends. He says it's serious. I believe him. Tell me."

She related the meat of the story to him, being careful to omit names.

When she finished he said, "I think I see what Will meant. Before we go further I should tell you I've worked with the police on several rape cases, so I am familiar with the territory. Let's start with the simplest first."

Laura started to bring out her tape recorder, but he shook his head. "I'm *not* talking on the record—I don't want to be in the paper or in court as a witness. I'm talking to you because Will Stuart is an old dear friend. We've played cards for over twenty years. You've got to be a good friend to manage that."

"Agreed," Laura said.

"Good." Softening his tone, he said, "Will has often talked about you. He's very fond of you, you know."

No, she didn't, but it pleased her to hear it. She doubted that Will would appreciate having such a confidence aired, though. Not good for the "Front Page" image.

Switching back to a more professional tone, he began: "In a case of rape, when you're dealing with a mature woman, the presence of sperm in the vagina is often the only way to verify that a sex act has actually taken place. With a virgin, of course, it's different—"

Laura's thoughts immediately went to Terri and Marie, both virgins until almost the moment of death.

"—But with a mature woman the vagina has sufficient elasticity to take the most vigorous penetration, and without the presence of sperm we're left with no medical way to determine that penetration has occurred."

When he began to go over what she already knew about secretors and non-secretors and blood types she became impatient . . . "Yes, I know about all that. What I need to know is, are there any tests that could *eliminate* Felix as a suspect? That could maybe prove he's innocent? Genetic factors that might not necessarily match him up with the killer?"

"Well, yes, there is. But it's a long shot. It's also rather complicated to explain. The ABH factors that determine blood types are part of a group called antigens. Antigens stimulate the production of antibodies. Which brings us to the Lewis factor."

"What's that?"

"The ABH factor is a red cell antigen. The Lewis factor is a plasma antigen. Like the ABH factor it's also water soluble and can be secreted into other bodily fluids such as sperm or saliva. The saliva or sperm is mixed with saline solution, boiled and spun in a centrifuge, then tested for the Lewis factor by its reaction to known chemical agents."

"What will this prove?"

"There are two Lewis groups that may show up: Lewis A or Lewis B. If he's a Lewis A he will be a secretor—not of the ABH factor, that's something entirely different, but of the Lewis factor. And if he's a Lewis B he will be a non-secretor."

"Let me see if I understand. You're saying that just because he matched before with the ABH test, it doesn't mean anything when you do the Lewis test. It's sort of a new ballgame. The killer could be a Lewis A, and Felix could be a Lewis B. If *that* happened they would have to let him go, because . . . genetically he couldn't be the killer?"

"That's correct," he said. "You're a quick study."

"You said something about a longshot. How long?"

"Is the subject black or white?"

"White. Does it make a difference?"

"Yes, about seventy-five percent of the black population falls into the Lewis A category. About *ninety-five percent* of the white."

they'll let us do it. They'll do it *for* us. If they didn't,
t that would sound like to a jury—police refuse to
it could clear suspect. No, they'll do it if we
ou say, it could backfire."

Laura felt her hopes sinking. "That means there's only about a *five* percent chance the two of them will be different—"

"And I'm afraid that's not the worst of it. If it turns out that both samples tested are Lewis B, then that in itself could be a damaging piece of evidence. Only five people out of a hundred will be Lewis B. I know enough about forensic medicine to say most juries would tend to believe both samples were from the same man . . ."

"There's nothing? A test with better odds?"

"I'm afraid not, Miss Ramsey."

Outside, she left the car in the parking lot and walked, trying to absorb what this new information meant. And no matter how she added and subtracted, it always came out the same . . . A five percent chance to clear Felix, and another five percent chance the tests would almost certainly backfire and convict him.

Moving down Sansom Street, looking in shop windows without actually seeing, to put things in more familiar terms she tried to liken it to a doctor telling you that you had one chance to live, one last dangerous painful procedure. What do you do?

But of course it wasn't the same.

Here, if they didn't take the chance, Felix would almost surely be convicted. Possibly even sentenced to death. It was to weight the odds except on the side of taking the gamble . . . ? She turned and began to walk toward Broad and Chestnut and the offices of Coleman Green.

It was after two when she arrived. His secretary told her that Coleman was still in court but expected back. She sat down to wait. The reception area was crowded and smoky. Most of the other people waiting were black, reminding her that criminal lawyers dealt more with the poor than the rich. She picked up an old copy of *Philadelphia* magazine and began to leaf through it, seeing but not reading.

About an hour later Coleman returned. He was carrying his briefcase in one hand and two paper bags in the other. When he saw Laura he managed a smile and ushered her into his cluttered office. He waved Laura to a chair while he cleared a place on his desktop for the two paper bags. One held a coffee in a cardboard container; the other a cornbeef on rye with coleslaw and Russian dressing.

"A late lunch, been in court. Would you like half?" Laura declined. "Suit yourself. The Cornbeef Academy makes a great sandwich." He took a bite, chewed for a minute. "This Missy Wakefield business is unfortunate—"

"*That* is a goddamn understatement. I *know* that she's lying. I'm not going to let her get away with it. She's not going to frame Felix and get him convicted for rape and murder."

Coleman took a sip of his coffee, did not reply.

"When I got back to the paper I talked this over with my editor, and he sent me to see a friend of his, a urologist . . . Have you ever heard of the Lewis test?"

Coleman shook his head.

Laura did her best to fill him in. "I'm surprised," she said, "that you didn't know about this test."

"It's no mystery, Laura. I almost never take a rape case. It's a part of the practice I detest. Too damn many unknowns, too messy—"

"Well, then don't you think Felix ought to have a lawyer who's a specialist in the field?"

"I do and I so advised him, but he said no, he wanted me. He was quite firm about it."

"Why?"

"Felix goes by the person, the relationship. Puts all his faith in it. Maybe too much. Anyway, he and I are friends; I'm involved in this project of his . . ." He shrugged.

That sounded like Felix, and she knew better than to try to reverse his decision. Back to business. "What do you think about the idea of this test? Will they let us do it?"

"Oh, they'll let us do it. They'll do it *for* us. If they didn't, imagine what that would sound like to a jury—police refuse to give test because it could clear suspect. No, they'll do it if we ask. But from what you say, it could backfire."

"I know, but what other choice do we have?"

"Let me call Felix's corporate lawyer and see what he thinks," he said, reaching for the phone.

The two lawyers spoke for several minutes, Coleman explained the test as he'd gotten it from Laura, but making the issues clearer . . . no wonder he knew how to get his point across.

When Green hung up, he looked seriously at Laura. "He feels that we should go ahead with it. I'll call Sloan and arrange it."

"He's not at the Roundhouse. He's home asleep," and she gave him Sloan's home number.

From what Laura could make out listening at one end of the conversation, Sloan was, as she'd expected, less than pleased at being awakened from a sound sleep, but in the end, Coleman reported, he agreed to have the test done.

"But Felix has already been taken to the detention center," Coleman told her, "and it will be several hours before the sheriff's people can bring him back for the test. I doubt we'll know anything until around eight tonight." Escorting her to the door, he said, "Why don't *you* go home now and get some rest? I'll let you know what happens, as soon as I hear."

Laura looked at him. "I have to believe it's going to work. At eight o'clock tonight I'll be at Lagniappe waiting for the two of you to join me for a celebration drink. Don't disappoint me."

"We'll be there . . . but if there should be a snag, I'll call you there and let you know what's up . . ."

She walked back through the crowded reception area and out to the elevator. The ride down, the walk back to the car, and the ride home were accomplished with her head in a different zone.

The phone was ringing as she walked through the door.

It was Missy.

"I've been thinking about what you said when you were here earlier, and you're right. I want to tell you what really happened but not on the phone. That's too impersonal. Besides, it's so complicated. Carl is having some people over tonight. Meet me at his loft at eight? I promise to explain everything then. Don't worry, I'm doing this for me, not you, dear, even if you do end up with what your little heart desires." She hung up before getting an answer.

It wasn't that Laura suddenly trusted her. But if Felix could take a life-and-death risk with that damn test, could she do any less?

She would be there.

A drink did no good. Neither did a hot bath. She dressed and by eight was at Lagniappe, where the decibel level was reaching full blast as the cocktail hour was at its height.

Lois and Justin were at their usual table, having a drink with the owners of nearby Sassafras, and waved her over.

"I'm glad you're here," Laura said, her voice tight. "I wanted to tell you—"

"We know," Lois said. "Felix has been arrested. Everyone's talking about it."

"Yes, well, we hope to have him free very soon . . . in fact, he'll be meeting me here with his lawyer for a drink." Her smile was quick and forced as she said it.

"But Missy . . . she says he raped her—"

"That's what she *said,* Justin, but it's a lie, and I'm going to get the truth out of her at Carl's loft. When Felix comes in tell him I love him and that I'll be back here to meet him."

She was out the door before they could ask how she expected to get Missy to tell "the truth"—whatever *that was* . . . And then the cocktail-hour din took over and helped blot out any more upsetting thoughts.

CHAPTER 29

Missy waited in the darkness surrounded by the unfinished sculptures in Klaus Knopfler's studio outside Carl's living quarters. Actually the darkness wasn't total, was altered slightly by a faint intrusion of the lingering outside light filtered through the dusty windows—enough to make out shadow and form—and by a thin yellow strip that showed under the door to Carl's loft.

The quiet of the room was broken by the sound of a Kurt Weill tape coming from Carl's quarters. Dagmar Kruse was singing "Surabaya Johnny." But Carl wasn't there. That, of course, was the beauty of it. Missy smiled into the darkness. He was at the Spectrum at a Flyers game. There would be no one to spoil her evening with Laura.

Coming to the decision to end Laura's life had been no bold stroke for her. Boldness had long since gone out of such decisions. Nor was panic a factor. No, it was a matter-of-fact decision, much like the solution to, say, a medical problem. Laura, fortunately, was vulnerable on account of her hang-up on Felix, but she was also smart. She was a real adversary. Now that she'd seen the car, it was only a matter of time before she would at least guess at Peter's real identity. And, of course, that wouldn't be allowed to happen.

Actually the boldness was in the means, not the end. With Felix in jail for Peter's crimes, she needed a new *modus operandi,* as the pretentious police liked to call it. And that was where Carl had, all unwittingly, come in.

As soon as he heard about her rape he called. No doubt in part because the idea excited him, but at least he called. No one else did. He had mentioned in passing that he was going to be at the Spectrum this evening and . . . there it was—the means.

All that was necessary was to get Laura to Carl's and arrive ahead of her. She had keys. She could open up his loft, turn on lights and music so it would seem as though people were already there, and wait.

After talking to Carl she dialed the number Laura had written on her card and was relieved when Laura answered—she did not want to call the paper and need to leave messages. Their conversation went as she had hoped. Above all else, Laura's voice made it clear she was eager to do anything she could to free Felix, much too eager to worry about a possible trap . . .

Laura was not like the others. For her there would be no act of love or awakening or the one-upmanship of making her body betray her, as had happened with Cynthia. No, this time it would be an act of revenge. No embellishments . . . no hand-cuffs, no chain, no gun. She would use a knife. Perhaps like old Jack the Ripper, she thought as she fingered the handle of the razor sharp boning knife she had taken from his kitchen.

The special piquance to this one had not occurred to her until after six, when she had gone to the lab for a sperm sample. She had found one in the tray marked "A-Positive"—Carl's type. When the police found Laura's body they would naturally turn to Carl, and it would serve him right for the way he treated her—

A sudden abdominal pain made her wince. She put her hands to her stomach and pressed. The pain had started earlier in the day and had progressed at irregular intervals, growing stronger with each recurrence.

She pressed harder, pushing back the pain as well as her own panic, still convinced she was pregnant. As soon as she was fin-ished with Laura, the instant she was back home she would call her gynecologist and check into the hospital. She wanted it aborted immediately. Tonight, this very night, before it could hurt her any more—

The sound of the elevator being actuated startled her. The pain slackened. She stepped deeper into the shadows and waited. From Carl's loft she could hear the sound of Lou Reed singing "September Song."

Downstairs, Laura waited as the old freight elevator clanked to a halt. She hitched her purse higher on her shoulder and muscled open the heavy horizontal doors. On board, she closed them again, lowered the picket gate and pressed the button for Carl's floor.

She felt a weary sort of elation as the elevator began to climb. No matter how the Lewis test turned out, after her confrontation with Missy, Felix would be cleared; they would be together . . . Her mind shut away, refused to allow into consciousness the truth of Missy . . . The future of herself and Felix would not allow it . . .

The elevator stopped some six inches short of its mark. She pushed up the gate, pulled hard on the rope to the outer doors, which now slowly opened, spilling light into the dark studio.

She stepped up and into Klaus Knopfler's studio. As she turned to look toward Carl's she heard the sound of "September Song," and seeing the yellow strip of light under his door turned back and reached up to close the elevator doors.

From the shadows Missy watched as Laura struggled with the heavy doors. It was working perfectly. Just like her father had taught her on hunting trips long ago. Nothing too elaborate, the minimum always worked best.

The elevator doors closed slowly, taking with them the light. Pulling their heaviness Laura could feel the unused muscles in her chest stretching under her scar. It was painful, but a good kind of pain, another sign that her body was finally waking up and beginning to function normally again.

She glanced over her shoulder at the shadowy sculptures and it occurred that they made the dark room look more like a graveyard or a warehouse than a loft. Adjusting her collar and purse she began to walk toward the strip of light showing under Carl's door. The sound of her heels on the wooden floor seemed unusually loud, an off-beat note to the music coming softly from his loft.

Missy watched her pass so close that she could reach out and touch her, but she kept still. To move now was to risk a shocked Laura reacting unpredictably. Better to wait a moment, use to her advantage the elements of distance and timing. There was, after all, no place for her to run.

Laura was only a few feet from Carl's door when she heard something behind her. But she was alone, the elevator hadn't come back with more passengers. She whirled around, terrified it might be one of those cat-size, inner-city rats.

What she saw, standing where she had just walked, was a bearded man wearing tinted glasses and a leather jacket. She looked quickly around, trying to stay calm, to figure her options. He hadn't come from the elevator, she was sure of that, and he hadn't come from Carl's. Which could only mean that he had been there in the darkness all the time. Waiting.

Now he stepped forward out of the shadows.

Don't run, she ordered herself. *Talk to him, pretend you assume he's going to Carl's, too, nothing out of the ordinary, no sweat . . .*

But she didn't. It would only come out as fear. She wanted to believe he was just another guest, but that didn't work either . . . The music was coming from Carl's, but there were no *people* noises to go with it. Soft as it was playing, she should be able to hear party noises, laughing and talking . . .

Well, for God's sake, Laura, she told herself, say *something* . . . But what? Hi, there, you waiting for me? Sorry, I have to see a lady about a man . . .

Missy watched Laura, saw with pleasure the fear. She could feel the wet beginning to seep into the crotch of her briefs. She could scarcely wait to get her hands on her. Revenge, inflicting pain were the objects, but she would be giving a special pleasure even through all the pain. Pleasure for both of them.

She said nothing, let Laura wait. She was establishing her control, her superiority. Laura would need to understand that.

Laura finally allowed herself a "who-are-you?" A ridge of uncertainty, fear was in her voice, and it infuriated her to hear it.

For Missy it was like a lover's sigh. She let it hang there for a moment. Laura's fear was fine-tuning every nerve in her body, drawing each one increasingly taut . . . Enough. For now. She moved a half-step closer to give Laura a better opportunity to see. "I'm Peter."

Laura backed away. No denying the obvious now. Carl was not here. *No one was here.* She was alone. Missy had set it up for Peter.

Missy took a step forward. She needed to see more fear. It made Laura so attractive . . .

Laura took a step backward, trying to keep the same distance between them. Death was staring at her, and it was worse, much worse, than when the doctor had told her about her breast cancer. Both cases were the same—death. But something had changed between then and now. Then, she had been alone, if she died it would have been almost a relief. Being alone did that. Now she wasn't alone. There was Felix. A most powerful reason to live. She wasn't about to roll over and die for this bastard. He could rape little girls and get away with it, but before they were finished tonight . . . She looked around for a weapon, anything to defend herself with. More important, to inflict damage with.

Outside around the corner on Second Street at Lagniappe, Tem opened the door for a weary Felix and his attorney, Coleman Green.

"Gentlemen, it's good to see you here tonight. Especially you, Mr. Felix. Everything is all right?" he asked, taking Coleman's coat and ignoring Felix's battered leather jacket.

"Everything is fine. Thanks to Laura," Felix said, managing a smile.

"*Good.* We were all worried . . . Lois and Justin are back there at their table."

As soon as Lois spotted him crossing the bar area she was on her feet, pushing waiters out of the way as she hurried toward him, Justin on her heels.

"Are you okay? Is it straightened out?"

Other customers at the bar turned to stare.

Felix was smiling broadly now. "Yes, everything's straightened out."

"But how? Tell us *everything*," Lois was saying.

"How about a drink first? We both could use one."

"You get it," said Justin. "Champagne for—"

"Jack Daniels on the rocks and a beer," Felix told him quickly.

Linking her arm in his, Lois said, "A two-fisted drinker; I like that. Wish more of the customers would think of it. A little sobriety can go a long way. I don't want to be reduced to hustling Shirley Temples."

"Heaven forfend," said Felix.

"Scotch on the rocks for me," said Coleman.

At the table Lois said, "*Goddammit*, I'm not waiting another minute. Last I heard they had an open-and-shut case. What happened?"

"Okay," Felix said. "You know the divine Missy accused me of raping her. I guess it's tied in to that pregnancy thing of hers, but what made it even worse was that whoever *did* do it had to be the one who killed the South Philly kids Laura has been writing about"—He turned to Coleman, "Laura . . . where is she? I thought you said she'd meet us here."

"That's what she said."

"Have you seen her?" Felix had turned to Lois.

"She was here, Felix. I'm sure she'll be back . . . But come on, I'm still waiting to hear what happened."

"Well, like I said, whoever raped Missy killed those kids . . . and Cynthia . . . Anyway, you can imagine how that looked for me—one woman says I raped her, and one of the other victims is my ex-wife I'm supposed to have argued with. To make matters worse, my blood type matched the killer's—"

"How did they know the killer's blood type?" interrupted Lois.

"From his sperm—"

"I didn't know you could tell blood type from *sperm* . . ." Justin said.

"Neither did I, but you can, and more. Laura was the one who researched it. She found this so-called Lewis Test. It's a saliva test, like the first one they gave me, but with a difference I don't pretend to understand. The police don't usually give it to rape suspects because it identifies such a small percent of people. Five, I think. But Laura and Coleman convinced them to make an exception in this case. Anyway I took it and I passed. It showed scientifically that the killer and I weren't the same person because our Lewis samples didn't match. There was *no way* I could have done it—not to Missy, not to Cynthia, not to the kids—"

"What about Missy's accusation?" Lois said.

"The police are on their way to her now. I'm afraid she has a lot of explaining to do," Coleman said.

"That bitch, she's flagged from here for life," Lois snapped.

Violet brought their drinks.

"*Now*, where's Laura?" demanded Felix.

"She's at Carl's," Lois said. "When she left she said something about meeting someone there. It was awfully noisy then, the cocktail hour . . ."

"You must not have heard that right . . . about Carl's, I mean," said Violet, setting Justin's drink in front of him.

"Why's that?"

"Because he was in earlier. You guys weren't here but he had a drink and said he was going to the Spectrum tonight for the Flyers game."

Felix felt his heart skip a beat. "Are you sure?"

"Yes, he said he'd stop in for a nightcap afterwards and tell me who won."

"I don't like the sound of this," Felix said, face tightening. "Justin, you know where Carl lives, don't you?"

"Sure, it's just around the corner."

"Take me there," Felix said, getting to his feet.

"I'm coming, too," said Coleman, but Felix was already at the door, trying not to think. It was time to act.

Missy as Peter thought she saw panic in Laura's eyes, a panicked searching for an escape route.

"Don't,' she said. "There's no way out of here. There's no one here but you and me. Real cozy."

Laura began to move away from Carl's door. If there was a weapon anywhere it would be in Klaus Knopfler's work area near the elevator. Moving slowly, carefully in that direction she tried to make mindless small talk, stall until she could get her hands on something . . .

Missy shook her head slightly. It was so cute the way Laura was trying to keep her talking until she thought she was in a position to make a mad dash for the elevator. Of course it wouldn't do her any good. Even though the car was still on their floor, the doors were so heavy that she'd never be able to open and close them in time.

Toying with her, Missy said, "First, we're going into's Carl's and make *love*. You'd like that, wouldn't you?" No answer. "Admit it, lovey, that's all you've thought about since you started writing about me. You're in love with me, you want to feel me inside you; you want to milk me dry, don't you?"

Laura had reached the nearest piece of sculpture, positioned herself so that it was between them. She would try to use the shadowy darkness and the other pieces the same way as she searched for a weapon . . . To keep Peter talking she said, "What happens afterward? Do you kill me like you did Terri and Marie and Cynthia?" She was amazed at the calm in her voice. Inside was near-hysteria. "And what about the other little girls, the missing ones? You killed them, too, didn't you?"

Missy took a step or two on the diagonal to intercept Laura. As she did, the gnawing pain returned. Once again she forced herself to ignore it. She would deal with it later . . . Concentrating on Laura now. "Ever the little reporter, aren't we. . . . Anything for a story. Well you can have it. Yes, I killed, but not all of them. Everything I touch doesn't die. If you're a *good* girl maybe I'll let *you* live—like Missy. But you'll have to be a *very* good girl. Do exactly as I tell you . . ."

The recurrent pain loosened voice control, it was no longer low, soft and smooth but subject to higher octaves as she said, "After you've been with me once, love, you'll never be satisfied with being dear Felix's whore again . . ."

Laura moved, noting without comprehending the change in tone as she continued to keep at least one sculpture between Peter and herself. The words seemed to . . . "Dear Felix's whore"? She had heard those words before, who had used them? Her mind flashed over the day's events—and then she remembered . . . Missy Wakefield had used those words, hadn't she? But why would Peter use them? Coincidence . . . ?

Missy moved with her, continuing on the diagonal, closing the distance between them though the pain kept her from moving as nimbly as she would have liked. This was not the time for foreplay. It was time to get it over with.

Wishing she had her usual set of handcuffs to make it easier, she closed the gap, step by step, readying herself to reach for the knife.

"I'll treat you like a queen, you won't go around looking like you shopped at Lad 'n Dad anymore . . ."

"Lad 'n Dad" . . . Missy had said those words as an insult earlier . . . one coincidence too many . . . She stared across the narrowing distance at Peter, not yet able to accept the thought . . . But as she was nearer the front of the room with the windows, and the faint light reflected up from the cars and streetlights below, she could see more clearly through the disguise of the tinted glasses and the beard . . . She could see those fine, high-fashion features . . . She could see that Peter was, unmistakably, Missy Wakefield . . .

The shock brought forth an "Oh, my God, Missy," followed by an instant realization that it was the worst provocation possible.

Missy, uncovered, felt an enormous relief. And then a new kind of excitement. She could now perform as double—as Peter and as Missy. And maybe a third person, a combination of the two. It was delicious.

"Well, it had to happen sooner or later. You're the first, but don't celebrate too soon, or give yourself too much credit. Seeing my car was just a lucky—unlucky really—break for you. You're not going to leave here to tell anyone. After I'm finished with you, and the police find you in Carl's bed with sperm that has his blood type *he's* going to be the one they arrest . . . Well, aren't you even curious about how I've managed it? Of course you are. Remember that my—"

"But how—" started Laura.

"—sainted father, whatever else he was, was one of this city's best urologists. And that I worked in his lab. I just took the sperm from the supply there."

Laura could hardly speak . . . "And that's what you did with the others, with yourself. That's the sickest thing I've ever heard—"

"Sticks and stones may break my bones . . ." Missy started the nursery rhyme in a child's singsong voice as her hand reached into her jacket and returned with the knife.

Laura backed away, hands groping for anything like a weapon.

Missy, knife in hand, took two steps and moved on Laura, who just managed to dodge away and duck behind one of the sculptures.

"Missy, for God's sake, you need help—"

"Not Missy, *Peter*, and *you're* the one who needs help because . . ."

As Laura tried to maneuver out of there she found herself bumped up against a partially finished sculpture of welded metal. She turned to face Missy, and as she did her hand brushed against something . . . She risked diverting her attention just long enough to see it was a hammer.

She grabbed it and swung. And missed. Missy now stepped back into a fighter's crouch. From Carl's came the sounds of Todd Rundgren doing "Call from the Grave" from *The Threepenny Opera*. Too damned appropriate, but Laura was in no position to dwell on it.

"They're playing our song, sweetie."

Nothing left for it but to brazen it out, provoke her out of her feeling superior and secure. "It's for you, Missy, not me. I could almost feel sorry for you. Poor Missy, a real loser . . . Felix is out of jail and waiting for *me*. You lose, all the way—"

It worked . . . Missy came to her now in a rage, slashing and stabbing air. Laura sidestepped, swung the hammer again, claw-end forward.

But Missy still had her superior reflexes . . . Out of her peripheral vision she saw, sensed, the blow coming, dropped her head and rolled her shoulder. The hammer whistled over her head, and the movement brought her inside Laura's guard.

She brought the knife up . . .

Laura saw the blade flash, could do nothing to defend herself. It seemed almost in slow motion as she watched the knife snake between the folds of her coat as she instinctively sucked in her stomach.

And then she felt the blade.

Missy, wanting to disfigure, slashed. Another clean stab was too easy . . .

Laura felt the blade rip across her stomach. It felt like a gigantic paper cut followed by a stinging and wetness.

Missy stepped back now to admire her work, prolong the pleasure. "When I'm finished with you the only way Felix is going to see you is in a box. You'll both be lucky if they get the pieces together right. Who's the loser . . . ?"

Laura's head was on her stomach. She could tell she was bleeding but had no idea how much or what the damage was. That last slash had, she hoped, been cushioned some by tummy fat, which up to now she had always hated . . . She tested the heft of the hammer in hand, tried to steady herself. "Come on, I'm waiting—"

Missy smiled. "But not for long. It's over—"

The sound of the elevator startled them. Laura, grabbing the opportunity to stall, said, "That's Felix. I left word for him to meet me here—"

"Good, because all he's going to find are body parts." And she came forward on the balls of her feet, slashing, driving Laura back.

Laura was more cautious now, giving ground, not provoking. She could hear the steady whine of the elevator. A sweet sound, but it stopped somewhere below . . .

Missy saw, sensed Laura's momentary diversion, she stepped across Laura's path and slashed again.

Laura was just able to grab Missy's arm as she felt the blade cut her a second time.

Missy pulled her arm free, scrambled to her feet as the elevator doors were opening.

"I'll be back, you can count on it, you bitch." And then as the light from the elevator doors began to widen she turned and ran into Carl's loft.

Felix was the first out the elevator. He stopped abruptly, seeing Laura bleeding on the floor and holding her arm. He tried to take her in his arms, but she backed away. "Peter . . . it was Missy dressed as a man . . . she tried to kill me . . . she's in Carl's loft . . ."

Coleman Green and Justin, who had joined him now, both told him to stay with Laura, that they'd go after Missy.

"Be careful . . . she has a knife . . ." Laura said.

Felix slipped out of his jacket and covered her. "Lie still, honey; you're bleeding. We'll get you to the hospital and stitched up; you'll be fine, but meanwhile just rest."

Justin and Coleman had gone to Carl's door, but it was bolted from the inside.

"Get something to break it down," Coleman said.

Justin got one of Klaus Knopfler's tools, a sledgehammer, and with the third blow the door gave way.

But the loft was empty, and the open window to the fire escape told why.

Looking out they could see nothing and quickly reported back to Felix.

"Never mind," he said, "what's important right now is Laura. We need to get her to the hospital fast." After a call to emergency, he turned to Coleman. "The police shouldn't have any trouble picking up Missy, should they?"

Coleman shook his head. "It's not going to be that easy. There's still no substantive evidence to connect her with the crimes. All *we* have is Laura's word. The police won't go for it. After what happened between Laura and Missy they'll figure Laura was the one trying to make a frame. No, I'm afraid she's going to get away with it," he said, looking out the window at the fire escape and into the night.

Inside the loft the Kurt Weill tape was still playing, and Sting was now singing "Mac the Knife."

CHAPTER 30

THE DARKNESS of the alley covered Missy's escape as she scampered down the fire escape from Carl's loft and headed for Third Street. *Move,* she told herself, knowing that whoever was on the elevator would be looking for her. She hoped she was far enough away so that the darkness would keep them from seeing her.

As she came out of the alley the lights of the Society Hill Hotel startled her after the thick darkness. Momentarily she froze, like a jack-lighted deer. Coming so close to being caught had shaken her. For a moment she felt disoriented, not quite sure who she was or where she was—and then she saw the knife in her hand and snapped back. "Get to the car," she muttered as she shoved the knife under her jacket.

No one paid any attention to her, she heard no alarm, but her heartbeat was tripled by the time she made it up Third Street to her parked car.

The sight of it didn't comfort her as she realized she didn't have her purse with her. Where had she left it? It had her money, credit cards, drugs, keys—her *identification*. She felt panicky. Did she leave it at Carl's? She tried the door, maybe she'd left it unlocked. No luck. Get a cab. If she could make it home before the police arrived it was still her word against Laura's and then she saw her face reflected in the window of the car. Of course . . . it wasn't Missy she saw, it was *Peter*. And Peter didn't carry a purse. She put her hand in her . . . his . . . trouser pocket. The keys were there.

She fumbled with the lock. "Steady now. Control." Finally she got the key in and the door came open. She got in, closed and locked the door.

"All right, you're fine. Settle down and get to business, but don't waste a minute doing it."

Hand unsteady, she started the engine, and the tape player came on with it—the sudden sound of Bob Seger's raspy voice singing "Turn the Page" made her jump. She reached to turn it down, heart pounding now, put the car in gear and out of habit glanced at herself in the mirror. The hardness of Peter's face in the dim light shocked her. Damn it, she didn't want to be Peter now. She wanted to be Missy again, the old Missy before . . . the Missy who dressed in her soft and pretty things, lounged in front of the fire and welcomed proper gentlemen callers with champagne. Most of all she wanted her father. With him she would be loved, safe . . .

She shook her head to clear away the fantasy. "Be careful, take it slow and easy. You know how long it takes the police to respond to a call around here. You have plenty of time to get home. All you have to do is get rid of these clothes and appear surprised when the police show up. There's nothing to connect *you* with what happened at Carl's . . ."

She thought of Laura . . . the way she fought back. She'd never known a woman so committed, so *crazy*. Women didn't act that way. They died quietly and with dignity as long as you didn't mess up their face, even young girls. Especially the young girls. They were so good at accepting the inevitable. When the time came all they asked was to be a pretty corpse, but not Laura . . .

She crossed Market Street and replaced the Seger tape with one of Miles Davis playing the Cyndi Lauper hit, "Time After Time." The soft sound of his trumpet helped settle her. By the time she turned onto Race Street by the Black Banana her heart rate had begun to slow down and she reached over and took out her flask from the glove compartment. It was still half-full from when she had waited outside Lagniappe for Felix and Cynthia on Halloween night. That time when she and Felix were still together seemed long ago, far away. Felix, he'd pay, oh yes . . .

She paused a moment at the stop sign on Delaware Avenue and took a drink. The bite, the burn, felt good, but quickly faded.

Replaced by a vision of Felix's face, so like a younger version of her father. Her father . . . she'd done everything for him, hadn't she? She'd loved him enough even to kill for him. She'd given him the deep love her mother had denied him. Well, Felix would miss her . . .

Her father, Felix . . . her nipples began to harden under the elastic bandages flattening her breasts. She wanted the bandages gone, her breasts free and swollen. She wanted to open her blouse to him, sit back with a brandy while he suckled and nursed at them . . .

She drove south on Delaware Avenue, the river shimmering on her left. Traffic was heavy but she'd soon be home, be Missy again. Get rid of Peter's things. Weigh them down with something, throw them in the river.

She put on her turn signal and moved into the left lane—and then she saw it, there in her driveway, a police cruiser. They were waiting for her, somehow they'd responded quicker than she'd imagined possible. Instinctively she pressed down on the accelerator, but caught herself in time. "What the fuck do you think you're doing? Take it easy. The last thing you want is to attract attention . . ."

She stayed with the traffic moving south until she came to Washington Avenue, took a right, driving slowly toward the Italian Market at Ninth Street. The neighborhood that once held such fulfillment for her with Terri and the other girls now made her uneasy, heavily patrolled as it was by police. *Get out before you're seen* . . . but to where? She couldn't go to her townhouse; she couldn't go to Carl's; even as herself there were no friends she could go to, not now.

The Italian Market with its streetside stalls was closed and almost deserted except for garbage trucks. Down the block she saw a police cruiser at the curb, but facing the opposite direction. She shook her head. Where could she go? Where could she find any safety? She had no money, no credit cards, no clothes, not even a purse. She was trapped, trapped in her Peter role, when what she wanted to be was Missy, to put all this behind her. And then the answer came—the one place where they had to take her, the one place where she was always welcome—home.

Her mother was still in Rio with Edgar, which meant she could have time to herself in the house, collect her thoughts. She knew she couldn't stay, the police would be there sooner than later, but at least she could catch her breath, figure out where to go and pick up some money. Her father had always kept ready cash in his study safe.

She stayed on Washington all the way to Twenty-second

Street before she took a right and headed north toward East River Drive. The pain began again during the ride out, but she did her best to ignore it, push it away. Too many other things to think about, like where was she going to live . . . not what house, but what city? She couldn't stay in Philadelphia any longer, needed a place where they wouldn't be looking for her, a place far away, with life and style pleasing to her. By the time she reached Chestnut Hill she had decided on it . . . the one place she wanted to live, that she could lose herself in, was Los Angeles.

The stone house, nearly hidden from sight by trees and bushes, was dark when she arrived. Good. She turned off her lights as she pulled into the driveway, being doubly cautious, and parked behind the house.

Looking about at the familiar grounds she already felt herself begin to relax, and reached for the flask, wanting to savor the feeling.

"Who was it said you can't go home again? Shows what *he* knows," she said, raising the flask to the dark house in a toast. "Old house, maybe when all this is over I'll even come back for a visit. You'd like that, wouldn't you? Well, goddamn it, wouldn't you? Come on, you old bastard, talk to me. It's Missy, your golden darling daughter . . ." And then she broke down, let loose, her shoulders shaking, tears flowing down her cheeks, wetting the beard, she was no longer aware of . . . "Daddy, *Daddy*, where are you? I need you, I do . . . please, please, Daddy . . ."

Finally she quieted, trying to dry her eyes without ruining her eye makeup, not realizing that she was Peter and wearing none.

Feeling shaky, she got out of the car and approached the house. Only at the door did she realize she didn't have the keys. Seldom used, they were back at her townhouse. And this house was wired with a security system, so she couldn't even pry open a window.

She slumped down at the picnic table, feeling undone, about to cry again . . . but in a moment stopped and heard the voice . . . "Stop that goddamn nonsense. Just *break* the window." Peter's voice. She shook her head, no it wouldn't work—"Yes, it will"—

Peter's voice. "It's the frame that's wired, not the glass. You can break the glass and the alarm won't go off. You just can't raise a window or open the door." She thought a moment, knew he was right. Wasn't he always?

She looked at the window. What to break it with? How to cover the noise? The latter was more serious . . . even though the houses were far apart this was still a neighborhood, and the sound of breaking glass could easily arouse someone to call the police. She needed something to muffle the sound but what? "Use your goddamn jacket," Peter said.

Which only left something to break the glass with. There was no loose brick or stone. "Use *yourself* . . ." *What? Oh, sure.* And she went to the window over the kitchen sink, stuffed Peter's leather jacket against it to muffle the sound and gave it a sharp hit with her elbow. The sound of glass shattering momentarily froze her. She waited in a half-crouch, expecting headlights at any minute, swarms of police cars.

Nothing came. She brushed away the glass and climbed through the window onto the sink and slid to the floor. The house was dark, but it had always been dark, all her whole life. It was a familiar darkness.

She didn't turn on any lights. They would only attract attention, and besides she didn't need them. She'd always thought of herself as a cat, a night person. Her instincts were all she needed.

She paused outside the door to her father's study. The night's strain had taken its toll; she felt exhausted. She needed a drink and five minutes to unwind, to escape the gnawing pain in her gut that had never left. She followed the dark hallway to the living room, where she poured herself a large brandy and flopped into an easy chair. She found a cigarette in a china box on the coffee table, sat back and blew a column of smoke toward the ceiling.

What a mess—what a colossal mess she'd made of it all. Just as her father had warned her . . . it was what happened when you let your heart rule your head. Stupid . . .

Well, she'd never again be taken in by a man like him . . . Like Felix. The two were so alike in her head she sometimes got them mixed up . . . He had used her, deceived her, rejected her even though she had offered him everything . . . And now, because of letting her feelings run away with her, it looked as though he was going to get away with it, go free after what he'd done to her, and *she* was the one who was going to have to suffer for it. Just as always . . . it wasn't fair, it wasn't, it wasn't . . .

And that bitch Laura . . . no question she'd milk her pitiful little cuts for all they were worth. She'd convince Felix she was Joan of Arc. The thought of them together was enough to make her want to throw up . . .

She took a long drink of the brandy, and half-smiled, her thoughts shifting to Cynthia. *That* was a bright spot. She'd really enjoyed it and knew Cynthia had, too. Maybe she'd try another older one, but not too much older. Like Cynthia, old enough to really appreciate her, before their body got wrinkled and saggy like she knew Miss Priss Laura's was.

Worse than all of that, here she sat, her body full of pain on account of a pregnancy she didn't want, feeling it tearing at her insides. And it was all *his* fault. Goddamn him. His? Felix's, yes Felix, who else? He had made her inseminate herself and go through this misery. Missy . . . Missy. Thanks to *him* and Felix and that wimp, Carl. All faithless, all users.

As she reached for the doorknob to her father's study the pain got worse. She would have liked to talk to him, to *tell* him about it, what he'd done to her . . . Then maybe he'd fix it, as he'd done when she was little. He'd kiss it and it would be all better.

"All better," that's what he used to say . . .

Standing at the threshold she looked at his big chair, and what had been pushed away for so many years, what she'd forgotten, needed to forget, began to come back . . . Her feelings that awful night had been like the ones now . . . that night, too, she had been pregnant, in pain, scared. "Well, I'm back, and I'm pregnant again. Only this time it's worse. I don't know who the father is, I don't even know what color he is."

She crossed the room to his desk. "I always seem to—" She was about to say "disappoint you," but something stopped her, her eyes widened behind the tinted glasses. The room, the circumstances, all too similar. She shook her head and began again. "No, doctor, I don't want to be a doctor, I *can't* follow in your footsteps like you want, I could never live up to you . . ."

Those long-ago feelings of the pain and shame—she'd let him down again as she'd done that night . . . He was behind the desk, doing something. What? Talking on the phone? No. Reading? No. Working on his stamp collection? Maybe . . .

Looking around the room, it was as if she were standing in the middle of a movie she'd seen and forgotten and now remembered. She knew the room—recognized it, rather, but didn't know it. She knew the actors' lines, though, or did she?

At least some of them. She'd stood there now in front of his desk. He'd been behind it. Yes, that's how it had been. And it *was* the stamp album. He was pasting stamps in it when she came in, didn't look up until he was finished—

She tried to shake off the past, told herself to "get busy, get the money, get *out* of here . . ." But this night the past wasn't so easy to exorcise. She'd opened the gates, let it come back, and it seemed to have a life, a will, of its own.

She set her drink down on the desk and walked over to the photo of Cyrus Wakefield's medical class that was hanging on a nearby wall. Behind it was his wall safe, his money.

The stamps . . . she had never remembered them before . . . Before she'd only remembered coming to his study door with the news of her pregnancy, then nothing after that until she'd come home from the hospital without the baby. And for a long time she hadn't even allowed that partial intrusion of the past.

She turned from the picture and looked at the desk. What happened after the stamps? What did he do? What did she do?

The scene focused. Maybe it was the pain, the pregnancy, that did it. Memories of his voice rising as he lectured about the dangers of trimester abortions . . . She could *hear* him now, even though his voice sounded far away, as though she was hearing it through water. Oh, God, he was calling her names, saying things that hurt her so . . .

She could see herself standing there in front of his desk. Was she crying? No. What then? When the answer came it brought back a humiliation long denied . . . She stood in front of the desk and lost control. The next sensation was the wetness, just as when she was Peter with those girls . . .

The scene changed and they were no longer at home. They were in his office. It was night—the same night? Yes. They were alone in the main examining room. He made her strip and get up on the table—

"*Enough.*" She turned to the picture, took it off the wall and put it on the floor, face-down. "Get busy, you've *got* to get out of here." And the urgency in her voice now had nothing to do with fear of the police. It was her father . . . he had forced her to do something in the office that night, something that had changed everything between them . . .

Frantically she started twisting the dial on the safe, trying to open the doors. It was no good. Her memory was like toppling dominoes. She couldn't stop it . . .

The examining room. She was on the table. The light was shining from above, the corners of the room dark. She was ashamed. Horribly ashamed. He made her lie on her side and draw her knees high up to her shoulders. She shivered with the memory of the cold liquid he had dabbed near the base of her spine, felt the burning that followed the cold.

She had looked up and seen him standing in front of her. He was gloved and gowned. Over the lower half of his face was a surgical mask, and above it the light glinted off his glasses. He was holding a huge needle.

"No, *please*, don't . . ." She mouthed the words in the darkened study, and they still did not help her. He was ordering her to lie still, to stay in that fetal position; then he was behind her, out of sight, and she felt the pain and burning as he worked the needle through her muscle layers and into her spine.

How could her daddy, her beloved daddy, do this to her? She asked it then—she asked it now. Why didn't he understand? Why was he hurting her?

The light over the table was hot. She began to go numb. He bustled about . . . affixed the catheter, turned her over, strapped her down, taped the syringe of anesthetic to her shoulder. And then he was talking to her through his mask. "I'm going to make a transverse incision; we call it a bikini cut. You'll like that; you can still wear a two-piece at the beach . . ." A stranger's voice. He shouldn't have been wearing green, should have been wearing black . . .

"Daddy, please, please . . ." Words that got you excused, but not this time—

Shake it away, she told herself, moving around the study. *This is all wrong. It didn't happen this way, he'd never do this to you, he loved you too much.*

Still the dominoes toppled . . . The aseptic solution on her belly. More coldness flittering through the numbness. She didn't want to look but had no choice. Her head was propped up to keep her from vomiting, he said.

The scalpel, its gleam and twinkle in the night. "*No . . .*" His hand moved, quick and sure. She felt a tugging. Then she saw the blood. Her belly was laid open—

Back in the study. "Brandy. Where's my brandy?" It was on the desk where she'd left it. She went to it, half-stumbled, picked it up with shaking hands . . . and there he was again, anchoring a shiny metal ring the size of a dinner plate to the side of the table, his hands positioning it over the cut, using it to hold the retractors as he opened the incision wider. He was tearing her apart with his bare hands, but she felt nothing. Not then, but now . . .

The cut for the uterus came next—" Get a *grip* on yourself," she said in the study. "You're acting crazy. So he did a C-section on you. It should have been done in a hospital, but you were too far along; that was your own damn fault for not telling him sooner. At least now you know what happened. It hurt, but that's medicine for you. He did what he had to do, no reason for you to have blocked this out . . ."

She gulped from her glass and looked back at the safe. "Now what was the combination?" She still couldn't remember.

All the dominoes hadn't toppled yet.

What she remembered was waking up in her own bed upstairs and not knowing how she got there. Her belly felt on fire. She was stiff, sore inside and out. When she moved she felt something against her breast and pulled back the covers to investigate. It was wrapped in a towel. She reached for it—"

"*No, don't*" It was the adolescent Missy's scream, trying to reach back over the years. And now she was there, memory replaced by crystal-clear vision. She didn't know what was in the package, didn't want to know. All she knew was that until now she had never been able to remember what had happened that night. And whatever it was, the C-section wasn't it. It was something worse, much worse—

She smashed her glass against the wall and ran from the room, without thinking going up the stairs to the one place that belonged to her. Years had passed since she'd been in her old bedroom but nothing had changed. One wall was still covered with ribbons from horse shows and trophies from camp. Barely visible in the darkness were pictures of a younger Missy, pictures of her with her horse, pictures from school. On another wall was a poster of Led Zepplin. Below it had hung a picture of Cher but it was gone now. Her father had made her take it down.

She crossed the room and sat on the window seat, wishing she dared to turn on some lights. Just one, that's all she needed to break up these bad memories, but she couldn't risk attracting attention. She sank down on the bed. It still had the same frilly girlish spread her mother had picked out. She'd always hated that damn spread. And looking at it, the past rushed in, not to be denied . . .

She was groggy from the shock of the C-section when she found the bundle in bed with her. The towel wrapping it was white, and the bundle was cocoon-shaped, the size of a bread basket. She remembered reaching for it, hoping it was a present from her father, to show that he had forgiven her . . .

Her fingers touched it. She unwrapped it near the top and peered inside. At first what she saw didn't register. And then, when it did, she began to scream.

Inside the white towel was the dead fetus. Hers? Her child? She shoved off the covers and tried to scramble away. She felt the pain in her belly from the strain on her stitches. Never mind, it didn't matter. She had to move, get away from it, not let it touch her.

"Daddy, help, help," she called out, over and over.

Seconds seemed like hours until the door opened and he was there.

But he didn't come over to her. He was like a stranger. And it was a stranger's voice that said, "Don't run from your baby. That's no way for a mother to act . . ."

"Bastard, bastard," the words coming now from Missy's huddled form on the windowseat, more a whimper than a growl. She uncoiled herself and moved toward the door.

Downstairs she looked for her drink before she remembered she'd smashed the glass when she'd run out of the room. She picked up the bottle and carried it to the French doors that opened out onto the brick patio and garden beyond. Staring into the moonlight, she turned the bottle up and took a long pull from it.

Her reflection was fragmented in the panes. The moon, the bricks, the light . . . Yes, it *was* so like that night. The house was dark. The moon was shining like now. Except it was warmer then. Summer. She remembered the moon, a bright reflection in the water of the swimming pool. And she saw him again . . .

He was carrying two candlesticks. Mom's candlesticks. "Get up. Bring it," he said. She sat up and swung her feet to the floor, the pull of her stitches again filling her belly with pain. She didn't resist. Whatever came next couldn't be worse than what had already happened.

The bundle felt so light in her arms. Funny how something as small could cause so much pain.

At the door he gave her one of the candles, and their eyes met for a moment. His seemed especially bright in the candlelight. She followed him down the dark stairs. At the bottom he told her to go ahead of him. They made a strange procession. She barefoot wearing panties and a Rolling Stones T-shirt, stitches burning with each step. He in madras slacks, golf shirt, looking like a gin-and-tonic ad. Step by step, they marched. Solemn. Step by step.

Outside, the night was warm, humid. The air smelled of fresh-cut grass. She thought that the gardeners must have been there. Step by step they marched across the patio bricks.

Ahead in the moonlight just beyond the pool was the gas grill. They moved toward it. He raised the lid. "Put it here," he said. She did as he told her.

"Now cover it with charcoal," he said, indicating a bag beside the grill. She picked up the charcoal and managed to shake out the briquets without having to touch them and get her fingers all black. When she was finished she stepped back, and he handed back her candle.

And then he turned on the gas.

Why? Still looking out the French doors, she tried to remember his answer. And then she remembered too well . . . "Because it was a boy." He'd said it so quietly, under his breath, she almost hadn't heard it, but she had, and remembering it now, it explained everything. She could never make him love her. She was not what he wanted. Never had been. And this bastard boy-child had been the final straw. Too cruel a joke for him to accept. Better to destroy it and make her suffer for the bitter disappointment she'd been to him. "Bastard, bastard . . ."

The next day she had tried to kill herself . . . and the day after . . . until at the hospital the drugs and the shock therapies erased her memory of it—at least of the birth and death of the infant "Peter," as her father had called it later that dark summer night . . .

She turned from the French doors and looked at the study. She had always been told by her father, and had believed, that the baby had been aborted at the hospital, that her loss of memory was from anesthetic shock.

She stood behind his chair and put her hands on the back, like it was his shoulders, and she was massaging away the tension in them the way she had done so many times when he was alive.

"Was I that much of a disappointment?" she said softly. "I did all I could to please you, even trying to be a boy, your son, as well as your daughter. Wasn't that enough?" No, it wasn't. "Well, screw you . . ."

She went to the safe, remembering the combination now. Turning the dial, she stopped at the numbers corresponding to the last four digits of the home phone number, with the last, the door opened. She reached inside and brought out five thick packets of hundred dollar bills.

Hefting them in her hand, she said, in Peter's voice, "Cyrus, you old bastard. There must be at least twenty-five thousand here. More than enough to get a smart fellow like me on his feet in Los Angeles."

She left the house the way she had come, pausing only to pick up a bottle of brandy and a bottle of vodka from the bar on her way out.

Inside the car she looked in the mirror and stroked her beard. "Los Angeles, land of angels and beautiful young women. Here I come . . ."

She maneuvered down the drive with the lights off, only turning them on once she reached the road. She waited for a car to pass, then pulled out. She did not look back at the darkened house.

The easiest route to take, she figured, would be the expressway to I-95 south and follow that to Delaware and points south, but she decided against it because the drive would take her back into the heart of the city. She also ruled out getting on the Pennsylvania Turnpike at King of Prussia because the turnpike was a toll road that offered little chance of escape if she were seen and identified. She settled on City Line Avenue to take her out of the city most quickly and into Delaware by less dangerous roads.

She took Lincoln Drive until she hit City Line near Bala Cynwyd. Traffic there was heavy and slow, and just past the Mariott she noticed a young girl wearing the pleated skirt and the blazer of one of the nearby prep schools, ambling toward the bus stop. There had been a time when she could have told the name of any nearby Main Line prep school by its colors . . .

The girl had blonde hair that reached her shoulders. She was pretty and wholesome-looking, but what especially caught Missy's eye were her shoes. The teenager was wearing brown-and-white saddle shoes with white socks . . . like a young teenage Missy—before that awful night . . . And suddenly she couldn't stand the feeling of emptiness, of being alone . . . she needed *someone* to give her a little affection. Why not this girl who reminded her of herself . . . ? She put on her turn signal and cut across to the curb. She would only take a couple of minutes more, then she'd drop the girl off wherever she wanted and be on her way.

As the girl approached, Missy lowered the window on the passenger side and leaned across the seat. "Hey, want a lift? It'll save you waiting for the bus."

When the teenager hesitated Missy reached for her police badge to reassure her, but then remembered that she didn't have it, that she had purposely left it behind when she went to the rendezvous with Laura.

She pushed open the door on the passenger side and smiled. "Don't be silly, it's cold out there tonight . . ."

The youngster looked so unsure, vulnerable, hesitated again, as if trying to decide whether to obey her overanxious parents, then smiled and shrugged and got into the car.

Missy quickly slipped in a tape of Paul Simon doing "Graceland." It was lively but calming at the same time. Just what the doctor ordered. The doctor . . .

They pulled back into traffic. "What's your name?"

"Julie," replied the blonde. "Actually it's Juliet but I don't use it. Gets me too much kidding."

Missy smiled. "Mine's Peter, but tonight maybe I'll be Romeo?" She laughed. "Just a joke, Juliet."

Looking into the night, Juliet said nothing until she spotted Missy's cigarettes and asked if she could have one.

"Sure, and would you light one for me, too?" Missy said.

After lighting up, Juliet settled back, watched the traffic, smoked. Quiet thing, and she didn't even say anything when some ten minutes later Missy pulled off into a wooded area and stopped.

"Come here," ordered Missy, and was pleasantly surprised when the girl came into her arms.

She kissed her hard, the false beard rubbing harshly against the youngster's face, thrust her tongue deep into the girl's mouth.

Juliet began to respond, sucking on Missy's tongue, kissing back until Missy, aroused, felt she had to touch her, slipped her hand under the pleated skirt and began to move it up the girl's thighs. Juliet kept her legs tightly closed, arousing Missy even more. This girl wasn't like the ones from South Philly. This one was different, and now she had to have her . . . Missy's exploring hand touched panties, and moved inside—and touched something else, something she did not expect. Her eyes opened wide, she started to speak—

Then she felt the pain.

It was a sharp pain, a breath-taking pain as Juliet drove the ice pick between Missy's ribs . . . once, twice, three times.

Slumped in the seat, semi-conscious but unable to speak, unable to protest as Juliet went through her pockets, relieving her of the five packets of hundred dollar bills.

The last sound Missy Wakefield heard before she died was Juliet's now clearly masculine voice saying, "Sweet dreams, *Romeo.*"

CHILLING TALES

FROM WARNER BOOKS

☐ **FEARBOOK** *by John L. Byrne*
(B34-814, $3.95, U.S.A.) (B34-815, $4.95, Canada)

A horror tale of supernatural surburban terror in
which a couple is stalked by a mail order catalog
with evil powers.

☐ **THE HUNTING SEASON** *by John Coyne*
(B34-321, $4.50, U.S.A.) (B34-320, $5.50, Canada)

A woman's anthropological studies of a mountain
community reveal a dark and nightmarish secret.

W **Warner Books P.O. Box 690**
New York, NY 10019

Please send me the books I have checked. I enclose a check or money
order (not cash), plus 95¢ per order and 95¢ per copy to cover postage
and handling.* (Allow 4-6 weeks for delivery.)

___Please send me your free mail order catalog. (If ordering only the
catalog, include a large self-addressed, stamped envelope.)

Name _____

Address _____

City _____ State _____ Zip _____

*New York and California residents add applicable sales tax.
364

From bestselling author

WILLIAM KATZ

☐ AFTER DARK

(A34-605, $3.95, U.S.A.) (A34-606, $4.95, Canada)

A psychological thriller about a young woman with insomnia whose nightly vigils at her window attracts the attention of a paranoid killer across the way.

☐ SURPRISE PARTY

(A32-778, $3.50, U.S.A.) (A32-779, $4.50)

One man's homicidal obsession turns a fateful surprise party into a bloodbath of terror.

☐ OPEN HOUSE

(A30-192, $3.95, U.S.A.) (A30-193, $4.95, Canada)

Young single women in New York are murdered in their apartments by someone they are apparently expecting.

**Warner Books P.O. Box 690
New York, NY 10019**

Please send me the books I have checked. I enclose a check or money order (not cash), plus 95¢ per order and 95¢ per copy to cover postage and handling.* (Allow 4 -6 weeks for delivery.)

___Please send me your free mail order catalog. (If ordering only the catalog, include a large self-addressed, stamped envelope.)

Name _____

Address _____

City _____ State _____ Zip _____

*New York and California residents add applicable sales tax.

326

William Goldman

THE CHILLING SEQUEL TO *MARATHON MAN*

Brothers

"Scintillating."—*Chicago Tribune*

"Wildly imaginative."—*Publishers Weekly*

"Compelling."—*Boston Herald*

"A cause to rejoice."—*Philadelphia Daily News*

"Unique."—*Cosmopolitan*

"A highly satisfactory novel."—*San Diego Union*

"A fine thriller."—*Cincinnati Post*

(A34-680, $4.95, U.S.A.) (A34-681, $5.95, Canada)

Warner Books P.O. Box 690
New York, NY 10019

Please send me ___ copy(ies) of the book. I enclose a check or money order (not cash), plus 95¢ per order and 95¢ per copy to cover postage and handling.* (Allow 4-6 weeks for delivery.)

___Please send me your free mail order catalog. (If ordering only the catalog, include a large self-addressed, stamped envelope.)

Name _____

Address _____

City _____ State _____ Zip _____

*New York and California residents add applicable sales tax.   314

SIDNEY SHELDON

WINDMILLS OF THE GODS

#1 BLOCKBUSTER BESTSELLER

"Fun!"—*Publishers Weekly*

"Fast-paced."
—*St. Louis Post-Dispatch*

"Entertaining!"—*Washington Post Book World*

"Exciting."—*United Press International*

(A34-749, $4.95, U.S.A.) (A34-750, $5.95, Canada)

**Warner Books P.O. Box 690
New York, NY 10019**

Please send me ___ copy(ies) of the book. I enclose a check or money order (not cash), plus 95¢ per order and 95¢ per copy to cover postage and handling.* (Allow 4-6 weeks for delivery.)

___Please send me your free mail order catalog. (If ordering only the catalog, include a large self-addressed, stamped envelope.)

Name _____

Address _____

City _____ State _____ Zip _____

*New York and California residents add applicable sales tax.

315